T0244665

ALL
SHOOK
UP

ALL
SHOOK
UP

A Novel

ENID LANGBERT

Copyright © 2024 Enid Langbert

All rights reserved. No part of this publication may be reproduced, distributed, or transmitted in any form or by any means, including photocopying, recording, digital scanning, or other electronic or mechanical methods, without the prior written permission of the publisher, except in the case of brief quotations embodied in critical reviews and certain other noncommercial uses permitted by copyright law. For permission requests, please address SparkPress.

Published by SparkPress, a BookSparks imprint,
A division of SparkPoint Studio, LLC
Phoenix, Arizona, USA, 85007
www.gosparkpress.com

Published 2024
Printed in the United States of America
Print ISBN: 978-1-68463-264-0
E-ISBN: X 978-1-68463-265-7
Library of Congress Control Number: 2024906650

Interior design by Stacey Aaronson

All company and/or product names may be trade names, logos, trademarks, and/or registered trademarks and are the property of their respective owners.

This is a work of fiction. Names, characters, places, and incidents either are the product of the author's imagination or are used fictitiously. Any resemblance to actual persons, living or dead, is entirely coincidental.
NO AI TRAINING: Without in any way limiting the author's [and publisher's] exclusive rights under copyright, any use of this publication to "train" generative artificial intelligence (AI) technologies to generate text is expressly prohibited. The author reserves all rights to license uses of this work for generative AI training and development of machine learning language models.

All Shook Up

Chapter One

I know what you're going to think. You're going to think I'm pathetic. I'm already fourteen years old. It's been two years since I first heard rock and roll. And what do I have to show for it? Nothing.

If I live to be a hundred, even two hundred, I know I will never forget the minute I heard my first rock and roll song. It was like waking up when I didn't know I'd been asleep. The drums pounded, and the melody kept going around and around. My body moved by itself. I felt as if I were lost in a world I'd never been in before but might have been born in and never wanted to leave—like all my life until that moment I had been inside a little cage, and the door just swung open.

"I said shake, rattle, and roll.
I said shake, rattle, and roll.
Well you never do nothin' to save your doggone soul."

You have to understand what music before rock and roll was like. Every song I'd ever heard before had music like a gentle horse that carried the singer on its back. Each word was like a bubble, round and perfect, floating into your ears. But this music was like a bucking bronco. It argued with the singer. It answered back. You couldn't even hear the words. The first few times I heard the song, I thought they were talking about a girl who had the "shape of Marilyn Monroe," until I heard the name of the song on the radio: "Shake, Rattle and Roll." It was the perfect name because it's what the music did. This music shook, rattled, and rolled, and it was going to shake and rattle and roll the whole world. It was going to change everything.

Well, it hasn't. Not yet, anyway.

Even though the next song Bill Haley and the Comets sang, "Rock Around the Clock," was the biggest hit record in the country and they played it on the radio constantly.

Grown-ups hate rock and roll. At least the ones I know—my parents and my friends' parents and probably my teachers, although they don't talk about it in class. It's amazing how all grown-ups say the same thing—like they had a meeting about what to say about this new thing that might actually make their kids happy for a change. They say it's a communist plot to undermine the youth of America. And my friends believe them. They believe everything our parents tell them, just because our parents have lived for such a long time and gone to college and stuff. My friends tell me I'm a dupe to listen to rock and roll.

Well, I don't believe them. For one thing, I figure the communists have kids, too, and they're probably so busy worrying about their own kids they don't have time to think about kids living in Queens, let alone plot to undermine us. Another reason is I hardly believe anything my parents tell me. And I have good reasons.

Take my father. He's what you would call an egghead. He

thinks you can't even call something music if it has words and wasn't written at least a hundred years ago. My father came into my room one night when the radio was playing my favorite song.

Oh yes, I'm the great pretender.
Dooey do.
Pretending that I'm doing well.
Dooey do.
My need is such I pretend too much.
I'm lonely but no one can tell.

I loved it because it talked about being lonely. I waited for him to smile and say what a beautiful song it was. Maybe even say he understood why I loved it so much because he was lonely, too.

But he just shook his head, as if something really sad had just happened, and asked, "Paula Levy. What is that racket?"

My father loves to call me by my whole name. As if we don't exactly know each other that well. Which is probably true.

Anyway, I looked into his eyes to see if he was joking. He wasn't.

"It's called rock and roll, Daddy. It's a new kind of music."

"Music she calls it! I thought the furnace had exploded."

And my mother. I don't know what you would call her. But she thinks all you need to be happy is to have enough to eat because when she was my age, it was the middle of the Depression, and no one had much money.

I thought maybe rock and roll could make her happy, like it made me, so I played "Shake, Rattle and Roll" for her on the jukebox when we were having lunch at Murray's Luncheonette.

Murray's sells soda and sandwiches with really big pickles. The best thing about Murray's, though, unless you are in love with white bread and big pickles, which I am not, is the jukebox. It is as tall as I am and blue and green neon with red and yellow flashing lights.

Ever since I was little, I loved to watch the metal arm reach down and pick out the record you wanted from the row of records lined up inside the glass dome. There it was, in the middle of all the corny songs my mother loved—"Shake, Rattle and Roll." I put in a dime and held my breath. Out it came, shaking and rattling.

Everyone in the luncheonette was a grown-up. And every one of their heads jerked up, looking really angry. Like this racket was ruining their baloney sandwiches. My mother was so embarrassed.

It was pretty cool, actually, seeing them so mad and my mother so embarrassed. And all because of rock and roll. It gave me a lot of hope.

Every night now, for months, after I come home from Chemistry Club or orchestra or the other dumb things I do after school to help me get into a good college so I can have a great life, and after I finish my homework, I listen to rock and roll on the radio in my room.

Pathetic, right? Well, not anymore. Because last month a miracle happened. A cool girl became my friend.

Chapter Two

*M*aybe that doesn't sound like a miracle to you. Maybe you have lots of cool friends and think miracles haven't happened for thousands of years. Well, if that's what you think, you don't go to my high school.

In my high school, there are two kinds of people: cool kids and us. And everybody knows which one you are the minute they see you. For one thing, we're younger than the cool kids because we skipped a grade. I don't know whose great idea that was, but somebody figured that we were so smart we didn't need to go to all the grades and we could skip one or two. So hopefully the reason I'm so short and, you know, younger-looking in a sweater is because I am in tenth grade instead of ninth, and I'm going to have an enormous growth spurt in every direction anytime now.

But as if being younger wasn't bad enough, you would know I wasn't cool the minute you saw me from the clothes I wear. My mother doesn't let me pick out my own clothes. Anytime you see me, I'll be dressed the way my mother thinks teenagers should dress. Saddle shoes. Fat white socks folded down over my ankles. Pleated skirts. Sweater sets. But if you saw a cool girl, you would know that she looks the way teenagers should really look. Tight black skirts with a slit up the back. Tight fuzzy sweaters. Bright red lipstick and bright blue eye shadow. And big plastic earrings in gold and silver and bright colors.

I don't think the cool kids even care about getting into a good college. But I don't know that for sure because they never talk to us. And we never go to the places where they hang out. Because if one time, by mistake, you went to the luncheonette across the street from school where the cool kids hang out, they would nudge each other and yell, "Hey, Brain, how're your cooties?" Or, "Cast your eyeball on the square."

So, you would leave as fast as you could and never go back. Even our parents seemed to know the cool kids would never have anything to do with us because, of all the things they warned us not to do, they never warned us about falling into "bad company."

But at night in my room, when I listen to my radio, I close my eyes and go back to the luncheonette wearing long plastic earrings and flat black shoes without socks. My sweater sticks out pretty far from my chest. Everyone smiles at me, and I sit down in a booth next to a boy with blond hair slicked back and a white shirt with the collar open. He puts his arm around my shoulder, and this strange feeling is squeezing my chest. We look into each other's eyes and listen to our special song, the song that was written just about us.

Why do birds sing so gay?
And lovers await the break of day?
Why do they fall in love?

"Paula!" My mother is banging on my door.
"What?"
"Did you finish your homework?"
"Yes."
"Then go to sleep. It's after nine o'clock."

Chapter Three

I wasn't kidding when I said it was a miracle for me to have a cool friend. You probably are wondering how it could have happened. I don't blame you because I can hardly believe myself.

It all started when a new kind of store that no one had ever seen before opened a couple of blocks from my house. A record store. It was like my radio was a pumpkin, and my fairy godmother waved her wand and turned it into a chariot filled with music. The first time I walked into that store and looked at the walls covered with little cubbies filled with records, I felt as if I were in church. Actually, I should say a synagogue because I've never been in a church. I've hardly been in a synagogue, either. But I figure it feels the same way, you know, all special and quiet and thrilling.

I hope God isn't insulted when I say this. Not that He probably pays too much attention to me and my family since we don't pay much attention to Him.

Unfortunately, it was like an announcement went out over the cool kids' public address system because they all started hanging out in the record store. Hundreds of them. So, of course, my friends wouldn't go there because their mothers told them good girls didn't go to places like that. Only tramps. I can't figure that one out.

What was trampy about going to a store and buying things?

Our mothers did that all day long. Of course, I knew the answer: "Trampy" was our mothers' word for "cool." It was like their secret code for making sure we never had fun.

So, I went to the record store by myself. I would have to pretend I didn't know the cool kids were staring at me and nudging each other, smiling mean smiles. I had to pretend I couldn't hear what they were saying about me, although I knew they weren't calling each other "brain" and "creep." I would keep my head down, so they never caught my eye, except when I was holding a record or paying for it. Richie, the guy who worked at the cash register, had the same face as the boy in my dream luncheonette, with his long blond hair slicked back at the side, and a white shirt with the top button unbuttoned. Whenever I paid him for my records, his blue eyes would look right into mine and he would smile and say, "Thanks, doll," in his deep, velvety voice.

When Richie spoke to me, when he called me "doll," my whole body felt like it was on fire, and I couldn't catch my breath. I figured if anyone looked at me, they would know how I was feeling, so I hurried out of the store even faster than I came in. But on this one day, I must've forgotten about keeping my head down. My eyes wandered up from the floor, as if they moved by themselves, and I found myself staring at a cool girl's back. I was shocked to see a skinny paperback book sticking out of her coat pocket.

I know. I know. You're going to say you've seen hundreds of people with books sticking out of their pockets, and you can't understand why I'm making such a big deal about it, as if I'd seen an iceberg in the middle of a desert or an elephant with wings. Well, I don't want to be a pest about this, but you don't go to my high school. If you did, you would know this was probably the first time in history a cool kid carried a book.

They don't walk around with big leather book bags, like the ones our parents gave us for the birthday before we started high school, filled with textbooks weighing about a half a ton each. They don't spend the first month of every term pasting little round paper doughnuts called "reinforcements" around the holes on every single page of loose-leaf paper in the big, blue-binder notebooks. Cool girls carry shiny little plastic purses that don't have room for anything as big and clunky as a textbook or a three-ring binder. A cool girl would no more carry a book than she would wear socks.

But there it was. And even though the book was squished and only half sticking out of her pocket, I knew what book it was from the gold-and-red cover. *Catcher in the Rye.* All beat-up, it looked exactly like my copy. Like the copy I always kept with me in my book bag because everyone thought it was a dirty book. My mother would've had a heart attack if she knew I'd read it even once, let alone four times.

Chapter Four

*C*atcher in the Rye wasn't like other books. It knocked me out every time I read it. Knocked me out. That's the way Holden Caulfield, the hero of *Catcher in the Rye*, talked. Holden felt like I did about life. He was the only person I knew who did. I guess you could say Holden was my only real friend. I would talk to him in my private thoughts and tell him things I couldn't tell anyone else because I knew he would understand. But if there was someone else who was carrying the book around, she must have felt the same way I did.

I turned back to the records on the wall and pretended to be searching for something else. But really, I was sneaking a peek at the girl who, at that very minute, turned around. She was beautiful. She had all this wavy hair with blonde streaks in it, red lips, and bright blue eyelids. She seemed to be like all the other cool girls, leaning against the wall, smiling at a couple of the cool boys who were talking to her. But I knew she wasn't like all the other cool girls. She had a secret. From everyone but me.

In my room that night, I started making a plan. I would search my high school. I would look at every single cool kid until I found her. I was thinking up excuses for leaving homeroom or going to a different period study hall. What if she didn't go to my high school? I would figure something out. I would find her.

My mind churned with plans the next morning. Churning so much that I almost missed her. In the hallway after third period, there she was, walking toward me talking to a boy with a black pompadour that stuck up about six inches off his head.

I couldn't believe it. It had taken my whole life to find another person who loved *Catcher in the Rye*. And she had been there all along. After third period. Everyone mostly had the same classes every day, so you passed the same people. But I still couldn't believe it had been so easy. Maybe she was only walking there that day and never would again.

I practically held my breath until third period was over the next day. But sure enough, there she was again walking down the hall. It was Friday. Then it was the weekend. For once, I couldn't wait for Monday because I knew exactly what I was going to do.

On Monday, when I walked in the hall after third period, I took out my copy of *Catcher in the Rye* and held it in front of me, like I was reading it. When I saw her coming toward me, walking with pompadour boy, I saw her see me. Her eyes opened wide in surprise, looking at the book and then at me. That afternoon I went to the record store. I saw her sneaking peeks at me. The next day I did the same thing again, walking down the hall after third period, with the book in front of me. I could see her look at me again. I knew what I was going to do next.

On Wednesday, when I walked down the hall after third period, I didn't take the book out. When she turned her head toward me, I smiled at her. She whipped her head back so fast I was afraid it might fall off.

On Thursday she smiled back. At least, I was pretty sure that she did. It was not a very big smile. But I already knew that cool kids didn't smile big smiles. Sure enough, at lunch my plans were rewarded. While I was standing in line waiting to pay for my lunch, she walked up to me.

"Hey, hi. Didn't I see you the other day, you know, at the record store?"

"Um, yeah, maybe." My heart was pounding so loud I was afraid she could hear it. A voice in my head was saying, *I'm talking to a cool kid.* Another voice was saying, *Shut up! It's not cool to say that.*

She was looking around as if she were a spy. "I'm going to be sitting over there by the door. Want to sit with me?"

She was pointing to the table behind a pillar.

"Sure. My name's Paula." She was walking away, and I didn't know if she heard me. She probably didn't care.

Chapter Five

S he looked up and nodded when I sat down.

She wore a fuzzy white sweater that only came up a little way over her brassiere. A lot of her chest showed. And she had a lot of chest.

She said, "You like rock and roll, huh? I mean, you're always buying records."

"Oh, yeah. I love it. More than anything." I'd said too much. Cool kids never said long sentences. Not that those were long sentences. There were just a lot of them.

"Yeah. You got some pretty cool records. We were surprised. 'Cause you know, I mean, you look like a cree—I mean, aren't you like in the smart kids' classes?"

"I guess so. Some of them." Only all of them.

"Well . . . you know . . . the thing of it is, Paula . . . Your name's Paula, right? My name's Barbara. Not Barbie or Barb."

"Hi, Barbara."

"Yeah. So, anyway I saw you reading that book. You know the one I mean? *Catcher in the Rye*."

"Yeah?"

"Yeah. Well, you know, I mean, I read it, too. I mean, do you like it?"

"It's my favorite book," I said.

I bet you think that was an easy thing to say. Well, it wasn't. I'd never told anyone the truth about how I felt about *Catcher in the Rye* or much of anything before. I had just said more truth to someone I'd known for about twenty seconds than to anyone else. Ever.

"Yeah?"

"Yeah."

"Well, it's mine, too," she said.

I had to ask her. "Did you . . . did you really read all of it? Not just the part in the hotel room?"

"Three times. I read it all the way through three times. How about you?"

"Four. I don't know anyone else who likes it."

"Me, neither. Everyone just reads the part about the prostitute."

I'd never heard the word "prostitute" said out loud. I felt cold. Then warm. Then cold and warm at the same time.

It felt like we were the only people in the cafeteria. Maybe in the world.

She didn't say anything for a minute. Then she asked, in a very soft voice, "Why do you like it?"

I didn't need anyone to tell me this was the biggest moment of my life. If I answered the question wrong, it would be over and I would never have a cool friend. I didn't know what would be cool to say or not cool to say. There was nothing I could think of to say but the truth.

"Because . . . I . . . you know . . . because I feel like he does. When he says how phony everyone is and how dumb and fake everything is."

I held my breath and waited to see what she would say. She didn't say anything for a while. Then she nodded a very little nod and said, "Yeah."

We sat quietly for a minute and then she said, "I always thought it was weird, you know, 'cause Holden, you know, he's like this rich kid, and he goes to this fancy school, but he's just as unhappy as I . . . I mean, he's unhappy. And he's rich."

"I never thought about that. I guess he's rich. But it doesn't seem to make much difference. Those schools he goes to don't sound great. And his parents. I mean, they don't understand him at all. Like mine."

"Yeah. Like mine. You must be rich. I mean, you buy so many records."

"Me? No. I'm not rich." Smart *and* rich. Two strikes and I am out. She would never be my friend.

"You could—" I stopped before I made the mistake of inviting her over to listen to my records. I wondered if being cool was like playing the violin, and if I kept practicing, I would get better at it. Not that I'd ever gotten that much better at the violin.

"I never talked about *Catcher* with anybody before," I said instead.

"Me, neither."

"My friends won't read it 'cause they think it's a dirty book."

"My friends won't read it 'cause it's a book."

She smiled her almost smile. I started to smile back. She stood up. "Yeah. Well . . . uh . . . I got to go. Do you want to . . . meet me here tomorrow?"

"Yeah."

"Okay. I'll see you. I mean, you know, maybe."

"Yeah. You will. I mean, maybe."

Chapter Six

*H*olden always says he doesn't feel like talking about where he was born and his lousy childhood and stuff like that. He calls it David Copperfield crap. I read *David Copperfield* to find out what he meant. And boy do I ever feel the same way. I mean, I know it was written a long time ago and in another country, but that's not a good reason for making every sentence half a page long and to begin telling you about his life before he was even born. It seems as if he tells you about every second of his life, which I don't think can be that interesting about anyone's life.

I know if I started by telling you about my life before I met Barbara, you would've fallen asleep. I mean, who would want to hear about a girl whose mother doesn't let her buy her own clothes and arranges for her to go to high school every morning with Margaret, the girl who lives down the block, because she thinks it's dangerous for a girl to ride the subway alone? Like she thinks the GG train is filled with maniacs who attack any girl who isn't standing next to another girl. But not just any old maniacs. These have to be maniacs who get up early enough to get to your first period class. But I have to tell you a little about how things were before I met Barbara so you'll appreciate what a miracle it was and how much it changed my life.

If I were David Copperfield, I would tell you about the first time I met Margaret, because it was before either of us were born. My father and Margaret's father grew up together in Germany and came to America at the same time and bought houses on the same block when their wives were pregnant. But I'm not David Copperfield, lucky for you, so I'll skip to the present.

Margaret's eyes were too large to stay neatly inside of her head, like other people's, and her frizzy black hair never stayed in her barrettes. Mothers loved her because she was always doing the stuff they thought their daughters should do—homework, Chemistry Club, and wearing shoes that made her feet look like a duck's. But they didn't know what she was really like.

On the morning I'm thinking of, Margaret's big brown eyes looked seriously at me, but if you knew her as well as I did, you would know deep down inside, she was laughing a mean laugh. It was the look she got whenever she was about to say something she knew would upset me. It seemed like upsetting me was her favorite hobby.

"Are you going to Marcia's party?"

Marcia was one of the girls Margaret and I had known since we were little. We'd been going to each other's birthday parties all our lives, so of course I was going to go, although I wasn't particularly looking forward to it. It would be the kind of party where only girls were invited, and Marcia's mother would organize games she thought we loved like charades and telephone. I'd been to a few parties lately where boys were invited, and we'd played kissing games like spin the bottle and post office. I liked those a lot better.

"Yes, Margaret. Of course, I'm going to Marcia's party."

"That's good," Margaret answered. "It would be so embarrassing if you didn't."

"What are you talking about? What would be embarrassing?"

"Well, it would be embarrassing for me if you didn't go because I told her to invite you."

"What do you mean you told her to invite me? She's my friend."

Margaret had a lot of annoying looks. But of all of them, the most annoying was the one she was doing now, acting like I was a sorry, silly person she felt sorry for.

"Oh, yes," Margaret said, "of course she's your friend. Forget I said anything. Actually, Marcia would probably be mad that I told you."

As if all by themselves, my hands curled into fists, and my teeth clenched together. Only Margaret made me feel this way. But she wasn't finished.

"It'll be fun, you know, because this is one of the last parties like this we'll have."

"What do you mean?"

"Well, you know, we're growing up. We'll be having grown-up parties from now on. I was talking about that the other day with my parents about my sweet sixteen party. It will be a completely different kind of party. It'll be formal, you know, at a hall. Maybe at the synagogue or a place like that. Everyone will be wearing formals, and we'll have a nice dinner. And a band. For dancing."

"Really. You're already planning it?"

"Well, you have to rent halls a long time in advance. If they're . . . you know . . . nice."

"Like a wedding."

"Well, I guess. A little. What're you going to do?"

"I haven't started thinking about it."

"No, I guess you wouldn't."

"What does that mean?"

"Well just that you don't plan so much for the future."

"Margaret . . ."

"And of course you'll have to bring a date. Everyone will have to bring a date."

"A date?"

"Yeah. But don't worry about it. I'll be able to fix you up."

"You. What?"

"I'll be able to fix you up. I'll have a boyfriend. And he'll probably have friends."

"How do you know I won't have a boyfriend?"

She gave me that same annoying smile again, like she was feeling so sorry for me for thinking I would ever have a boyfriend, let alone in only two years. Because at that very minute she was looking into a crystal ball and knew for sure I would not have a boyfriend by the time of her not-very-sweet-sixteen party.

"It's not like I've never gone out with a boy, you know." Why was I even bothering? It seemed as if I couldn't help myself.

"I remember. You went to the movies with that boy. Wasn't his name Dennis? Of course. He was in ninth grade."

She said "ninth grade" like it was an incurable disease. We were walking toward a tree with a thick branch hanging over the sidewalk. In my mind, I saw my hands grow bigger and stronger until they reached up and yanked the branch off the tree and beat Margaret's head with it until she cried and begged me to stop.

Chapter Seven

I figured the worst was over. Now that Margaret thought she'd made me feel like I had no friends and I would never have a boyfriend, the rest of the trip would be peaceful, especially since we had reached the subway. We walked slowly down the stairs, being careful not to trip on the wads of crumpled newspapers. It was hard to see at first, going from bright sunshine to gloomy station.

But I was wrong. Even while she was holding onto the dirty wooden banister and looking down at her feet, Margaret continued talking.

"I'm really worried about you, Paula. Ten whole days without rock and roll."

What now?

"What are you talking about, Margaret?"

We were walking toward the turnstiles and Margaret looked over at me. Her smile spilled out of her big eyes and spread all over her face. Even her nose was smiling.

"Well. You won't be able to listen to rock and roll while you're staying at my house."

"While I'm . . . what?"

"When your mother goes to Cleveland. What did you think you were going to do when she went away?"

What a good question. But here's an even better one. Did I even know that my mother was going to Cleveland? *No!*

A couple of weeks ago, my mother said she was *thinking* about going to Cleveland to help her sister, Carol, after her baby was born, not *making plans for me while she was away* going. Actually, when she said it, I wished I could go with her. Aunt Carol was the best grown-up I knew. She used to come over and play with me and take me to the movies. She seemed to really like being with me. But she got married and moved to Cleveland and was having a baby of her own, so she probably wouldn't care about me anymore.

I looked back at Margaret, who was grinning like she just won the World Series, just because she knew something I didn't. I couldn't let her think she was right.

"I . . . um . . . didn't really think that much about it. I thought I would just, you know, stay home."

"For ten whole days? My mother is right. You do have your head in the clouds. My parents borrowed a bed. You'll be sleeping with me. In my room. It'll be like being sisters."

Talk about a terrible thought. Margaret as a sister. But here's one that was even more unpleasant. Storing me in Margaret's house like I was a plant that had to be watered every morning. What would my mother have done if Margaret hadn't blabbed? Tape a note to the door? *I went to Cleveland. Your clothes are at Margaret's. Love, Mama.*

Chapter Eight

I knew Margaret thought I was going to spend the day worrying about whether Marcia was my friend and why she knew more about my life than I did. But she didn't know I had much more important things to think about. So, as soon as we sat down in our first period geometry class, I forgot all about Margaret, Marcia, and Cleveland and thought about my new friend, Holden, and being cool. I couldn't wait for third period to be over.

I pushed my way out the door and walked down the hall, feeling like I was floating on a cloud. And sure enough, there she was. My beautiful new friend. Walking with the girl I'd seen her with before. The mean-looking one with the penciled-in eyebrows and sneering mouth. She wasn't as pretty as Barbara, although she had the same blonde streaks in her hair and wore a fuzzy white sweater similar to the one Barbara had worn the other day.

I smiled and waved. "Hi, Barbara."

Barbara's eyes and mouth opened at the same time, and her cheeks turned even redder under her makeup. It was like she was robbing a bank and the police walked in. She turned to the other girl, but she was staring directly at me. She squinted her eyes, like she was examining something very closely, and pulled one corner of her mouth to the side until I thought it might touch her ear. And then they turned and were gone. Past me down the hall.

How could I have been so stupid? Waving, like a complete jerk, like some old lady calling, "Yoo-hoo! Yoo-hoo!" across the hallway. I even said Barbara's name, so there was no doubt in anyone's mind who the creepy girl was waving at.

I scarcely heard a word in my next two classes. They were boring even when I didn't have anything important to think about. And now I had something very important to think about—how totally miserable I was. How I'd had what I wanted in the palm of my hand and dropped it.

At lunchtime, I took my tray to the table behind the pillar—our table—even though I knew Barbara wouldn't eat there or even talk to me again. I ate alone and thought about Holden, who generally didn't have anyone to talk to or eat with, either. But that was mostly because when he did have someone to talk to, he was rude and nasty and they stopped talking to him. Waving wasn't nearly as bad as some of the stuff Holden did. It just wasn't cool. Holden never thought about being cool.

All of a sudden, Barbara stood next to me, looking down angrily.

"Don't ever, ever, ever do that again, okay?"

"Okay. I won't. Definitely."

"You better not."

She was gone. I wanted to cry again, but this time in relief. She would still be my friend. And I swore an oath to myself that I would never look at her again when the other kids were around.

Chapter Nine

Reporters all around me are calling, "Miss LaVie. Miss LaVie."
"Tell us about your new movie."

"Is it true that you're going to shoot it in Paris?"

I smile and wave from the top of the steps outside the airplane door. "Yes. Paris. Needless to say, Natalie Wood and I are very excited to be going to Paris. I've been there before, of course, but it's Natalie's first time."

"Everyone's excited about this one, Miss LaVie. Hollywood's biggest teen stars, Natalie Wood and Paulinha LaVie in one movie."

"Yes. It will be a—"

"Paula. What's wrong with you? I would appreciate an answer when I'm talking to you."

The airplane had vanished. The reporters were gone. I was not going to Paris or any place else. It was the evening after the morning Margaret had let me in on the secret Cleveland plan, and I was sitting at the kitchen table in my house in Queens. I waited for my mother to bring me my frozen dinner cooking in the oven. Turkey in thick gravy with mashed potatoes. My mother was at the stove making dinner for my father. He liked food from Germany, where he was born, like Wiener schnitzel and cabbage. I liked food from America, where I was born, like turkey, stuffing, fried chicken, and mashed potatoes. And especially the newly invented frozen food, which tasted so much better than food in cans or anything my mother had ever cooked.

"I'm sure," I answered my mother's back, hoping the last thing I remembered her saying was the last thing she said, that "ninety-four was one of the highest marks on the French midterm."

She didn't turn around. "I thought you said you didn't know the other kids' grades."

I had made the mistake of showing my mother the French midterm, and she wouldn't stop talking about it. Like it was the most important thing in the world. Like it was the cure for cancer or the key to world peace. What was so important about a French midterm? Holden was the smartest person I knew, and he flunked out of school. More than once. Not that I could say that to my mother.

She brought me my dinner, which came in a metal tray divided into sections—turkey, mashed potatoes, peas, and dessert. I started to cut the turkey, but the tray slipped because my mother had brought it on a dinner plate. The plate was round and the tray was rectangular, so it stuck out on the sides and hung over the middle of the plate.

"Can I put the tray on the table? It keeps slipping."

"No. It will burn the tablecloth. Don't change the subject."

"What do we need the tablecloth for anyway? It's ugly. I like the table better without it."

"You know we have to protect the table. It came from Germany."

"Is it the table Daddy ate on when he was little?"

"How would I know? They probably had lots of tables. It was a big house. Don't forget your milk."

I spooned the last peas into my mouth. All the compartments

were empty except the one with the cherry cake. The best part. I forced down the rest of my milk. I didn't want the sourish taste to spoil the sweetness of the berries.

My mother's back asked, "What did Margaret get?"

I was expecting that question. But I wanted to talk about it while I was eating peas or mashed potatoes, not the best part of the whole dinner. I had already put a spoonful of the wonderful berries in my mouth, so I closed my eyes and pushed the syrupy berries to every part of my mouth, tasting them on my tongue and my gums and my lips and the roof of my mouth. I wished I could taste them with my teeth. I wished I could keep them in my mouth forever. I wished I could be eating bowls of syrupy berries and listening to rock and roll.

When the taste was gone, I answered, "I think . . . um . . . I think it was maybe ninety-six or ninety-seven."

My mother's back sighed.

"I got one of the best grades in the class."

She turned around and looked at me with a sad smile.

"I know, Paula. But you know that it . . . disappoints your father when Margaret does better than you do." She turned back to the stove.

"It doesn't happen very often. Is Margaret's father disappointed when I get a better grade than Margaret?"

"I'm not German. I don't know how Germans think. I only know what your father always says." She turned around, lowered her voice, and said in a mock-German accent, "I got better gradesss than Leo on efry test ve efer took, from kinderrgarrten to medikol skul."

We laughed. She was so pretty when she laughed. It was too bad she didn't do it more often. I wondered if she used to smile more, before she was married, before she met my father. I knew she had another boyfriend before she met my father. She told me she was really in love with him, but her mother made her stop seeing him because he didn't go to college. It seemed like I was full of wondering tonight. I wondered if my father noticed my mother didn't smile so often anymore. I wondered if I would ever be as pretty as she was. Or as tall. I looked like my father. And I was even shorter than Margaret.

"Margaret said that I was going to stay at her house when you were away. How come you didn't tell me?"

My mother stopped laughing.

"Well . . . uh . . . it's not for . . . uh, a couple of weeks yet."

"Is it true?"

"That's the arrangement we've made."

"Why can't I stay home with Daddy? He'll be home."

"Stay home with Daddy? What a silly idea. You know he's too busy to take care of a little girl. He wouldn't have the first notion of what to do. Who would get your clothes ready for school? Who would make you dinner? Gertie said they would be more than happy to have you. You'll have a wonderful time."

"No, I won't. I'll have a terrible time. I'll hate every minute of it. Every second."

"Look, Sarah Heartburn. Spending a few days with the Feldmans should be the worst thing that ever happens to you."

"Don't call me that. I hate it when you call me that. Sarah Bernhardt was the greatest actress in the world. You shouldn't make fun of her name." Sarah Bernhardt was_Paulinha LaVie's idol. But I didn't mention that.

"All right, Paula, all right. Calm down. You're so melodramatic. Everything is a tragedy. You have no idea how fortunate you are. When I was your age, it was—"

Oh no! The middle-of-the-Depression speech.

She continued, "The middle of the Depression. I worked every day after school and gave all the money—"

"To your mother."

My mother looked at me in surprise. It was like she had amnesia and didn't remember she'd told me this story a hundred times already.

"The question in my family wasn't what college I should go to. The question was—"

"If you could go to college at all. Because you had to work to help your family."

"Oh, very good, Paula. You're so smart. You know everything. Everything except how lucky you are. Why you're always so unhappy is a complete mystery to me. Moping around. Feeling sorry for yourself. Your father and I try so hard to give you a good life. You should be so happy. Anyway, it's all arranged. I'm going to help Aunt Carol, and you're going to the Feldmans'. It's too late to change your mind."

I started to say it wasn't my mind that needed to be changed. My mind never even knew about the plan. But we heard the front door open. My father was home.

Chapter Ten

I waited to leave the kitchen until I heard my father hang his coat in the closet and walk to the living room. He was sitting in the soft armchair reading his newspaper when I walked into the living room. The lamp was shining on the bald part of his head. I walked over to his chair and kissed him on the cheek.

"Hi, Daddy, how was your day?"

"Delightful. Only two patients died."

He was a surgeon in a cancer ward.

My mother was walking toward us, carrying my father's dinner. She put it on a little metal table and moved it in front of him.

My father said to me, "I know you have no time to waste on a chitchat with your old father with all the studying you have to do."

"I finished my homework."

"Already? Why don't you do tomorrow's homework. Then you can be ahead of the class."

"I don't know what tomorrow's homework is."

"Too bad. If you did, you could excel."

"Excel?"

"Be the smartest."

"I am the smartest."

"You are? Well, I suppose it's possible. It is a family tradition that goes back many generations."

He turned to my mother, and they began to talk about me as if I weren't there.

"Quite a scholar they're training at that school. Seven o'clock and she's finished with her homework."

"It's not her fault, Martin. It's the teachers."

"Really? Leo told me Margaret has some very fine teachers, especially in French, I think he said. You are in Margaret's French class, aren't you?"

My stomach started to sink toward my knees. But fortunately, my father didn't wait for me to answer or for my mother to tell him about the French midterm.

"That's what Leo said. I don't suppose she's doing as well as Margaret. After all, Gertie speaks French, so Margaret has the advantage of having a mother who can help her."

My mother sighed. "You've told me that several times. I studied Latin."

"I'm sorry if I repeat myself. But you, of course, are also repeating yourself. You told me that you studied Latin the first time we met. That was why we met a second time. But it doesn't help Paula with her French, does it?"

My mother looked like someone shut off her light switch. She turned her head from left to right as if she didn't know where she was and walked toward the kitchen without saying anything. I escaped to my room. I walked past the paintings my father had brought from my grandparents' house in Germany. Huge pine trees covered with snow and ugly people in old-fashioned, velvet clothes. I thought about how quiet my house was in the evenings. If they turned off the TV, people walking by would think there wasn't anybody at home. They might even think no one lived here.

Chapter Eleven

O f course, Barbara and I didn't cut our fingers and let our blood flow together. We didn't have to. I had taken a solemn oath, and I never broke it. Every day, Barbara and I passed each other in the hallway and stared straight ahead, like we had never seen each other before. A few times the other girl pointed at me and tugged at Barbara's sleeve like she wanted to ask her about me. But Barbara paid no attention to her, as if she couldn't understand what she was talking about, and after a while she forgot.

At least once a week, Barbara and I would be at the record store at the same time. We completely ignore each other.

A few times the other girl, whose name I found out was Sheila, tugged at Barbara's sleeve and asked if that wasn't the girl she knew.

Barbara said, "What girl? Nah."

I knew they were talking about me.

Barbara and I were so busy ignoring each other that one day we smacked into each other in the middle of the record store. I dropped my book bag and the records I was carrying. Barbara helped me pick them up, and we mumbled, "Sorry, sorry," and walked away. We spent the next day at lunch laughing about how even when we smacked into each other, no one could ever guess we even knew each other, let alone that we were friends.

I was afraid Barbara would get tired of having lunch with someone who could only talk about two things: *Catcher in the Rye* and pretending we didn't know each other. I tried to think of other things to talk about. But it was hard.

"We learned something really interesting about valences in chemistry yesterday." Yeah, right. "Did you hear about Betsy Ross making the first flag?" Even worse. And then Barbara solved the problem.

Barbara leaned over the table. "You know what I think?"

I could hardly answer, I was so excited.

"No, Barbara. What do you think?"

"I think that you don't have enough fun."

"Well, yeah, genius. That's not very hard to figure out. I don't have any fun."

"Well, genius. I think we should change that. Don't you?"

My heart started that loud beating I was always afraid she would hear. I took a deep breath and asked her in a voice that sounded like I didn't really care one way or another, "What do you have in mind?" I practiced that voice every day.

"Well, you know, I can't take you anywhere with me because you look like a creep."

"Thanks." I twisted my mouth into what I hoped was a sneer.

"I know. It's not your fault. Your mother makes you dress like that. But you know I could never face my friends again if they saw me with you."

Since I had met Barbara, I stopped buttoning the top button of my white blouses and putting a scarf or a pin on the front of the collar. I pulled the back of my collar up. It was definitely cooler, but obviously not cool enough. I didn't know what to do about the socks—I didn't have any shoes I could wear without them, except the fancy flats with the flowers, which I wore to dances. My mother would never let me wear those to school.

"So, how about coming over to my house this afternoon."

"This afternoon. But . . ." I stopped myself before I said that there was a Chemistry Club meeting that afternoon. Extracurricular activities were important when you were applying to college, which I would be in a couple of years. Missing them could jeopardize my whole future, not to mention my parents would have heart attacks if they found out I skipped Chemistry Club and went home with someone they didn't know. I could see them grabbing their chests and falling to the floor next to each other.

My mouth answered all by itself. "Sure, Barbara. I'll meet you by the gate."

I felt like I was Columbus sailing into unknown seas. It would be the first time in my life that my mother didn't know where I was.

Barbara made a funny face. "No. Don't do that. Meet me at my house. I'll write down the address. Give me a piece of paper."

"Hey, Barbara. You . . . Never mind. I see you're busy."

A deep voice rumbled from somewhere behind me, startling us both.

In about a second, Barbara's face changed from surprised to embarrassed to happy. "Hey, Andre. Wait up. I'm not busy. You got any butts?" She threw down the paper and walked around the table.

I wanted to see the owner of this deep voice, but I didn't dare turn around. And I didn't dare take the paper to see if she'd written her address or if Mr. Andre Deep Voice had just ruined everything.

He laughed. "I figured you had some."

"You figured right."

They both laughed. As their voices got softer and softer, I slowly turned around. It was pompadour boy. I reached for the paper. It had her whole address written on it.

Chapter Twelve

A secret rendezvous.
An exciting idea, but not easy to do for a person who was never alone. Or at least it seemed like I was never alone. The first thing I had to do was get away from my friends. We usually walked together from our last class to the chem lab. I pretended I had to go to the bathroom and waited in the stall until I was sure they were gone. Waiting was hard. I was anxious to get to Barbara's house before she changed her mind. I had no idea what was going to happen, but I knew it would be the greatest day of my life. First, I had to stand in the smelly stall, staring at the peeling paint.

When it sounded like there wasn't anyone in the hall anymore, I crept out and left the school. No one I knew was on the street, since they were all in Chemistry Club. I drew a couple of deep breaths because it felt like I hadn't been breathing for a long time, although I knew that if I really hadn't been breathing, I would be dead.

I worried about running into my friends' mothers, not that I'd ever met any of them in the subway coming home from school before. But it would be just my luck. I could hear them now.

"Paula. What's the matter? Why didn't you go to Chemistry Club? Are you sick?" And then the telephone call to my mother as soon as they got home from wherever they were going. "Helen, I saw Paula this afternoon. Why isn't she going to Chemistry Club anymore?"

My house was two stations away from school. Barbara lived a few blocks away, so it was the same train stop. I was terrified when the train stopped at the station before our houses until the doors closed and nobody I knew had gotten in.

Once I got out of the subway, I had to walk a few blocks. Even though I had never been to Barbara's house before, it was easy to find because the streets in my neighborhood are numbered. In order to get to Barbara's house, I had to walk past the supermarket and the dry cleaner, where my mother and her friends went. So, as I walked, I looked around in every direction. This wasn't just pretend hiding, sitting at a table by a pillar where everyone could still actually see you. This was for real hiding. Like a spy. Whenever I came to a corner, I pressed my back against the building and stuck my head around to see who was there.

Sure enough, I saw Marcia's mother up the block, walking toward me. I ducked into the supermarket and ran through the vegetables to the back of the store. I was halfway through the canned goods before I realized how stupid that was. Marcia's mother was probably coming to the supermarket and some of the clerks knew me, although I doubted they would tell my mother they'd seen me hiding in the canned vegetables aisle. I went over to the counter where they sold fish—my mother never bought fish—and I could see the front doors. The fish lined up, on crushed ice, seemed to be watching me with their glassy eyes.

Marcia's mother walked by the door to the supermarket without coming in. I almost cheered, but the clerks would probably remember that. "Mrs. Levy, is your daughter all right? She snuck in here this afternoon and cheered in the fish department. We were all surprised. Nobody ever cheered in the fish department before."

I quickly left the store and turned the corner onto Barbara's street. It didn't have any trees on it or yards, like my street, just apartment houses pushed together and fallen garbage cans. We never went into the front or the backyard, except maybe once or twice in the summer. But the yards made a lot of space around the houses and something nice to look at, like flowers in the summer and snow that wasn't slushy and gray in the winter. When I got to Barbara's building, I was exhausted from sneaking around. You can imagine how I felt when I discovered Barbara lived on the third floor and there wasn't an elevator. Barbara opened the door as soon as I rang the bell. She smiled and let me in.

Chapter Thirteen

T here were toys everywhere and glasses on the table with left-over milk in them. A newspaper had fallen open on the floor, and a shirt was crumpled up on the sofa. I tried not to look around because I didn't want Barbara to be embarrassed. I mean, my mother was embarrassed if a guest came over and her book was open on the table. Nothing ever stayed on the floor longer than it took to bend down and pick it up. But Barbara didn't seem embarrassed. She didn't even seem to notice.

"I told you, right, that I had this little brother and sister. Real brats. Can you imagine walking around with your old lady and she's pregnant? Never mind. I know what you're going to say. You're going to say that Holden had a little brother and sister and that he loved them more than anything. He went crazy when his little brother died. But I don't feel that way, okay?"

"Yeah, sure, it's okay. I always felt bad I didn't have a brother and sister like he did, but maybe it's not so great as he makes it seem."

"It isn't. Take it from me. They make noise and break stuff. And Tony acts like they're the greatest things in the world and whatever happens is always my fault because they're his kids and I'm not."

"But what about your mother? You're her kid."

"Yeah? So? She's too busy to really . . . Never mind. Luckily, none of them are here. The old lady is at work, and the brats are at the sitter's. C'mon. Let's go to my room."

I was in the house of a strange person my mother had never heard of, and we were alone without any grown-ups. I had landed in a new world.

I followed Barbara down the hall to her room like the brave explorer I was. The bed was unmade, and there were about twenty pictures of movie stars torn out of magazines and taped to the walls. Torn. Not cut neatly. My mother would never put Scotch tape on the wall. It would spoil the paint.

We had to step over a pile of dirty clothes to walk over to the bed and sit down.

Barbara said proudly, "My mother hates my pictures."

I didn't know Barbara's mother, but I couldn't imagine anyone liking Barbara's room.

"Mine would, too. She only likes things she picks out."

I stopped myself from saying any more. That was so creepy. Fortunately, Barbara wasn't paying attention to me. She opened a drawer in her night table, and a stale smell came out. The drawer was full of ashes and cigarette butts. She pulled out a pack of cigarettes, a book of matches, and a dirty ashtray.

Barbara lit a cigarette, breathed in deeply, and blew a cloud of blue smoke out of her mouth. I felt like there was a hundred miles between me and my eyes. Barbara blew a perfect smoke ring. It floated into my face and burned my eyes. She took another cigarette out of the pack and held it toward me. My arm wouldn't move. I wanted to say no. But I had to find a reason.

My mother would kill me? No. That wasn't cool. It'll stunt your growth? Or was that coffee?

"Come on. Take it. Don't be afraid."

I shook my head. "I don't really think—"

"Come on. It's not like it's going to get you pregnant."

"Pregnant? Barbara!"

"What a good girl. Take the stupid cigarette."

And for the second time in my life, I had to make an important decision. Either I took a cigarette, or I gave up the chance of having a cool friend. There were my parents lying on the floor again, the ambulance on its way. But one cigarette probably wouldn't stunt my growth that much. I was short anyway. It was probably coffee that stunted your growth.

I took the cigarette and held it between my fingers.

Suddenly, I wasn't me anymore. I was Paulinha LaVie. I was beautiful, and I was grown-up, and everybody loved me. I tossed my head back and smiled. A secret sexy smile that spread over my whole body. The room was filled with golden light. Slowly, like a ballet dancer, I made a circle in the air with the hand holding the cigarette.

"This feels great."

"It'll feel even better when it's lit, genius."

I put the cigarette between my lips, which formed around it like a kiss. Barbara struck a match and held it to the tip.

"Breathe the smoke in deep, past where it catches in your throat."

I breathed in. The smoke hit the back of my throat like a burning punch. I began to cough. Nausea rose from my stomach into my throat, and a sharp pain moved from my eyes toward the back of my head. The room was rolling like a boat. Barbara took a deep drag and blew the smoke out of her mouth. She wasn't sick.

"Don't feel bad. My first butt made me real sick. I didn't tell you that 'cause I knew you wouldn't try it if you knew how sick it was going to make you."

I ran to the bathroom.

When I came back, Barbara was smiling and putting a record on the record player. "Don't sweat it about the butts. It'll go away. You'll see." She pointed to a pack of gum on the table. "You'd better chew this chlorophyll gum, so your parents won't smell the cigarette on your breath."

I took a piece, although I figured if they smelled anything on my breath, it would be vomit.

"Anyway," Barbara said, "that wasn't what I wanted to show you. This is what I wanted to show you. It's going to make you forget all about being sick. It's going to make you forget all about everything."

I still felt dizzy, and there was a sour-bitter taste in my mouth. The gum tasted like medicine. I couldn't figure out why Barbara was making such a big deal about a record. I had lots of records.

"I thought you didn't have money to buy records," I said.

"I didn't exactly buy this."

"You didn't? But how . . . ?"

Barbara sneered. "What a good girl. Remember the day I was carrying a big purse?"

Suddenly, I saw my mother looking into a magic mirror and seeing me in Barbara's room. Next to the ashtray. Listening to a stolen record. Forget the ambulance. Take her body right to the cemetery. She'll never recover. And then the music burst into my brain and chased every other thought away.

"Well, since my baby left me

Well, I found a new place to dwell.

Well, it's down at the end of Lonely Street
At Heartbreak Hotel.

Where I'll be, I'll be so lonely, baby.
Well, I'm so lonely.
I'll be so lonely, I could die."

The music wrapped itself around me and hugged me. My heart pounded. I listened to rock and roll every day. I knew every new singer. But this was different. This was as different from all the other records as rock and roll was from all the other music.

"Who is that?"

"His name is Elvis Presley."

"What?"

"El-vis Pres-ley."

"What kind of name is that?"

Barbara shrugged. "Who cares? He's the greatest singer in the world."

Chapter Fourteen

I 'd been right. It was the most important day of my life. But not for any reason I had imagined. It was the day I first heard Elvis Presley. And Elvis Presley was all that mattered now. He filled my life. There were so many Elvis things to do. I had to go to the record store to buy "Heartbreak Hotel" and to the candy store to look for magazines with pictures of him and to Barbara's house to listen to records and smoke cigarettes.

I didn't have to worry Barbara would get tired of being my friend. She never got tired of talking about Elvis because she was always trying to figure out how to meet him. I sort of thought she was crazy, but I wasn't sure if that was me thinking or my parents, so I didn't say anything. Even if it was a crazy idea, it was exciting to think about. I went to Barbara's house every day and read every magazine we could find to see if he was going to come to New York. No matter how hard I tried, Barbara always found some magazine I hadn't seen.

"Where did you find this? I have all the ones they sell at Sammy's."

"Sammy's stinks. I got this in the store in the subway."

"You went in there? But it's so dirty and full of creepy guys. My mother told me never to go there. Does your mother let you?"

"I didn't exactly talk to her about it. But if you're afraid you'll get cooties . . ." Barbara pulled the magazine out of my hands and hid it behind her back.

I yelled, "Don't be a spaz!" trying to grab it back. Barbara pushed me away and opened the magazine on the bed so that we could both see it.

"Ohhh. These are cooool pictures. He is soooo cute. Are you sure he's only twenty-one? He looks . . . grown-up."

Barbara had this special look on her face when she talked about Elvis—all serious and grown-up—not like the rest of the time when she seemed mad or bored.

"Definitely. Only twenty-one." She said it like Elvis's age was the most important fact in the world.

"Eight years older than us."

"Eight years older than *you*, genius. You keep forgetting I'm a lot older than you are."

"Not a lot. Do you really think he would go out with a girl almost seven years younger than him?"

"Why not? If she's cool," Barbara said.

"I don't know. It seems like he would go out with girls who, you know, finished high school. Who's this girl with him?"

"Her name is Linda something. But she's not his girlfriend. He doesn't have a girlfriend. I know that for a fact. If I could meet him . . ."

"I bet he goes out with girls who are really, you know, fast."

"With him. I'd do anything. Anything."

"Barbara, if you went out with him, would you . . . do it?" I was nervous mentioning "it." I didn't want Barbara to know how little I knew about "it."

"You're such a baby. Do you want to live in Nowheresville all your life?"

Chapter Fifteen

"**G**oot morning, gehls!" Mrs. Feldman sang from the doorway. "Breakfast is ready."

Oh, yeah. The Feldmans. Talk about living in Nowheresville.

It all turned out just like Margaret said it would. My mother was in Cleveland. I was sharing a bedroom with Margaret. And I was having the dream.

I don't remember when I started to have the dream. It seems like I always had it. It's always the same. I'm in the subway station, and a train pulls in. But it is not a regular subway train. It is one long car painted black, without any windows. The doors open, and hundreds of people are trying to get out. All of a sudden, there are men on the platform pushing them back in. I try to run away, but somebody pushes me into the train. The doors close. It is dark. Elbows and shoulders are pressing into me, and I cannot breathe.

I wanted to open my eyes and see my room. It was the only way to make the dream go away. But I wasn't in my room. I was sleeping on the metal cot my father and Dr. Feldman had moved into Margaret's room last night.

"Good morning, sleepyhead."

Margaret's voice exploded in my ear. I could feel her breath on my cheek, and little drops of water sprayed my ear. It was disgusting. I opened my eyes. Her face was practically touching mine.

"Hurry, my parents are waiting."

I tried to push her away. "Waiting for what?"

"For us to come to the breakfast table, of course."

I'd never heard of anything called a "breakfast table" before. My father went to work before my mother woke me up. I made my own cold cereal and ate it by myself until my mother came in to tell me to stop dawdling or I would be late for school. I would say I wasn't dawdling. I was almost done.

"But I have to wash and get dressed."

"After breakfast. Put on your robe and hurry. My father usually has his first patient at eight."

Dr. Feldman's office was on the side of their house. He usually had funny stories to tell about his patients who didn't die all the time like my father's. When we came into the kitchen, Dr. Feldman was already sitting at the table, shaved and dressed, wearing the cleanest white coat I ever saw over his shirt and tie. He wasn't handsome like my father and spoke with a heavier accent. Margaret's mother was German, too, and they spoke German to each other. She was taller than her husband and worked as his nurse. She wore a white dress, white stockings, and white shoes, without a wrinkle or stain or speck of dust anywhere.

The table was set with brightly colored bowls and napkins made out of cloth.

Did they go to all this trouble to make a breakfast party for me?

Dr. Feldman smiled. "Goot morning, goot morning. How did you sleeeeep?"

No one had ever asked me that before.

I shrugged. "I slept okay."

"Thank goodness. Your father was so worried."

"He was . . . worried? About me?"

A warm feeling started to fill my chest.

"Oh, yes. Very worried. After we moved your bed into Margaret's room, he said, 'With a bed like this, the princess wouldn't need a pea to keep her awake.' And I said, 'It is a good bed. It was army surplus.' And he said, 'What army? Frederick the Great?'"

Dr. Feldman laughed. Mrs. Feldman didn't.

"Typical Hans," she murmured. Margaret's parents were the only people who called my father by the German name he didn't use in America.

The warm feeling vanished. My father wasn't worried about me. He was just making fun of Dr. Feldman, as usual.

Mrs. Feldman brought in steaming bowls of oatmeal covered with carefully cut slices of apple, brown sugar, and cream. The sweet smell of the oatmeal and the apple brought the warm feeling back.

Dr. Feldman continued, "As I'm sure your father has told you, Paula, Frederick the Great was the king of Prussia, where Mama and I and your father are from, during the eighteenth century. That would make your bed two hundred years old!"

I really didn't care about Frederick the Great. I wanted to eat this delicious-smelling oatmeal.

Margaret smirked. "Did your father tell you who Frederick the Great was?"

The spoon was almost in my mouth. I slowed down for a second and then decided to keep going. Frederick the Great had been waiting two hundred years. Margaret could wait two minutes.

"Yeah, sure. Lots of times," I answered after I swallowed, shrugging my shoulders. The oatmeal tasted as delicious as it smelled, and I wanted to eat it without talking about some dead king I'd never heard of before and, with luck, would never hear of again.

"I'm sure he did," continued Dr. Feldman. "He published an article about him when we were in high school. It was quite a feather in his cap."

Margaret was quick on the trigger. "Did he show you the article?"

The idea of my father telling me anything was ridiculous, let alone showing me an article that he wrote in German when he was my age, which must have been about a hundred years ago. Anyway, why would anybody care? There were probably a hundred million dead kings. But I had never tasted anything as delicious as this oatmeal, especially compared to the cold cereal I ate every day that tasted like cardboard. The cold milk I took out of the refrigerator to pour into the bowl made me shiver on winter mornings. Frederick wasn't greater than hot oatmeal with apples and brown sugar.

I answered quickly, between bites. "Yeah, sure, his article."

Margaret wasn't finished, but Dr. Feldman smiled and said, before she could say anything else, "And now you must tell me, my young scholars, what do they have in store for you today in school?"

Margaret sat up very straight in her chair. "We have tests in biology and in English. The biology test is about photosynthesis. That's what they call how plants breathe. The English test is about *Julius Caesar*, the play by Shakespeare."

Margaret was acting like she was in school instead of the "breakfast table." Her parents were looking at her like she was some kind of precious jewel. She was so busy showing off, she wasn't even eating. I wondered if I could have her oatmeal.

Dr. Feldman beamed. "Two very worthy subjects of study. Don't you think, Paula, that it is interesting that we breathe in oxygen and breathe out carbon dioxide, while plants do just the opposite? They breathe in carbon dioxide and breathe out oxygen."

Why on earth would I think that was interesting? It was like saying, "Don't you think it's interesting that we bought Louisiana from France instead of from Guatemala?" "Yeah, I guess. It's pretty interesting," I lied.

Without even raising her hand, Margaret said, "It's more than interesting, Papa. There wouldn't be any oxygen for us to breathe if plants didn't put it into the air."

"You are one hundred fifty percent correct, my young biologist. Perhaps even two hundred percent."

Mrs. Feldman looked at her watch and stood up. "Time to leave, girls. Don't forget to take your lunches."

Mrs. Feldman was holding a lunch box and a paper bag. She looked at me and smiled. It wasn't a phony smile. It was a really nice smile. As if she really was glad I was there and that she had the chance to make lunch for me. Gladder than my mother ever looked to make me lunch and kiss me goodbye. It made me want to hug her.

"I'm sorry about the paper bag, Paula, but the only other lunch box I had was Margaret's old Bugs Bunny lunch box."

She had made me lunch. She knew a kid's lunch box would embarrass me. She cared about embarrassing me.

"Thank you for everything, Mrs. Feldman. It was really nice of you to invite me to stay with you."

It was something my mother would have told me to say . . . except that I meant it.

"It's our pleasure, Paula."

That was something my mother would say, too, except it sounded like she meant it.

Chapter Sixteen

arbara and I were having lunch behind the pillar. A delicious
Mrs. Feldman lunch with homemade cookies.

"It's crummy, you know. Your parents making you stay someplace you don't want to go. What's it like there, anyway?"

"Well, it's weird. They all talk to each other all the time."

"What do you mean? Who talks to each other?"

"They all do. Dr. Feldman and Mrs. Feldman ask Margaret
what she did in school and then they talk about Shakespeare and
photosynthesis and Mrs. Feldman bakes cookies and makes this
delicious oatmeal. And they eat together on pretty dishes with napkins made from cloth. Do your parents do that?"

"Do what? Talk about photosynthesis? No. Why would my old
lady talk to me about plants breathing?"

I was surprised Barbara knew what photosynthesis was.

"Does your family eat together?"

"At dinnertime. But no one talks. I mean, not like a conversation. My mom feeds the kids, you know, and they always fuss, so
Tony gets mad because they're making noise, and she's a lousy
cook, and he worked so hard all day. And she gets mad at him for
getting mad at her. And if I say *anything*, they both get mad at me
and start bugging me about my grades and my friends. And I yell,
'Shut up!' and run to my room and slam the door. So, I try to wait

until I finish eating before I say anything because I don't want to have to run into my room when I'm still hungry."

"Tony?"

"My mom's husband."

I forgot he wasn't her father, so I changed the subject. "Nobody ever gets mad at the Feldman house. Especially not Dr. Feldman. And my father always makes fun of him."

"I figured him for a creep. I mean look at his daughter. Does Margaret have good records?"

"She doesn't have any records. She says that rock and roll is a communist plot."

"Sounds like a family of creeps. Phonies that can't even see their own phoniness. Holden would know what they were."

"Yeah," I answered. But for some reason I didn't understand, I felt like a traitor. I had no time to figure out why I felt that and who I was betraying because Barbara changed the subject.

"You know what I was sort of thinking about yesterday?"

"How can I know before you tell me, Barbara?"

She laughed. "Yeah. Good one, genius. I was thinking about how Holden is so nasty all the time. You know what I mean? I mean, he's so lonely and sad, but then he's so mean to everyone who likes him, and he makes them go away."

"That's true. He does it all the time. He's really mean to everyone that likes him."

"Yeah, right. But it doesn't make any sense, you know. I mean, why does he do it? If he's lonely, you'd think he'd be nice to people so they'd be his friend. And if he purposely makes people not like him, how can he feel bad when they don't like him?"

It was at times like this when I realized Barbara was smart. Her question was the kind of question teachers asked in class, not the kind of question kids usually thought up by themselves. Take me, for example. I read the book so many times, and I never thought of it that way.

"That's a really good question, Barbara."

"My friend, the honor student. I know it's a good question. What I'm looking for is a really good answer."

"Well, maybe it's because he's like scared, you know what I mean?"

"No. I don't know what you mean. Scared of what? The bogeyman." She waved her hands at me like she was trying to scare me.

"Scared of being like everyone else. I think it's really important for him to think he isn't like everyone else, like all the phonies. That he's different. But maybe he's afraid that it's not true. So, he does stuff to make himself different. He wears a stupid red hunting cap in the middle of New York City. He's rude to people who like him. If people liked him, then maybe he'd see he really isn't so different from them. Maybe if he was really different, he wouldn't need to wear a weird hat."

I felt like these thoughts were unrolling themselves. Like they were hiding deep inside my brain waiting for me to let them out.

Barbara was paying close attention to what I was saying. She actually looked thoughtful. She paused for a minute and said, "Is that what you do?"

"Yeah," I answered, "that's what I do. I never thought of it before. But you know what? This is so interesting. You do the opposite. You're nice to people, the cool kids, so they'll be your friends and won't know that you're really different from them."

"I told you not to talk about my friends."

"I'm not talking about your friends. I'm talking about you."

"So, you're saying I'm a phony."

"And you're saying I'm a phony."

"And we're both saying Holden was a phony, too."

"I guess he was. I guess that's why we're friends."

"Yeah, but we're a bunch of phonies who know we're phonies and that makes us different from all the people who are phonies and don't know they are phonies."

Chapter Seventeen

*A*fter I realized Barbara was really smart and could think about
Catcher in ways I'd never thought of, I tried to share other
books and stuff with her. I mean, there weren't any other books like
Catcher, but there were still other books I liked. And I really liked
poems. At least the ones that said things I knew were true but
couldn't have said myself as clearly.

One time I tried telling her about a poem by Lawrence Fer-
linghetti that was about "wonder." Just saying the word to myself
sometimes made me almost cry with excitement. I told her this
poem I really liked talked about waiting for all these different kinds
of things. It even mentioned Elvis Presley and said he was waiting
for him and Billy Graham to exchange roles.

"Billy who?"

"Graham. He's this famous religious guy. Like a minister."

"A religious guy?"

"Yeah."

"And he's waiting for him to change places with Elvis?"

"Yeah."

"That's dumb."

"No. It's not dumb. I mean, don't you think it's cool for a
poem to mention Elvis? I'll bet this is the only poem ever written
that mentions Elvis."

"Poetry is for creeps. Even a poem that wants you to think it's cool by talking about Elvis."

"But . . . I mean . . . that wasn't even the part I really wanted to tell you about. What I really wanted to tell you is after he talks about all these different things in the poem that he says he's waiting for, he says he's waiting for a rebirth of wonder."

"A rebirth of wonder. You think that's cool?"

"Well, yeah. Don't you? Doesn't it sound exciting? A rebirth of wonder."

"You want wonder?"

"Yeah."

"Ask your mother for another sandwich."

"What?"

She pointed to my sandwich. "What's that?"

"Tuna fish."

"On the inside. What's that mushy white stuff on the outside of the tuna fish?"

"Wonder Bread. Oh God, Barbara. I don't think that's funny."

And I didn't. But she did. She laughed until the lunch period was over.

Chapter Eighteen

"Where is your next trip, Miss LaVie?"

"Memphis, Tennessee. I'm leaving tomorrow."

"Any chance you'll be meeting Elvis Presley there?"

"I certainly hope—"

"What're you doing after school tomorrow?"

Margaret threw this sentence at me from across the room. This was my fourth night at the Feldmans'. I was starting to get used to being there. Except for sharing a room with Margaret at night when I crawled into bed and wanted to crawl into my mind and fall asleep. I'd never shared a room with anyone before. I hoped I never would again. At least not with anyone like her. Blah. Blah. Blah.

"Can we talk about it in the morning, Margaret? I'm tired."

"How come you're so tired? I guess it takes a lot of energy to hang out with juvenile delinquents."

I felt like someone poured freezing water into a hole in the top of my head and let it run though my body to my feet. Paulinha LaVie was definitely not going to meet Elvis tonight. I sat up and looked at Margaret.

"What're you talking about?"

"Don't pretend to be stupid. Everyone sees you two hiding behind the pillar. And you haven't been to Chemistry Club in a month. So, we figured you were out doing, you know, gang stuff."

"That's stupid, Margaret. I don't even know what you mean by 'gang stuff.' All we do is eat lunch."

"All afternoon? During Chemistry Club?"

It was like I was on trial, and Margaret was trying to convict me of a crime. *Doing gang stuff when you should be in Chemistry Club. Off with your head.*

"Margaret, come on. Let's just go to sleep, okay? It's late."

"None of us can figure out why you would be friends with someone like her."

None of "us"? Who was this "us," and why were they talking about me?

Margaret didn't wait for me to answer. "And. Anyway. My parents said . . . I mean . . . I thought that when you were living here, we would be like sisters. And now you don't even eat lunch with me."

She sounded hurt. I couldn't believe it. I couldn't believe that she wasn't as sick of me as I was of her. Cool kids didn't care about other people's feelings. But I did. I mean, Margaret was a big pain in the neck, but I didn't want to purposely make her feel bad. And anyway, if Margaret got mad at me, she could tell her parents about Barbara and Chemistry Club. And anything her parents knew, my parents would know in about ten minutes or less.

"Sisters don't always eat lunch together. Look at Diane. She has a sister. And they don't eat lunch together."

"They go to different schools. How can you be friends with someone who bleaches her hair and wears tight clothes and plays hooky and makes out with boys who are in gangs and carry guns and—"

"Stop it. You don't know anything about her."

But Margaret didn't stop. Not even to take a breath.

"She steals stuff. She's in a gang. Maybe you'd rather be in a gang than go to college."

"Oh, Margaret, that is so stupid."

"You called me stupid."

"No. I didn't. I just said that you said something stupid."

"It's the same thing."

"No, it isn't. Anyway, you call me stupid all the time."

"That's because you are. It was stupid of you to call me stupid. I know lots of things. Things that you don't know and they're about you."

Margaret's high, squeaky voice was angry.

"What are you talking about?"

"That's for me to know and for you to find out."

Margaret had finally stopped talking and was letting me go to sleep in peace. But it was too late. I couldn't stop thinking about what she had said. Was she just showing off, or did she really know something I didn't know? Was it important, and was she ever going to tell me?

Chapter Nineteen

J was eating a frozen fried chicken dinner with mashed potatoes and gravy and corn. My mother was home. No more breakfast tables and discussions of photosynthesis. No more oatmeal and dishes that matched.

My mother was facing the stove, cooking my father's dinner.

Without looking at me, she said, "You haven't told me about how it was staying with the Feldmans. I take it you didn't hate every second of it like I seem to remember somebody saying they would."

"Yeah. I didn't hate every second. It was okay. Mrs. Feldman makes oatmeal with apples and brown sugar and these really delicious sandwiches for lunch out of raisin bread with cream cheese and—"

My mother banged the mixing spoon on the stove and turned around.

"Don't tell me there's going to be another member of this family comparing me to Saint Gertie all the time. Too bad your father didn't marry her. If Saint Gertie was your mother, you could have wonderful sandwiches all the time."

I stared at my mother. She looked really angry. I couldn't believe it.

"Why are you mad? You asked me what it was like there. So, I told you about oatmeal and raisin bread sandwiches."

"One week with Saint Gertie, and Wonder Bread isn't good enough for you anymore."

"Of course, Wonder Bread is good enough for me. It helps build strong bodies eight ways, doesn't it? I just said that there was this other bread that I'd never tried before, and I liked it. I wouldn't have said anything if I knew you were going to go crazy."

"Don't you dare talk back to me, Paula Levy. I'll tell your father."

"Tell him what? That you called Mrs. Feldman 'Saint Gertie' and said he should have married her? You always told me that she wanted to marry him, but he didn't want to marry her."

The angry look rolled off my mother's face. In its place was the sad look she got when my father said things like knowing Latin doesn't help with French. I hated when I made her feel that way, although lately it seemed harder and harder not to. I finished dinner without saying anything else.

My father was sitting at his desk with the television on, looking at his stamp albums. Instead of walking past him to my room, like we both expected me to do, I stopped in front of his desk. He looked up with a frown.

"Dr. Feldman said you published an article about Frederick the Great when you were in high school."

He looked surprised. I didn't blame him. We didn't usually have little chats about Prussian kings after dinner. Or anything else.

"Leo always talked too much."

"Is it true?"

"Yes. But it was long ago. Why the sudden interest in Frederick the Great?"

"Dr. Feldman said it was a big deal publishing an article when you were in high school."

"Maybe it was a big deal to him. He didn't publish anything.

My father didn't think it was a 'big deal.' He said, 'You have a great career in front of you, bringing honor to famous anti-Semites. Who's next on your list? Savonarola?'"

"But that's so mean. Who's Savo . . . what you said?"

"Savonarola. An Italian monk who burned Jews at the stake before they burned him."

"He got burned at the stake?"

"Hanged actually. Then burned."

"He got hung because he killed Jews?"

"No. He was hanged because he tried to make the Florentines moral. Why this sudden interest in world history? Americans don't study Europe."

He called me an "American." Like I was from a different country from him. Which I guess I am.

"We study England."

"That isn't Europe."

I started to turn away. I didn't have anything else to say. So, it was pretty surprising to hear my father say, "By the way. What's the name of that singer you listen to all the time?"

I turned back. "Singer? What singer?"

"You know. The one you play all the time. Alvin something?"

"Elvis Presley?"

The name felt strange in my mouth. I never talked about him with anyone but Barbara, even though everybody had heard of him by now. "Heartbreak Hotel" was the number one song in the whole country. At least, that's what they said on the radio. I didn't know anyone besides Barbara and me who bought his records or even liked rock and roll. Margaret never got tired of reminding me that rock and roll was a communist plot, and I was a dupe being undermined by the minute.

Whenever she said it, I would ask her, "How did you find that out, Margaret? Did the communist plotters call you? Long distance from Russia? What an expensive call."

And every single time, she would get angry and answer, "Ha. Ha. Very funny. You think everything is a joke. Well. This isn't a joke. It's the truth. My mother told me."

"Oh. Your mother told you. Did the communist plotters call her?"

"No, birdbrain. She read it in the newspaper. And do you know what else she read about that Elvis Presley singer you love so much?"

"Elvis Presley is a communist?"

"No, Paula. Elvis Presley is not a communist. He's a dope fiend."

I hoped my father was not going to tell me Elvis was a dope fiend. I wondered if he even knew what a dope fiend was. I wasn't sure myself.

"Yes," my father was saying, "that is the name of the singer you listen to all the time, isn't it?"

I nodded.

"Well," he continued, "it seems that one of my patients does something or other in television, I believe. When I told him I had a fourteen-year-old daughter, he asked me if you'd heard of this . . . Alvin Preston. I told him you had already worn out his record several times. So, he said to be sure to tell you that Alvin . . . whatever . . . is going to be on television in a couple of weeks. On *The Milton Berle Show.*"

I didn't know which part of what my father had just said was the most amazing. My father talked about me to his patients. I wanted to ask him what he said about me. Did he say I was smart?

And pretty? He was too proud to admit to anyone that he had an ugly and stupid daughter, even if that was what he thought. But I would have to think about it some other time. Because right now the fact that I was going to be able to see Elvis on television was the most amazing, unbelievable, incredible thing I had ever heard in my life.

I asked, "Are you sure?"

"I don't believe he had any reason to lie to me."

"Milton Berle?"

"Yes. Isn't that what I just said? Is there more than one Milton Berle?"

"I don't think so."

"Nor do I. I suppose you'll want to watch."

Everybody in America watched *The Milton Berle Show.* Even my family. Every Tuesday night. So many people watched him they called him Mr. Television.

"Don't you?"

"Only a fool resists the inevitable."

Chapter Twenty

I t was the news of the century. Even cool kids would want to know about this. I knew a sacred vow was a sacred vow. But this was different.

Barbara and Sheila were coming toward me. I crossed over the hall and stood in front of them. Barbara saw me the second before I started to talk and looked at me like I was a truck about to run her over.

"Guess what? I have the most incredible news. You're not going to believe this. Elvis Presley is going to be on Milton Berle's show."

They just stared at me. Without a word. A smug look spread over Sheila's stupid face. Her skinny pencil-line eyebrows rose up and disappeared into the streaky greasy hair hanging into her eyes. She turned to Barbara and pointed at me.

"Well if it ain't Miss Seven-a-Clock Nooz. Look who thinks she knows sompin' we don't know ten times more."

A great black hole opened in the floor underneath me, and I started falling. Except I was still standing in front of them. Given the choice, I'd have chosen falling.

I stammered, "You knew about it? You knew he was going to be on television?"

"Of course, *we* knew," Barbara answered. She had recovered

from her shock. But she wasn't my friend Barbara. She was Sheila's friend Barbara. You could tell by the matching sweaters, matching blonde streaks, and matching sneers.

"But. How did you find out?" Could her father have a patient who did something in television? I didn't think so.

Barbara grinned at Sheila. "Some of us don't waste all our time doing homework."

I saw a prize fight in a movie once. Now I knew how the loser felt. Punch. Punch. Punch. Sheila was pulling on Barbara's sleeve, trying to get her to leave. I had to talk fast.

"What are you talking about? Why didn't you tell me about Elvis?"

"You found out. Everyone knows about it."

And then. The most crushing blow of all.

Barbara continued, "He's been on TV a bunch of times. Sheila and me, we tried to get in to see him, but they didn't let us in."

"He's been on television before?" I turned away because my eyes were burning with tears of betrayal and rage.

Was she ever really my friend?

Barbara and Sheila kept smiling at each other like no one else in the world mattered to them.

"Yeah. A couple of times." Barbara shrugged, like what she was telling me was the most ordinary thing in the world, like brushing your teeth or doing math homework. Not that she did math homework, but she probably brushed her teeth.

"There were like a hundred girls there. But they didn't let us in. They said we needed tickets. And that we had to be with a grown-up. Then they called the cops to get us away from the doors."

"You were chased by the police?"

I tell her everything, and she never told me anything.

"Don't you hate that?" Sheila interrupted. "When people think you're a kid?"

"You are a kid."

"What are you, a cop?" Sheila said nastily. "Who says so?"

What an idiot. What would Holden think of Sheila? Nothing. She was too stupid for him to even notice. But she was my friend's friend. The friend who loved Holden as much as I did.

It was too late for me to say anything but the truth.

"Everyone says so. How come you didn't tell me? I could have come with you."

"Yeah, right. Mommy and Daddy would let you come with us. What's with the twenty questions? What're you writing a book? I can't tell you everything in the world, you know."

Twenty Questions was a game show on TV. Barbara said that whenever I was annoying her with too many questions. I usually felt bad when she said it and stopped right away. But this time I didn't care.

"I don't want you to tell me everything in the world. But you could have told me that Elvis was on TV. I mean, I could have seen him."

"Yeah, well we didn't see him, either. So, we're even. You can see him on *The Milton Berle Show*. Sheila and I are going down there, and this time we're going to get in."

"How will you get in this time?"

Sheila actually moved in between Barbara and me. "Don't waste your time, Barbara. She ain't coming with us." They walked away.

I shouted at their back, "Fine. Go get yourself arrested. I don't care. Don't come crying to me to come bail you out."

Yesterday, seeing Elvis on TV seemed like the greatest thing that could ever happen. Today, I knew it was only the greatest thing that could ever happen to squares. Barbara wasn't going to be watching *The Milton Berle Show* on television in the living room with her parents. Barbara and Sheila were going to see Elvis in person. Maybe they would even sit in the front row, and Elvis would see how pretty Barbara was, and he would ask her out. Barbara would be the coolest girl in America. She would never be my friend again.

I watched Barbara and Sheila walk away. I didn't want to live another minute. Until Barbara turned around and winked.

Chapter Twenty-One

"This is it. This is my big chance."

I didn't know what to expect when I went to Barbara's house that afternoon. Was she my friend or Sheila's friend? Would she even let me in? But it was my friend who opened the door and gave me a big grin.

"You know I had to say that stuff, right? I mean, what was I supposed to do? You come running up to talk to me in front of everyone. What did you expect?"

"It wasn't everyone. It was only creepy Sheila."

"Creepy Sheila tells everybody everything. Telling her you're my friend would be like putting it on the front page of a newspaper. Worse. 'Cause no one I know reads newspapers. But they all know Sheila."

"How come you never told me about Elvis being on TV before?"

"Tell you what? That I didn't meet Elvis? I didn't want my old lady to find out I went there."

"But. I don't even know your mother. Why would I go to some woman I never met and tell her that her daughter snuck out to see Elvis? It's ridiculous. You mean, you went out at night and your mother didn't know?"

"Right, genius, my mother didn't know."

"How did you go out without her knowing?"

Barbara shrugged. "I told her I was sleeping over at Sheila's. Sheila told her old lady she was sleeping over at my house. When we got back from the city, we both went home and told them we had a fight and didn't want to stay with each other anymore. So, they both thought we were at the other person's house when we were trying to get into the TV show. We do that all the time. They always fall for it. My old lady even asked me one time how come I keep doing stuff with Sheila when we're always fighting."

"But you could have told me."

"You didn't even know who he was. You were still listening to Perry Como. But this time we have a plan. And we're going to get in."

"Why can't you tell me? How did you find out about it, anyway?"

"You know, you're starting to bug me. It's not like you can come with us. Mommy and Daddy would never let you."

All of a sudden, I had the worst thought I ever had in my life. Ever since I heard rock and roll for the first time, I was waiting for it to change the world. I kept thinking that it hadn't happened yet. But what if I was wrong? What if rock and roll had already changed the world and I'd missed it? What if I'd been left behind with all the other people whose mommy and daddy would never let them? And what if there wasn't even any way to find out whether I'd missed it or not?

Chapter Twenty-Two

I was having the dream. I was in the train station being pushed into the car without windows when my mother woke me up for school. My head felt like it was filled with crumpled paper.

I tried to walk quickly past Margaret's house because I wanted to be alone. But she came running down the path to meet me. It was like she had X-ray vision. It seemed like if I left for school in the middle of the night, Margaret would come running down the path in her pajamas.

"Where were you last week?" Margaret cried in her hysterical, opposite-from-cool voice.

"Last week when?"

"You know very well when. You missed Chemistry Club and orchestra. Where were you?"

It was true. I'd missed them both.

"What's with the twenty questions? What're you . . . I mean. I was busy. There was a lot of homework."

"No, there wasn't."

"Well. I was working on a special project."

"No, you weren't. You weren't even home."

"You mean you checked? Are you a detective? Did you use a magnifying glass?" *Not that you need them with your giant bug eyes.*

"Ha. Ha. Everything with you is a joke. Well, colleges care a lot about extracurricular activities. Or don't you care about going to college anymore?"

"Why are you always accusing me of not caring about college?"

"You hang around with kids who are in gangs. You don't go to any extracurricular activities. It seems pretty obvious, if you ask me. But what I would like to know is if your parents know that you missed Chemistry Club and orchestra?"

"Why? Are you going to tell on me like a dirty snitch?"

I certainly didn't want my mother to find out. I didn't mean to insult Margaret. But it slipped out.

"You called me a dirty snitch."

"No, no, Margaret. I didn't. What I meant was that a person who tells on another person might be considered, by some people, not necessarily by me, to be a snitch. And some people, not even necessarily me, for example, might think that being a snitch is not a nice thing. But . . ."

"Don't give me that. It's the second time you called me a bad name. You think I'm a real dope. You can just go around doing whatever you want and calling people whatever you want. Well, you'll see."

She didn't say one more word for the rest of the trip to school. If I hadn't seen it with my own eyes, and heard it with my own ears, I would never have believed Margaret could be quiet for so long. I spent so much time wishing she would shut up that I should have been happy. But I wasn't. She was up to no good. I could just feel it.

Chapter Twenty-Three

*I*t was ten days until *The Milton Berle Show*. It was a long ten days. Barbara never shared her "big plan" with me, even though I kept going over to her house and talking about Elvis, Elvis, and more Elvis. I had to keep pretending I wished her luck and didn't care that she didn't tell me because I was so happy to be seeing him on TV, which was going to be the best thing that ever happened in my world.

The night finally came. *The Milton Berle Show* started at eight o'clock, but I went to the living room early and pulled open the big wooden doors of the television cabinet. I was glad we'd bought a new TV with a seventeen-inch screen. The picture was so much bigger than the twelve-inch one we had before. Of course, the TV was much bigger, too, and we had to move all the furniture around to make room for it. Our furniture was big and carved out of dark wood, so even though the TV was new and from America and the rest of the furniture was old and came from Germany, it fit in pretty well. As far as color was concerned—not space. There wasn't a lot of room to move around in.

I wiggled into the sofa. It came from Germany and wasn't very comfortable. The cushions were hard and slanted, and I had to keep my feet on the ground to keep from sliding off. The striped material had ridges in it, like a fat corduroy, which made dents on the back of my legs if I sat on it too long.

You may think from what I just said that I didn't like our living room very much, and you would be right. I thought the living rooms people from America had were much nicer—small, light, wood tables and soft cushions on the sofa. Margaret's living room looked just like ours, although the sofa was comfortable.

My mother came in and sat down next to me.

"Well, tonight's your big night, eh, Paula? I hope you're not disappointed."

"Disappointed? How could I be disappointed?"

"Well, you're always so dramatic about everything. The best this. The worst that. I don't know how anything can ever live up to your expectations. I shudder to think about what will happen the first time you fall in love. Romeo and Juliet and Hamlet and Madame Butterfly all rolled up in one."

That was the kind of mean thing my mother said a lot. But I didn't have time to answer because my father came into the room and sat down next to her.

"Are you sure you want to watch Berle tonight? I understand there's a very interesting program on another channel."

I looked at him in horror. But he was smiling. And so was my mother. They even smiled at each other like they were sharing a joke.

"Maybe next week, Martin. It seems your daughter has suddenly become a big fan of Milton Berle."

The theme song began.

"We are the men of Texaco, we work from Maine to Mexico . . ."

The announcer interrupted the music. "Tonight's program is being broadcast from the deck of the USS *Hancock* docked in the naval air base in San Diego, California."

"What? What did he say?"

California? No. It couldn't be. California was thousands of miles away. Elvis was thousands of miles away from Barbara and her secret plan. She wasn't going to be the coolest girl in America. She—

But I couldn't think about that anymore because *there he was.* Oh, my God. It was Elvis. In our living room, a few feet away from where I was sitting. Elvis was holding his guitar and smiling. How could I ever have thought this wouldn't be the greatest moment of my life? I tried to keep from screaming. I held my breath and pressed my fingers into my mouth. I knew I was making funny little moaning sounds, and my parents were looking at me. But I couldn't help it.

And then he was singing "Heartbreak Hotel." There was never anything like this before. The way he moved his hips. The way his long dark hair fell over his eyes. I wanted to dance. I wanted to feel the music in every part of my body. Maybe my parents would scream, too. Maybe we would all get up and dance together.

My father's loud voice drowned Elvis out. "Good God, it's even worse when you have to look at him."

My mother answered, "I don't know why Milton Berle would have such a person on his show. Do you?"

"No idea. Berle is not exactly high drama, but this is beneath even him."

My breath caught in my throat. How could these people be my parents? Why do I even know them?

When the song was over, Elvis came out to talk to Milton Berle. And suddenly I didn't care about not being able to smoke or having to wear saddle shoes and knee socks. There was only one thing in the world that mattered. I wanted what Barbara had wanted all along. I wanted to meet Elvis. I wanted to talk to him and look into his eyes and feel him looking into mine. I wanted to hear him say, "Hello, Paula," in his silky velvety voice that was different from anyone I knew because he came from the South. I had never met anyone from down South. I imagined him touching my hand, or even, oh, my God, putting his arm around my shoulders and walking with me like he was my boyfriend.

My body was tingling and numb at the same time, and my heart felt like it was too big to stay inside my chest. There was hardly any room for my breath to get around it.

The minute the show was over, I went to my room and closed the door. I didn't want to hear a single word from my parents. I didn't want to let them spoil the most perfect moment of my life. I closed my eyes so I could still see him, as if the television were inside my brain, and his picture would never go away.

Chapter Twenty-Four

J didn't remember falling asleep. Elvis was in my mind when I woke up as if he were waiting there on my pillow for me. I couldn't remember feeling so happy. Then I remembered Barbara. Where was she last night? What if she didn't find out Elvis wasn't in New York until it was too late to get home in time to see him? What if she was the only person in America who didn't get to see him? No. That was impossible.

I hadn't talked to Margaret since I called her a dirty snitch, so I was surprised to see her waiting for me in front of her house, all smiling and friendly.

As soon as she started to walk with me, I knew why.

Before even saying, "Good morning," or "How are you?" she said, "My parents and I always watch *The Milton Berle Show*. We look forward to it every week because we enjoy it so much. But we didn't enjoy it last night. Not at all. My father said, 'What is that caterwauling?' I said, 'He's that singer with the strange name. Elvis Presley.' And my mother said, 'Is *that* the singer Paula likes so much?' I said, 'Yes.' My mother shook her head and said, 'Helen says she plays his records constantly. Over and over again. Can you understand that?' I said, 'No.' And my mother said, 'Thank goodness I have a sensible daughter. Poor Helen.'"

It was like a slap and a punch at the same time, and I lost my breath and felt stinging in my eyes. My mother complained to Mrs.

Feldman about me. She complained that I listened to Elvis all the time. I didn't know she noticed. And Mrs. Feldman felt sorry for her because listening to Elvis was such a tragedy. Did that mean my mother wished she had a daughter like Margaret? A daughter who never listened to rock and roll and loved shoes that made her feet look like a duck's? What would she say if she knew I missed Chemistry Club and smoked?

I didn't want to fight with Margaret. But I couldn't help it.

"He's the most popular singer in the country. So maybe there are more people who think like I do than who think like you do."

I got ready to be attacked about communists and delinquents. But Margaret only said, "Do you remember the story about Cinderella?"

I thought I heard her wrong. "What?"

"The story about Cinderella. Do you remember it?"

Was she playing a trick or had she lost her mind? Probably both, knowing her. "Ye-es," I answered slowly. "I remember the story of Cinderella."

"Cinderella had stepsisters, right?"

"Right. Ugly ones." I stopped before I said, "Like you."

"Did they have the same father as Cinderella but a different mother? Is that what a stepsister is?"

"Step? No. I don't think so. I think if you have the same father and different mothers, you would be half sisters. Stepsisters are where you have different parents but one of your parents is married to one of their parents."

"Yeah. That's what I think, too."

I couldn't stand it any longer. "Margaret, have you gone crazy?"

Margaret's face was smiling and mean.

"You just called me crazy."

Chapter Twenty-Five

I couldn't wait for lunch. My mind was a television set that played only one program over and over. *The Milton Berle Show.* I could watch it whenever I wanted and wherever I was. Social studies. Biology. Intermediate Algebra. All I saw was Elvis. All I heard was Elvis.

I wasn't going to talk about him with anyone but Barbara. Not after what Margaret said. I waited at our table. Barbara never came. I couldn't understand it. Wasn't she dying to talk to me about the most important thing that ever happened? By the time I finished my sandwich, I knew I had to face the terrible truth. Barbara wanted to talk about Elvis with her cool friends, not with me.

I carried my tray to the window and walked toward the door. And then I saw her. Barbara. Sitting alone. I looked around but didn't see any cool kids. They always finished early. It takes less time to throw your lunch at people than to eat it, and they were always in a hurry to sneak a cigarette. I started to walk toward her. She got up and hurried away in the opposite direction.

Then I knew. She hadn't seen Elvis. She was at the studio in New York, where she thought he was going to be, but he wasn't there. By the time she found out, it was too late to go home and watch him on television. She told everyone she was going to meet Elvis and wound up not even seeing him on TV. All this time I was afraid I would lose Barbara as a friend because she was too cool. I never for one minute thought I could lose her because she wasn't cool enough.

Everybody in America saw Elvis. Margaret saw him. Margaret's parents saw him. Only Barbara didn't see him. And Sheila, I guess. But who cared about Sheila? If she hadn't been with Barbara, I would have been glad she didn't get to see him. It was like in the movies when someone bets all his money on one thing. Except in the movies, the person always wins in the end. In the movies, Barbara would have seen him, maybe even met him.

I knew why Barbara didn't want to eat with the cool kids. They would've laughed like crazy about her trying to sneak into a building in New York when Elvis was in California. But I wouldn't have. I would never laugh at her. Didn't she know that? Didn't she know I would've sold my soul to make it yesterday so I could tell her not to go to the studio?

Chapter Twenty-Six

I sat alone all lunch period at our table every day, even though Barbara was ignoring everyone else, not just me, from what I could see. She wasn't sitting with the cool kids at lunch, and she was never at the record store. Finally, one day, as I was staring into my soup, trying to figure out what the mushy little things were, I heard someone sitting down. It'd probably only been about a week, but it felt like forever, so this really happy feeling made my chest feel warm. Until I looked up and saw Margaret.

I asked her, "How come you're sitting here?"

She squinted her big eyes, which made them look the size of normal people's eyes, and hissed, "How come you're sitting here?"

"I always sit here."

"So I can, too. It's a free country."

People say, "It's a free country," all the time. It sounds like they're being patriotic. Like you should stand up and sing "The Star-Spangled Banner" for them. But it really has nothing to do with the land of the free and the home of the brave. It has to do with them telling you they're going to do something they know you don't want them to do. So, what they're really saying is, "Shut up and mind your own business because I can do whatever I want."

Which, as you already know by now, is pretty much Margaret's attitude toward life as far as I'm concerned.

Margaret carefully put her tray down on the table and arranged the plates and silverware as if they were fragile. Or valuable. She looked up at me and smiled, like she was proud of what a good job she did with her tray, took a blue envelope out of her book bag, and handed it to me. I recognized it right away. It came from the box of stationery I gave Margaret for her birthday last year. I told my mother it was a stupid present because Margaret never wrote any letters, but when you have to buy a birthday present for someone every year, you start to run out of ideas. My mother said you never knew when Margaret might want to write someone a letter, and she seemed to be right, although I'm sure she never thought it would be me that Margaret would write to since I saw her every single day.

"Margaret. For heaven's sake. Why on earth are you writing me a letter?"

"I . . . Open the envelope."

"Why can't you just tell me whatever it is you want to tell me? I'm sitting about three inches away from you."

"Just open it."

I picked up my knife, slid it into the back of the envelope, and carefully opened it the way my father always did. He collected stamps and was the most careful envelope opener you could imagine. When I looked inside the open envelope, at first I thought it was empty. I expected to see a letter written on the matching blue paper, but there wasn't one. I squeezed the sides apart, and a small white card was stuck in the corner. It was a snapshot. I pulled it out and squinted because it was pretty small. It was a picture of a man and a woman holding a baby. He had his arm around her shoulder, and they were smiling at the camera. Her body leaned against his. You could tell it had been taken a long time ago from the old-fashioned clothes they wore and the big square car passing by. I didn't think they were in New York. Maybe not even in America. The buildings around them were small and had spiky roofs and archways. There was a tower with a clock in it. They looked like buildings in a book of fairy tales.

I looked up. Margaret had the weirdest look on her face. Like she could hardly wait for what was about to happen because it was so exciting. Like Elvis was going to walk into the cafeteria and sit down at our table.

"Why are you showing me this?"

"Look at the man, Paula."

The man was young and wore a checkered cap with a brim set at an angle. His sweater was made out of the same checks, and his loose-fitting pants had the same checks, only smaller. They had big cuffs at the bottom. I'd never seen a man dressed in such snazzy clothes. I'd never seen a man smiling such a snazzy smile, either. All the muscles in my body pulled into a knot in the middle of my stomach. Underneath that happy young face was my father.

I felt Margaret watching me. Whatever it was she thought I was going to do, I didn't want to do it. I wanted to keep looking at the picture, but I figured that's what she wanted me to do, so I handed it back to her and said in the most casual voice I could manage, "Why are you showing me this?"

"Don't you know who that is?"

"No," I lied. Maybe she didn't know who it was.

"You dunce, it's your father."

She knew. Maybe she wasn't sure. Maybe I could raise a doubt in her mind.

"It is not."

"It is so. Just look at him. It's so obvious. Did you ever see a picture of your father when he was young?"

"Yeah. Of course. Maybe."

"Yeah, right. Maybe not. Because if you had, you would rec-ognize him."

"How do you know he's my father?"

"God, Paula, I have to tell you everything. For one thing, it looks like him. And for another, look on the back."

I'd seen Mrs. Feldman's handwriting before, on birthday cards and stuff. It was very neat but had big flourishes on capital letters. So, I knew she was the one who'd written on the back of the picture: *April 12, 1934. Hans and Lena Levy with baby Sophie.*

Well that made it pretty definite. Hans Levy. My father.

"Who are Lena and Baby Sophie?"

"What do they look like, dumbbell?"

The muscles in my stomach pulled tighter. I was glad I hadn't eaten my lunch yet because I felt like I was going to throw up.

"Stop calling me 'dumbbell,' dumbbell. If you're so smart, you tell me who they are. Are they friends of yours?"

"Oh, you're really funny, Paula. Funny like a crutch. What do they look like to you? I know what they look like to me. They look like his wife and his daughter."

The words "wife and daughter" sounded so loud when Mar-garet said them that I thought she had shouted them. But when no one turned around to see where the noise had come from, I knew they only sounded loud inside my head.

"His . . . But . . . What are you talking about?"

Margaret continued talking like she was reciting in a class. "She would be your half sister, not your stepsister. Remember Cinderella?

"Cinder—But how do you know that? That they're his wife and daughter. Do you know them?" I asked her. She seemed so sure of what she was saying.

"Know them? No, I don't know them." Margaret shrugged.

"You never met them?" I demanded again. "Then how do you know? Did your parents tell you who they were?"

"My parents?" Margaret shrugged again, like she didn't see the point of my question. "No, they didn't tell me anything. They don't even know I took the picture out of the picture drawer."

I was desperate. "So, then you don't really know who they are, right?"

But she was insistent. "Right. I mean wrong. That's not true. Just look at them. Isn't it so obvious?"

"No. I don't think it's so obvious at all. I mean, it's not even possible. My father doesn't have a wife and daughter. I mean, except for me and my mother."

"Pictures don't lie."

"Well, this one does. Or at least I mean pictures don't talk, either. The picture doesn't say who they are. Maybe she's his sister. Or someone else named Levy. It's a common name. His cousin, maybe."

"A sister? He doesn't have a sister. Does he? And anyway, he has his arm around her. And he has his hand over her hand holding the baby. Look at how he's smiling at her and how they're smiling at the baby. They look like a family. A happy family."

"They look like a family? What does that mean? That's the dumbest thing I ever heard. It's not what they look like to me. They just look like some people in a park who took a picture."

My voice was getting louder and louder as I said this, as if the louder I said it the more I would believe it. Because I didn't believe it. I believed Margaret. The word "family" echoed in my head like my head was a giant empty cave, louder and louder, moving out toward the shadows where I didn't dare to look.

One time, when I was about four, a little dog bit the leg of my pants and wouldn't let go. My mother had to rip the cuff off my pants to get me away. That's what this felt like. How could I rip off a piece of myself to get away from Margaret and that word? *Family.*

I stood up, grabbed my book bag, and started to walk away. Slowly and deliberately, I placed one foot in front of the other. It took all my strength to walk because I wanted to run. I wanted to run back to the morning. Back to English composition and intermediate French and my life before I saw that picture.

Margaret's voice faded into the lunchroom noise. "Hey, you didn't finish your lunch. Can I have your cake?"

Chapter Twenty-Seven

I stumbled forward, not really paying attention to where I was walking. I wasn't thinking about anything except getting away from Margaret. I saw the door to the girls' bathroom across the hall. It suddenly seemed like a good idea, and I turned to walk toward it. I turned so fast that I slammed into a boy walking next to me. Pain shot through my shoulder where it hit the corner of his books, and I looked up into his shocked face.

We both mumbled, "Sorry, sorry," as I ran into the bathroom and into a stall and sat down on the toilet and locked the door. It would probably have felt funny to be sitting on a toilet with my clothes on if I were paying attention. But I wasn't. My shoulder hurt. I wasn't paying attention to that, either.

I looked down and was amazed to see that the picture was still in my hand. I opened my fingers and pulled them away, like I'd touched something hot. It fell face down. The white curly paper with the neat writing was looking up at me. I wanted to leave it there. I wanted to leave it where people would step on it and the janitor would sweep it up and dump it into a big bucket and take it to wherever they take garbage that no one wants.

My mother had told me stuff about my father and his family and how his parents got killed by Hitler. She never told me about anyone named Lena or Baby Sophie. Where were they? How could my mother marry someone who was married to someone else and never tell me? How could she tell me over and over the story of how she met him? About how she fell in love with him the minute she saw him and told her mother she'd met the man she was going to marry and didn't even know his name? And when she told him she was pregnant, he had tears in his eyes. Was she making it all up? Maybe she didn't know about Lena and Sophie. My father never talked about his childhood or his friends. He could be keeping a secret. Maybe they lived in another part of New York. Maybe when my father said he was working or going to a meeting, he was really visiting them.

I picked the picture up and brushed it off. I looked at my father disguised as a young man. A happy man. Smiling a big dopey smile I'd never seen him smile. Was my father's real face hidden under that mask? Or was the face I knew the mask hiding his real face, his happy face, underneath?

I tried not to look at the woman. But I couldn't help it. She was so pretty. Even with her hair curled under in a way no one would wear now and with her clunky shoes. She sort of looked like the actresses in old movies I had seen pictures of. Her arms were curled around the baby wrapped in a blanket. You couldn't see it. Her. My . . . sister.

A wave of sickness like my first cigarette grabbed me.

It wasn't like I thought my father's life started when I was born. I mean, I knew he did stuff before. But I didn't know he was somebody else's father. Why didn't he tell me about her? Did he tell her about me? Is he lying to both of us, not telling either one of us that we have a sister? Who does he love more, I wonder? Probably her. She's a German.

Chapter Twenty-Eight

*U*p until a few months ago, my life was so boring I thought nobody could have a worse life. Well now I knew that having problems is worse than being bored. I had so many problems, I didn't have a second free for boredom.

I needed a friend.

That afternoon after school, I was standing outside of Barbara's apartment ringing her doorbell. It was Thursday. Hopefully, Barbara's mother would be at work. And hopefully, Barbara would be home. She hadn't talked to me in almost two weeks. As far as I knew, she hadn't talked to anyone in almost two weeks.

Barbara opened the door and looked at me. She looked surprised. Not delighted exactly, but she didn't slam the door in my face.

"What're you doing here?"

I knew she would say that. So, I was prepared.

"Chemistry Club is this afternoon. If I didn't come here, I would have to go."

She started to smile but stopped herself immediately. "Well come in, for Chrissakes. I don't want the whole world to see you standing outside my house in your pleats."

We walked to her room and sat down. She reached for a cigarette. Everything seemed normal, like we could just start being friends again where we left off. I wanted to tell Barbara about the picture. But I didn't want to bring it up right away. I didn't want to bring Elvis up right away, either. Barbara wasn't going to start the conversation. I knew that. If you took the picture *and* Elvis out of my life, there wasn't much left to talk about.

I asked her for a cigarette. It was stupid because she always gave me one and I never wanted it. I took a deep breath and pretended to be enjoying it.

"So," I said. "How've you been?"

"How've I been? Why? You some kind of damn doctor?"

I tried laughing. She didn't even smile. What would Holden do? Be . . . honest?

"I missed you."

"Missed me? When? Did you try to shoot me?"

Okay. Chitchat was out. It was Elvis or the picture.

"I'm sorry you didn't get to see him."

Barbara's eyes opened wide in shock. And then filled with tears. She tried to twist her mouth into her usual sneer. It didn't work. She turned her face away, so I wouldn't be able to see if any tears actually slid out of her eyes.

"It's not important."

But even with her face turned away, I could hear the tears in her voice. Suddenly, it was like she totally stopped caring about being cool. She spun around to face me and grabbed my arm. "Was it the greatest? The greatest ever?"

She was blinking to keep the tears from rolling down her cheeks.

I nodded. Blinking didn't keep the tears from rolling down my cheeks.

I told her. I told her every single minute of *The Milton Berle Show*. We took out magazines so I could show her what his shirt looked like and how his hair fell over his face and how he held the guitar and how he moved his hips.

Suddenly, Barbara jumped up and shouted, "Show me! Show me!"

"Show you? What are you talking about? I can't . . . show you."

"You have to."

"I c—"

"Heartbreak Hotel" burst from the phonograph. It was turned up to the loudest volume. Barbara stood over me holding the cardboard cover of a Monopoly box I'd never seen before. She held it against her stomach and moved her hand up and down in front of it.

"Here's your guitar. Now, show me."

I stood up and moved to the middle of the room. I cradled the box in my arms. The way Elvis held his guitar. Like a baby. I closed my eyes and let the music come all the way into my body. Into my feet. Into my fingers. I sang all the lyrics of "Heartbreak Hotel," which, of course, I knew so well, I might be able to sing them backward.

I swayed from side to side. I pushed my right arm up and down hitting the box with my fingers. Hard. The way Elvis hit his guitar. I felt strings under my fingers. I could hear chords. Filling my head. Filling the world. My shoulders moved by themselves. Back and forth. My hips swayed. Back and forth. I saw him move. And I moved with him. Back and forth. Back and forth. Me and Elvis. Alone in the world. Banging our guitars.

Suddenly, the music stopped. I was breathing fast. I couldn't catch my breath. I just kept moving back and forth. I opened my eyes. Barbara was looking up at me. Barbara? But I thought Elvis . . . I mean I felt Elvis . . .

I drew my breath in as deep as I could. Down to the floor. What was I doing? Did I just look like the biggest jerk in the history of time?

Barbara was smiling the un-coolest smile I ever saw a cool kid smile. She didn't look like Barbara. She looked . . . happy. Like my father in the picture. I had forgotten the picture. But I couldn't stop looking into Barbara's eyes.

"You know," she said, her voice hushed and respectful, a voice I'd never heard her use before, "I swear to God. I really mean it. If girls could be rock singers, you could be a rock singer."

Chapter Twenty-Nine

I f girls could be rock singers, I could be a rock singer.

Those words sat in the front part of my brain, waiting for me to wake up the next morning. When Barbara said those words to me, she'd looked at me in a whole new way, like it was the first time she had ever really seen me and she thought I was great—the greatest thing ever.

Barbara made fun of the principal when he yelled at the kids during lunch hour. And she'd shrugged when the giant assistant principal with the red face pulled her out of the line because he saw her cigarettes. But she'd looked at me with respect.

As I walked to the subway, I hummed "Heartbreak Hotel" softly and to myself, but I heard it plainly. I started to do a little dance from side to side until I got to the subway steps.

And, because I had finally forgotten about the picture for a minute, I had an idea. Ever since I'd seen the picture, the question that kept going around and around in my head was, "How do I find out where Lena and Sophie are?" It wasn't like I could look them up in the encyclopedia or the *World Almanac*. Or ask the librarian for a book about them. I had to ask people who knew them. The only people I knew who knew them were my father and Margaret's parents. They'd been keeping them a secret all these years, so I didn't think they were going to start talking about a secret they had kept for so long.

I was pretty sure my mother didn't know about Lena and Sophie because if she did, she would have told me. She was the one who told me about Germany and my father's parents and showed me all the pictures of his house and stuff. Anyway, I felt really sorry for her, having a husband and friends like the Feldmans who were keeping such a huge secret from her. I knew how I felt, finding out I wasn't an only child. Imagine how she would feel to find out she wasn't an only wife. I was definitely not going to be the one to tell her and ruin her life like Margaret had ruined mine.

Margaret. The more I went over our conversation in my mind, the more I kept thinking of questions I could have asked her. I mean, she didn't even tell me where she got the picture. It was a place to start. There was no time to waste because now that Barbara and I were friends again, I would be able to tell her about the picture and she would for sure ask me questions.

Margaret and I had PE second period. Margaret took so long to get dressed after PE that nobody waited for her, which gave me exactly the chance I needed. I waited in the next row of lockers where Margaret couldn't see me until everyone left. I walked around to where she was still standing in her slip with her skirt and blouse neatly spread out on the bench. She looked like a real spaz, in a stiff white cotton slip that was like an old-fashioned dress, with lace on the top and along the bottom and a little bow in between where her breasts would be if she had any. And as if the slip all by itself weren't bad enough, she was wearing fat white socks and saddle shoes. She put her shoes on first, before she put on her clothes. *Typical Margaret*, I thought. She did everything backward. Everyone knew you should put your shoes on last, so you wouldn't be standing there in shoes and a slip.

Although I was ashamed of myself, I was glad when I saw

Margaret wasn't wearing a brassiere, not even a 32AA like me. While I walked toward her and before she saw me, she picked up the white cotton blouse. It had so much starch it looked like someone was already wearing it.

"Where did you get the picture from, Margaret?"

Margaret jumped about a hundred feet in the air. But she found her smirky face pretty fast.

"What are you still doing here? You usually throw your clothes on and run to class barely buttoned up."

"Where did you get the picture, Margaret?"

She gave me the pitying look she loved so much and shook her head slowly. "That's for me to know and you to find out."

"You're right, Margaret. And I'm going to find out because you're going to tell me. You're going to tell me everything you know."

"You wish I'm going to tell you anything."

She was trying to talk tough, but I could tell she was getting nervous. She'd started to realize we were alone in the locker room where no one would hear her scream, like in a horror movie. Not that I was going to stab her or beat her up or anything, but maybe she didn't know that. She kept backing away from me. Of course, she couldn't go anywhere in her slip, and she was moving away from her clothes. It was perfect. She had fallen into my trap. I moved in front of her locker and her clothes on the bench. She was my prisoner.

"Okay, Margaret. Let me guess. Your parents gave you the picture and told you to give it to me. Right?"

"No, birdbrain. Of course that's not right. You better let me get dressed."

"Do they even know that you have the picture? They don't, do they? You said that. So how did you get it?"

"Oh, all right. I don't know what you're having such a cow about. I found it, okay? In the drawer in the cabinet in the living room that's full of pictures from Germany."

"Yeah, we have one, too."

"So, I like to look through them. One day when I picked up one of the albums, that picture fell out. It wasn't glued in, I guess. I never saw it before. So, I took it to my father and asked him who it was. And he went crazy. He started yelling, 'Where did you get this? What are you doing with this?' I never saw him like that before. He never yells at me. He grabbed the picture and left the room."

She looked at me and smiled like she had just given the right answer to a hard question. I wanted to hit her.

"What else did he say?"

"Nothing. He went to the kitchen and started talking to my mother. When I came in, they stopped talking, and he put his arms around me and said he was sorry he yelled at me, and it wasn't my fault, and we would forget all about it and never talk about it again."

"And then what?"

"And then, nothing. We never talked about it again."

The words rattled around in my head.

"But . . . what happened to the picture?"

"I don't know. He wasn't holding it anymore. Maybe he put it in his pocket."

"But. You found it again."

Margaret burst into tears. "I never disobeyed before."

What a baby! I started talking to her like my mother talked to me when I was little and fell down or squeezed my fingers in a door.

"Don't worry, Margaret. Everything is going to be okay. Just tell me what happened."

That was when I learned something I had never known about

Margaret, even though I had known her my whole life. She was the queen of crocodile tears. She looked up and smiled and her face wasn't one bit wet, and her eyes weren't one bit red.

"You're right. It's not like I actually disobeyed him. He didn't say not to look for it. So, when you started acting like such a brat, I went looking for it. I figured if he saved it all this time, he probably didn't throw it away."

"But is that it? I mean, you don't know who they are. You don't know where they are. And you never talked to your parents about them again."

"No. No. And yes. Now can I please get dressed? We're going to be late."

She tried to reach around me to get into her locker. I pressed my back against the door and squeezed her hand into the edge.

"Ow!"

Margaret looked ready to cry again, but now that I knew she was such a Sarah Heartburn, I wasn't the least bit impressed. She wailed, "We're going to be late for social studies."

She said it like it was a fatal disease, which is probably how she felt about it. She couldn't imagine a world where people didn't get to every class on time. It was true I had never been late to a class before or missed a class when I wasn't sick, either. But that was before I knew if girls could be rock singers, I could be a rock singer. On the other hand, I didn't really want to be caught cutting class, either. Not until girls could become rock singers, which I figured wasn't going to be anytime soon and certainly not before social studies.

"Okay. Get dressed. I'll see you there."

Chapter Thirty

R eporters crowd around me. Flashbulbs blind me. This was real news.

"Miss LaVie. Is it true? They say you're studying the guitar? They say you sing rock and roll like Elvis. Will you—"

"Wake up, girlie. Thez a hunert starvin' kids behind you tryin' to pay for lunch."

The reporters and photographers disappeared, and I was in the school cafeteria, standing on the lunch line, looking into the angry face of the cash register lady who hated kids. The person behind me pushed the edge of her tray into my back to get me to hurry. It felt like the whole cafeteria was staring at me. Like they had all seen the reporters and photographers and wondered where they went. Or why they were there in the first place.

I pulled my wallet out of my book bag, trying to act like an ordinary person who couldn't imagine why anyone was staring at her. I dropped my wallet, and change spilled over my tray and rolled onto the floor, adding sound to the *Paula Is a Jerk Show*. By the time I picked up my money and paid for my lunch, I felt like I had been standing by the cash register for an hour. I hurried to my table, glad it was behind the pillar for more reasons now than just that Barbara and I didn't want to be seen together.

Barbara was already eating. *Eating!* The whole world had

changed, even Barbara who used to throw away her lunch every day. When she looked up, she was smiling.

"Well, well. If it isn't the famous rock and roll singer."

I thought it would be cool to pretend I didn't know what she was talking about.

"Who? Me?"

"Yeah. You. Did you fall on your head or something?"

"No. Why?"

"Because you're acting like you have omnesia, that's why."

"Om . . . ? Oh. No. I remember, of course I remember." Wrong again. Amnesia definitely did not sound cool. "What're you doing this afternoon?"

"This? What do you think? I keep a book? For my appointments? Like the dentist? 'Let me see. Yes, I think I can squeeze you in this afternoon.'"

She pretended to be turning the pages of an invisible book and wrote my name in the air with an invisible pencil. Was it me, or was she getting funnier? I couldn't imagine Barbara making a joke like that before.

"You are fortunate, Miss Levy. The doctor can see you this afternoon."

Chapter Thirty-One

*W*alking to Barbara's house that afternoon, I knew how an invading army feels as it approaches the enemy. How a lion feels as it stalks its prey. I had a mission. Nothing was going to stop me. I was going to tell Barbara everything.

I knew it wouldn't be easy. She never made anything easy, and I would happily have spoken to someone else if there was anyone else I could talk to.

Before I could say a word, she stood up and walked over to where I sat. She said, "So, Miss Levy, why did you ask for this appointment? Do you have a cavity? Open wide."

In all the time I had known Barbara, she had hardly ever smiled and never laughed. I figured that being funny wasn't cool. But here she was making a joke! Under ordinary circumstances, I would have been happy to play along. But this wasn't an ordinary circumstance. The last thing I needed now was for Barbara to become a comedian.

I pulled the picture out of my pocket, and while Barbara stared at it with a puzzled frown, I told her the whole story. When I finished, she put the picture down and looked at me with her mouth pulled all the way over to the side. I knew that when she pulled her mouth to the side like that, it meant she was thinking seriously about something.

"Paula, will you get mad if I ask you something?"

"No, no. Go ahead."

"So, I mean, Margaret gave you this picture of your father from a long time ago, and in the picture, he's standing with a woman and a baby."

"Yeah."

"And you never met these people, right?"

"Right."

"And you never even heard of them before, right?"

"Right."

"So, this is a picture of people you don't know anything about. Right?"

"Well, I told you what I know."

"Which is pretty much nothing."

"I guess so."

"And you believe Margaret told you the truth because you made her fear for her life."

"Yes." I smiled proudly.

"So, then, I mean, I don't get it. Why are you flipping out over a picture of some people you never met and probably never will meet because you don't know who they are or where they are or where they've been for like a hundred years or however long it's been since people wore goofy clothes like this."

"Well, can't you see how upsetting it would be to find out after fourteen years that your father has another family?"

"Can't I see how upsetting that would be? No. Actually I *can't*, birdbrain."

Barbara almost shouted the word "can't," and her eyes narrowed as she looked at me. She looked really angry. But it also seemed like there was the beginning of tears in her eyes. How could she be so upset about my father? It didn't make any sense. She'd never even met him.

Barbara started fumbling with her cigarettes. I thought of something I'd never thought of before. In all the months that we had been friends, Barbara had never once mentioned her father. I didn't know anything about him, except that she didn't live with him. Had she ever met him? Did she think about him? Did he have another family? Maybe this was a really stupid thing to talk to her about. I didn't want to make her feel bad and talk about stuff she didn't want to talk about. Although that was probably almost everything. Barbara was the only kid I'd ever met whose parents were divorced, so it was hard to know how to talk about it, even if the person wasn't Barbara.

Luckily, Barbara seemed to forget all about whatever it was that she remembered. She lit her cigarette, and asked, "Do you think your old man has two wives? Like he has some kind of harem or something?"

"No. Yes. I don't know. I don't think he has two wives."

"Well, I mean, he is married to your old lady, isn't he? I mean your mother."

"Yeah. I mean, I think so. They have an anniversary every year when they go out to dinner, and there are pictures of the day they got married. She's not wearing a white wedding dress or a veil or anything. Just like a fancy dress. But yeah, I'm pretty sure they're married."

"Then how can he be married to someone else? Isn't it against the law to have two wives?"

"Yeah."

"So, you think your old man is a criminal? You want to go to the cops and get him arrested?"

"No. Of course I don't want to have him arrested. That's ridiculous. Why would I want to get him arrested?"

"Ha. If I could get Tony arrested, I would do it in a minute."

"Well, I don't want to get my father arrested. Anyway, I'm sure he's not a criminal. They must've gotten divorced."

Barbara stared at me, and the anger came back on her face. I'd said another dumb thing. Reminding her that her parents were divorced. Barbara turned her face away from me and took a drag on her cigarette. When she turned back, the look was gone.

"Well, then what's the problem?" Barbara shrugged. "I mean, when people get divorced, they don't see each other anymore. So probably your old man never sees them. Hasn't seen them in years."

"It doesn't make any sense, Barbara. Even if he didn't want to see his wife again, he would certainly want to see his daughter."

Barbara jumped up and started to walk around the room, keeping her face turned away from me no matter what direction she was walking in. It was obvious now that I should never have talked to her about the picture. Or at least not about my feelings about my father being divorced and having another daughter. I was trying to figure out if there had been any way I could have known beforehand that she wouldn't want to talk about fathers leaving their daughters. She came back and sat down.

"So, I guess you're thinking your old man knows where they are."

"Yeah. I was thinking maybe some of the times he says he's going out to do stuff, he's really visiting them."

"So, what are you going to do about it? Try to find them?"

"Yeah."

"How?"

"I don't know. I was hoping you would have an idea."

"You were hoping I would have an idea." She shook her head and blew air through her closed lips. It made her look like a duck.

"Great plan, Paula. Great plan. The honor student was hoping the school dummy would have an idea."

"Oh, shut up. You're not the school dummy. You're really smart. You could be an honor student if you wanted to be."

Barbara looked at me in surprise. "You really think so?"

I'd never said anything like that to her before. I'd never even said it to myself before. "Yeah. I do. If you cared about school and did your homework and stuff."

"Well, then. Let me turn my great brain on and start thinking."

She pretended to be studying the picture closely. "Hey, you know, your old man was pretty cute. Is he still?"

"Cute? No. He's old. I mean, he's more than forty. What a stupid thing to say."

"Sorry. I was just trying to cheer you up."

"I don't need to be cheered up. I need to find out about Lena and Sophie."

"Uh-huh. Okay. Well, did you ever think about looking them up in the phone book? Or don't detectives do anything that simple?"

"I don't even know their name. Or where they live. The phone book only has people in it who live in Queens. What if they don't live in Queens?"

"You don't know their name? Their name is Levy, like yours. It even says that on the picture. Are there schools for detectives? Maybe you could go to one. Because you don't seem to be very good at it."

"Thanks, Barbara. You're really helping me."

Barbara sighed. "But you're asking stupid questions. If they don't live in Queens, they won't be in the phone book. But you'll never know unless you look."

Maybe it wasn't such a bad idea.

"You know the drugstore on the corner?" I asked. "They have phone books from all over, you know, Brooklyn, Manhattan. I think even like Staten Island. That could be a good place to start."

"Yeah," Barbara agreed sarcastically. "Especially if you think they live in Staten Island."

Chapter Thirty-Two

T he next afternoon I stopped at Singer's drugstore on the way home from school. Mr. and Mrs. Singer came from Germany and were sort of friendly with my parents, so I had to be careful and let them think it was an ordinary day and I was there for my ordinary cherry Coke.

I liked going to Singer's because I could get almost everything there. They sold makeup and books and even jewelry. And they made really good cherry Cokes, malteds, ice cream sodas, and sandwiches. When you walked in the front door, there was a glass counter full of pills and lipstick and stuff on your left and the soda fountain with a long shiny black counter on the right. The store always had a funny smell of aspirin and melted cheese.

Mrs. Singer was behind the soda fountain when I came in. I hoisted myself up onto the round, cracked, red leather stool and smiled at her.

"Hello, Paula, what can I do for you today?" She spoke with a slight German accent, so the "what" sounded more like "vat."

Mrs. Singer's face was very pale, sort of yellow, with big black circles under her eyes. The skin under her chin hung loose and wobbled when she spoke.

"A cherry Coke, please."

"Of course. How is your mother and father?"

"They're fine, thank you."

Mrs. Singer held a glass under the faucet in front of her and pressed down on a flat, silver handle. Dark-brown Coca-Cola syrup squirted into the glass. She pressed the handle next to it for the reddish cherry syrup and then put the glass under the tall seltzer faucet. The syrups began bubbling, and Mrs. Singer smiled as she put the glass on the counter and handed me a straw. As I drank, I drew circles of water on the counter with my glass. When I was little, I thought the glass was leaking and couldn't figure out why the leaky water wasn't sticky with syrup.

I looked up and Mrs. Singer was still standing near me. I had an idea.

"Mrs. Singer?"

"Yes, dear?" She smiled.

"Did you know my father in Germany?"

Her smile froze, and her eyes opened wide in shock. Her pale skin became even paler. She opened and closed her mouth as if she started to say something and then changed her mind.

She backed away from me and shook her head, stammering, "Germany? No! Of course not! Ve meet here. In dis country. On dis street. Fritz and me. Ve open a store. Your fater comes in. He is doctor. He is German. So ve are friendly."

Mrs. Singer suddenly moved toward me and stuck her face close to mine. "Why? Why do you ask such a thing? About Germany?"

The way she said it made it seem like it was a really important question. Important enough that she would tell my parents that I asked it. I had to make her calm down. I smiled and shrugged my shoulders.

"Oh, nothing. No reason, really. I just wondered. You know. I just wondered if you knew my father before. You know. Like Dr. Feldman and some of their other friends who knew each other in Germany. It's not important." She seemed to calm down and tried to smile.

"It was. I was surprised. I'm not meaning to scare you."

I gave her the biggest smile I could manage.

"Oh no. It's fine. You didn't scare me. It's nothing."

Me and my big ideas. I wanted the day to be ordinary. Instead, I had turned it into a big drama.

I decided to drink my Coke slowly, to give Mrs. Singer the chance to forget about the question. I didn't want her to watch me leave and see me checking the phone books. I was in luck. A group of four grown-ups came in and ordered sandwiches, coffee, and pie for dessert. That was going to keep her busy.

I changed to drinking quickly so I could finish the Coke before she finished the sandwiches. I coughed because the Coke went down too quickly, so I got down from the stool, left a nickel on the counter, and walked toward the back of the store where I could cough without drawing anybody's attention. If Mrs. Singer heard me coughing, she would think I was sick and call her husband to recommend medicine.

Mr. Singer was where he usually was—behind the window that divided the Pharmacy Department from the rest of the store. He must have been filling a prescription because his back was turned. I was in luck.

There were two phone booths next to the back door with a rack of phone books between them. I started with Queens and turned the pages of the heavy book to "Levy." I almost groaned out loud. There were about a million of them. Well, not a million, but almost a whole column in the tiny little print they printed phone books in. It was like they really didn't want you to be able to find anything. The little print was so hard to read.

This is going to take longer than I thought. I told Margaret that Levy was a common name, but I didn't think it was this common. We don't have any relatives named Levy.

I moved my finger down the column to the *L*'s. I moved it past "Lana" and "Lawrence" until I got to "Leonard." There was no "Lena."

"Sophie" took longer because there were more names that started with *S*. But when I got to "Spencer," I knew there was no "Sophie." I smiled.

One down and four to go. I put the Queens book back on the shelf and took Brooklyn. There were even more people named "Levy" in Brooklyn. But no "Lena" and no "Sophie."

I put the Brooklyn book back and took down Manhattan. It was much thicker than Queens or Brooklyn. The Manhattan phone book was so thick that when I was little, they would put a Manhattan phone book on the chair for me to sit on when we ate in a restaurant so I could reach the table.

People named "Levy" took up two columns on two separate pages. I finished the *L*'s and was moving toward the *S*'s.

"Paula? Is that you? What on earth are you doing?"

Mr. Singer must have finished filling the prescription because he was walking toward the back door with the delivery boy holding a bag.

I covered my face with another big smile. I wondered if I was using them up or if people had an infinite number of dopey smiles to fool grown-ups into thinking they were not doing anything important.

"Hi, Mr. Singer. How are you?"

"Good, *Liebchen*. For what are you looking so hard?"

I pretended to laugh.

"Well, you know, I have this friend, you know, and uh . . . she moved to . . ."—I glanced down at the book I was holding—"Manhattan, and I wanted to find her phone number so I could call her."

He frowned thoughtfully. "When did she move?"

"Um. A month. A couple of months ago."

"I see. But I am afraid, *Liebchen*, that you are wasting your time. The number will not yet be in the book. I think that you will have to call the operator. Are you knowing how to do that?"

"Oh, yeah. Yeah. I do. Thanks. That is a great idea. Bye."

I put the book back on the shelf and started to run out the door, until I remembered I was trying to look ordinary. I walked instead.

I had finished exactly one half of the searches I needed to do. And I was never going to finish them in Singer's drugstore. *But of course*, I thought, as I walked slowly down the street, *this had been a really stupid plan.* There was another drugstore a few blocks away where my parents never went and nobody knew me. They probably had phone books. Why didn't I think of it sooner?

This detective business was really hard. You had to think of everything.

Chapter Thirty-Three

"They're not in the phone books," I reported to Barbara the next day at lunch.

"So, that's good, right? It means they don't live in New York. That means you can forget about them, right?"

"Wrong. I mean, that's what I thought at first, too. But then I realized. Sophie is a grown-up. She could be married. Her name could be anything. She could have been right there in any one of those books, and I would never have known it. I didn't learn anything."

"I guess. Maybe she isn't married."

"Maybe. But there is no way to know. And anyway, she probably is. Everybody gets married."

Barbara shrugged. "Except for nuns."

"Nuns? What a stupid thing to say. If there's anything I know for sure, it's that Sophie isn't a nun."

"So, see? What're you biting my head off for? You said you didn't learn anything. But you did. Sophie's not a nun."

"I didn't learn that. I already knew that. Jews don't . . . Oh, why're we talking about nuns? We need to come up with another idea."

"*We* have to come up with another idea? Who is this *we*? It's not like I care about some old picture."

"What're you saying, Barbara? Are you saying you don't want to help me? Well, fine. Don't. I just thought you were my friend. And I thought friends help friends. I guess I was wrong."

I started to stand up. The silly smile froze on Barbara's face.

"Sit down, for Chrissakes. It was just a joke. I am trying to help you. It's just . . . I mean, I don't really know what else to do. I thought of the phone books. And you said that was a good idea, right? Even if you didn't find anything."

"Yeah. It was a good idea."

"I can't think of anything else. It's not like you can look them up in a dictionary or in those books. You know the ones I mean? I forget what you call them. Those books that are all the same color in the back of the room?"

"Books that are all the same color in the back of the room?"

"Yeah. You know. The first one is *A* and the second one is *B*."

"The encyclopedia?"

"Yeah," she said, smiling, "the encyclopedia. You can't look them up in the encyclopedia. So, I guess I am out of ideas."

"Me, too." I sat back down.

"You don't think you could just ask your old man, right?"

"Right. I can't. In my house, anything you're supposed to know you do know. And if you don't know it, it's because you're not supposed to. My father never talks about his family. He never told me anything about when he was a kid and stuff. Mostly my mother told me stuff. But only when he wasn't around. Because when he was there, he got angry if she mentioned his family or school or anything."

"What about Margaret's parents? I mean, they know, right?"

"Yeah. But they told her to forget she ever saw the picture."

"Maybe they would tell you."

"No. I'm pretty sure the reason they got so upset was that they were afraid she would tell me. I mean, what difference would it make if she knew?"

"And you don't think your old lady knows, right? So, you can't ask her."

"I don't think she knows. I mean, how could she know that my father may have another wife?"

And then it hit me. I knew just what to do. It was so obvious, I didn't know why I hadn't thought of it before.

"I know what I can do, Barbara. I'll follow him."

"Him who? Oh, you mean your father. Follow him? You mean, like to work?"

"No, no. Not to work. But on Saturdays, he almost always goes out by himself. He tells my mother he's going to buy stamps or going to a meeting. Different things. But he almost always goes. So maybe he's lying. Maybe that's when he goes to see them. This Saturday he told my mother he was going to some kind of doctor's conference. Maybe he's lying. Maybe he really visits them on Saturdays. I can follow him and see."

"Sounds hard. And dangerous."

"Dangerous? How could it be dangerous?"

"He could see you."

"I'll be careful."

Chapter Thirty-Four

*T*here were a lot of reasons why it would have been better to have Barbara with me on Saturday when I followed my father. For one thing, he didn't know her, so it didn't matter if he saw her. For another, I was so nervous, I didn't want to do it alone. But she absolutely refused to go with me, for reasons she never explained to me, so the reasons I had for wanting her to go with me were irrelevant.

I pretended to be reading in my room. But I was really listening for my father to leave. When I heard the front door open and close, I walked into the entry hall, which led to the door. My mother was standing alone by the door. I was about to tell her I was going to the library to do research when the door opened and my father came back in, carrying an empty garbage can. They both looked at me. I stared back. We were silent.

"What is it, Paula?" my mother finally asked.

"Um. Could I have a glass of milk?"

She looked at me strangely. I hated milk and only drank it when she forced me with threats about never getting any taller and guilt about children starving in Europe. But it was the first thing that I thought of.

"I'm thirsty," I explained.

"Shall I ring for the downstairs maid," my father asked sarcastically, "or can you manage to get it for yourself?"

"I'll get it."

I fled into the kitchen, my face feeling like it was on fire. I had to tell myself over and over that just because I had been in the entry hall for no reason didn't mean my parents would figure out I was planning to follow my father to see if he had a secret family. I poured a tiny amount of milk into a glass and drank it. I didn't actually have to because when I left the kitchen, the entry hall was empty. My parents weren't around, so I went back to my room to wait.

I didn't want to put on any music because I wouldn't be able to hear the door opening. And I certainly wasn't going to start my homework because I might start paying so much attention to it, I wouldn't hear the door opening. So, I just sat there. Listening. It seemed like forever. Finally, I heard the door open and close again. I hesitated. He had to be leaving this time. He had already taken out the garbage, and there wasn't any other reason I could think of for him to go out and come back. I took my purse and walked to the entry hall. I shouted to my mother, who must have been in her room, that I was going to the library and left before she could answer.

My father was already almost a half a block away. He was a fast walker, but his hat made it easy to pick him out, and I was pretty sure he was headed toward the subway. I ran a little so I would not be so far behind him. I had to be able to see which train he was going to take.

I caught up in time to see him go down the stairs into the Roosevelt Avenue subway stop, go through the turnstile, and walk down the stairs to the trains going to Manhattan. I carefully went down the stairs and saw exactly what I expected—my father sitting on a bench reading the *New York Times*. There were a lot of people on the platform waiting for the train. I was able to hide behind a group of people before he looked up. When the E train pulled into the station, I was careful to get into the same car that he did, but far enough away where he didn't see me. There was a very fat couple standing by a pole, and I moved behind them. So far, everything was going perfectly. I wondered if girls could become detectives when they grew up. Contrary to what Barbara had said about going to detective school, I seemed to have a talent for it.

Chapter Thirty-Five

*T*he train stopped at Queens Plaza and more people got on. No one got off, so it was easy for me to stay hidden. The train stopped next at Twenty-Third Street and Ely Avenue, the last stop in Queens. I'd never seen anyone get on or off at this stop, and this time was no exception. I stayed very still. My father looked up for a second to check the station. Then he looked down and went back to reading his newspaper. I let out a deep breath.

The first stop in Manhattan was Lexington Avenue. A group of passengers who were surrounding me got off. The fat couple seemed to be staying, and I moved a little to keep them between me and my father. Unfortunately, they had no reason to warn me that they were leaving. When they walked out, they left me searching for a place to hide. I pulled my coat up over the back of my head and started to run toward the door that led to the next car when a deep man's voice yelled, "Scouts forward!" and an unruly bunch of Cub Scouts ran screaming onto the train. They surrounded me. But since they were only about eight or so, they were even shorter than I was.

The noise attracted the attention of everyone in the car, including my father. Before I could duck down or think of anything except that maybe I didn't have a talent for detecting, my father looked up from his newspaper, and we were staring directly into each other's eyes.

As the train began moving, my father folded his newspaper

and beckoned me with his finger. I had been holding onto a pole to keep from falling as the train jerked and swayed. I walked slowly toward him and forced my face muscles into a smile.

"Hi, Daddy," I said, trying to sound as if running into each other on the subway was something that happened to us a few times a week.

"What are you doing here? Where do you think you are going?"

"The Museum of Modern Art," I answered, "and the Donnell Library."

It was a brilliant idea, and it came to me in a flash. The next stop on the train would take me to the Museum of Modern Art, and I was anxious to get away from my father as soon as possible. The Donnell Library was across the street from the museum. So when my father would tell my mother about meeting me on the train to go into Manhattan and she said that I hadn't said a word about it but was going to the library, it wouldn't be a total lie.

"Alone?" my father asked. "You are going to the museum alone? When did you become an art lover?"

"Oh, no," I assured him. "I am meeting a bunch of people there. We are working together on a project, and we need to do some research."

He didn't exactly seem like he believed me. But we had already reached the next station. I smiled and started for the door. He stood and began to walk with me.

"I'm going to a conference. The hotel is around the corner from the museum."

"Really?"

He looked at me strangely. "Yes. Really. You could come along if you like. Perhaps you will find talks on the current state of renal and colonic oncology interesting."

"Ren . . . I doubt it. But thanks anyway."

We got off the train and walked upstairs. My father walked fast for an old guy, and it was hard for me to keep up with him. We climbed up onto the street. We were on the corner of Fifth Avenue and Fifty-Third Street. The museum was on Fifty-Third Street, halfway down the block toward Sixth Avenue. I walked toward the curb to cross the street.

"I'm going just here," my father said, pointing to the hotel door on Fifth Avenue in the middle of the block between Fifty-Third Street and Fifty-Fourth Street. I smiled and hugged him.

"See you later. At home," I corrected. I certainly didn't want to have to meet him later.

"All right. Be careful."

I crossed the street and turned back to wave at my father. He stood where I had left him, watching me. I waved. He nodded and walked into the hotel. I walked past the museum and around the block very slowly, studying all the shop windows, even if they didn't have anything very interesting for sale. It was ten minutes before I came back to the hotel entrance. I walked to the front desk.

"Is there a conference here for doctors today? Cancer doctors?"

The man behind the desk scanned a sheet of paper and asked, "Current Trends in Renal and Colonic Oncology?"

"Yes," I answered miserably, "that's the one."

"The ballroom. Third floor. Elevators on the left of the lobby."

"Thanks."

It was exactly what he had said. A conference for cancer doctors. Unless Lena and Sophie were cancer doctors, too, he wasn't seeing them this afternoon. Tears burned my eyes. My throat felt like it was closing shut. I'd been so sure that he was lying. I was sure this would be the day when I found out everything about his horrid secret. I was even planning what I would say when I caught him.

But I was the one who was caught. And I was the one who was lying. I couldn't go straight home. It would be weird if I came home too soon. I decided to go to the museum. Maybe I would turn into an art lover. At least there were benches there.

Chapter Thirty-Six

J'd seen this new Barbara, the Laughing Barbara, several times now, but it still seemed weird. And pretty annoying. By the time I finished telling her about what happened on Saturday, she was bent over the table, holding onto the edge and gasping for breath. When she finally looked up, there were black smudges of mascara running down her cheeks. Barbara had cried with laughter! Did she ever laugh at anything but me? I wondered.

When she had caught her breath, she said, "That is the funniest thing I ever heard in my life."

"It wasn't that funny."

"Yes, it was, great detective."

"Well, maybe I wasn't so good at following somebody, but I was very good at thinking up an excuse when I got caught."

"Okay. So even if you aren't a great detective, at least you're a great liar. What are you going to do next?"

"I don't know. I don't think I should try to follow him again."

"No, genius. I would definitely say that is not a good idea."

"So, I'm back where I started. I don't know what's left to do."

"What's left to do is forgetting about the stupid picture and listening to Elvis. That's what's left to do."

"I wish I could forget it. Really. I just don't think I can. There must be something. Something we haven't thought of yet."

"Well, maybe there is."

"What? You have an idea?"

"Maybe. Didn't you say your parents have a drawer of old pictures? Like Margaret's parents?"

"Yeah."

There were dozens of pictures of Germany in the drawers of the big wooden cabinet my father brought with him from Germany.

"So why don't you look through them and see if you can find more pictures of Lena and Sophie."

"I've seen the pictures in that drawer lots of times. I used to play with them when I was a kid. And sometimes my mother showed them to me and told me what they were. I never saw any of Lena and Sophie."

"You were never looking for them."

"I guess. I guess it's possible I missed something."

And then I thought of something. "Hey, you know what? There are actually a bunch of drawers in the cabinets that I never even looked at. I don't know what's in them."

"There you go."

"Help me."

"Huh?"

"Come over and help me."

Barbara said all the time that she couldn't be seen with me because I dressed like a creep. I never told her I couldn't let my parents meet her because she dressed like a tramp. She seemed to know that was how I felt because she was shocked when I said it . . . maybe even as shocked as I would be if she had said to me one day at lunch, "Come with me to the luncheonette where we hang out and meet the gang."

"You mean, you want me to come over to your house?"

"Tomorrow. On Thursdays my mother goes to the beauty parlor. She doesn't get home until five thirty. So come over for a little while."

She was shaking her head slowly. "It's not a good idea, Paula."

"Don't sweat it. I can't get through all those drawers by myself."

"It's a really bad idea, Paula."

"Puleeze."

She shrugged. "Okay. It's your funeral."

Chapter Thirty-Seven

I t was like running a movie backward. Well, not exactly backward. But instead of Barbara giving me her address, I gave her mine. And instead of her telling me she would meet me at her house so no one saw us leaving school together, I told her I'd meet her at my house.

I could have started sorting the pictures by myself while I waited for her. But I had my heart set on doing it with her. The doorbell finally rang, and there was Barbara, standing outside my door. She stared at everything as we walked into the living room.

"Nice house," she said, nodding. "Clean, you know what I mean?"

"Thanks. You want to see my room?"

"Nah, we have to . . . Okay."

I thought Barbara would make fun of my house. Call it square and creepy. But she didn't. She didn't say anything. She walked funny, like she was being careful where she put her feet down, and she was quiet like she was in church or something.

Barbara nodded when we got to my room. "Nice room, Paula. Lots of room for records and stuff."

"Thanks. Do you want to—" I walked over to the record player.

"Not now. We got to go through the pictures. Nice poodle lamp."

"Yeah, thanks. I love poodles. I'd like to . . ."

She may not have made fun of my parents' part of the house, but I realized she was definitely being sarcastic when she complimented my poodle lamp. I said, "Yeah, okay. Let's go through the pictures."

As we walked back to the living room, the house seemed unfamiliar to me, as if I were seeing it through Barbara's eyes, not mine. The dark heavy furniture made out of ornately carved wood that came from Germany. The rugs with Oriental designs of dark reds and blues and greens that came from there, too. Everything was polished and vacuumed.

I had told you Barbara's house was always a mess and that my mother picked up everything the second after it fell if she didn't catch it on the way down. But now, the house was more than just clean. It was unfriendly. I always liked my friends' houses more, the ones that had American furniture made out of light wood with straight lines and solid-colored carpets. I thought it was just because I liked light colors and straight lines. Now I knew that wasn't it. I liked their houses because they felt friendly. Even Margaret's house, filled with German furniture, didn't feel unfriendly in the same way. I couldn't explain it and decided I would have to think about it the next time I went over there.

Barbara followed me to the living room, and we sat down on the floor in front of the drawer of pictures. It was the top drawer in a cabinet of three drawers.

"See," I said, opening the drawer and taking out the wooden boxes crammed with photos. "My mother showed me this drawer when I was little. I've been through them lots of times. They're all from Germany. Pictures of my father when he was a little boy. Pictures of my grandparents and their house. Some are pictures of trips they took to places like Italy."

"Wow. There must be about a zillion pictures in here. Have you seen all of them?"

"Probably. I used to like to look at them."

"And you never saw any pictures of anyone that looked like what's their names?"

"Lena and Sophie. I don't think so."

"But you can't be sure. You said there are pictures of a lot of different people, relatives and stuff."

"Yes, so maybe I could have missed a picture of them. But I'm sure there weren't any pictures of them with my father, smiling. I sure would have noticed that."

I started to open the boxes to take out the pictures.

"What's in the other drawers?"

"I don't know. Papers and stuff."

"Pictures?"

"I don't think so."

"But, I mean, why don't we look in the drawers where you don't know what's in them?"

I closed the top drawer and opened the one underneath. It was like I thought—filled with papers. I took out a bunch of letters tied together with a ribbon. They were written on thin paper, like tissue paper. The writing was unfamiliar and spidery. I didn't think I could read it, even if it had been written in English, which I knew it wasn't. I put them down on the floor next to me and started turning over other stacks of papers. Barbara was frowning and examining papers in a folder.

"Isn't any of this stuff written in English?"

"I don't think so."

"So, for all we know, these papers could be telling us Lena and Sophie's whole life story. Do you know anyone who knows German?"

"No one besides my father and Margaret's parents."

"Too bad. We may as well go back to the pictures."

She was right. I turned over a few more batches of papers to see if there was anything underneath them in English when from somewhere behind me came the worst sound I ever heard in my life.

"Paula. What on earth?"

It was my mother's voice. I didn't want to turn around. Maybe I was hallucinating, or maybe I fell asleep and was having a nightmare.

"Paula!"

I spun around. She was really there, standing in the doorway in her coat with a bag of groceries in her arms.

Chapter Thirty-Eight

"**M**ama. What are you doing here? How come you're not at the beauty parlor?"

She was staring at Barbara.

"Grace was sick," she said without taking her eyes off Barbara. "But—"

Before she could say anything else, I said, "This is Barbara, Mama. Barbara Montalvo. She . . . um . . . just transferred from another school, and Miss Polatsek asked me to help her, you know, to catch up. She came over for me to start, you know, helping her with her homework."

Barbara twisted around and stared up at my mother like she'd never seen anyone who looked like her. And maybe she hadn't. My mother wore a dark-red hat with a small gray feather on the side. Under the hat, every hair on her head was in its proper place, even though she'd missed her beauty parlor appointment. She wore pearl earrings, which matched her pearl necklace, and a dark-red woolen dress and low-heeled black shoes. Not a crease or a stain or even a little piece of thread was on her anywhere. Barbara's head jerked up and she stared at me. And then something clicked. I saw it in her eyes. She stood up and smiled at my mother and started talking like she was reading words someone had written out for her to say.

"Hello, Mrs. Levy. It's very nice to meet you. It was very kind of your daughter, don't you think, to invite me over to help me to get caught up on my study work?"

My mother stared at Barbara without moving, as if she had been turned to stone, but it wasn't hard to know what she was thinking. She wanted to get this girl with blonde streaks in her hair and bright-green eye shadow and fake gold earrings out of her house as fast as she possibly could.

When she answered, her voice sounded like cracking ice. "It's very nice to meet you, too, Barbara. If you'll excuse me, I have to put my groceries down. Paula, what are you doing in the living room?"

I looked back at the open drawer, and the papers piled on the floor.

"Oh, that. Well, see, Barbara is, um, really interested in antiques. So, I was showing her pictures of Daddy's house in Germany with all the beautiful antiques in it."

My mother didn't exactly seem convinced. She turned back to Barbara and talked in this really cold way:

"So, you and your family just moved into the neighborhood, Barbara. How nice. Where were you living before?"

"Move? We didn't move. Oh, I mean, I just transferred schools."

"I see. And what school were you in before?"

"Precious Blood."

"Precious . . . um-hum. That's a parochial school, isn't it?"

"Paro . . . um, yeah, I think, it's a, you know, it's a Catholic school, with nuns and stuff."

My mother nodded. "Nuns and stuff. I see. Those are generally very strict schools. Why did you leave? Did they ask you to leave?"

"Mom," I started to interrupt, but Barbara kept answering.

"Oh, no. They wanted me to stay. Yeah. They practically begged . . . I mean, my old . . . my parents and I, we decided I should . . . um . . . change schools."

"And you transferred directly into the honor classes? Well, you must be a very smart girl. A very smart girl indeed. Paula, why are those papers on the floor?"

"I was showing Barbara the pictures of—"

"Daddy's house in Germany. But why are the *papers* on the floor?"

"Well, I—"

My mother interrupted and continued in her ice-cracking voice, "You've been told, more than once, not to touch those papers. Haven't you?"

"Yes, but—"

"And you've made a total mess. Look at them. Strewn all over the floor like garbage. You had better get them back into the drawer where they belong."

She'd never gotten mad at me when someone else was around before. She was always saying you shouldn't air your dirty linen in public. But she sure wasn't hiding any linen now. She was shaking her head and not smiling at all. I was embarrassed. I sat down on the floor and started to put the papers back in the drawer. Barbara sat down next to me to help. I could see my mother turn toward the kitchen and started to breathe a sigh of relief. But she stopped and turned around. She looked at Barbara with an expression I had never seen before. Her eyes and mouth were narrowed and slit-like, and her lips almost completely disappeared into her mouth. Her voice sounded like she was pushing it through a throat filled with crumpled paper.

"Barbara. It's after four o'clock now, and Paula has a lot of homework to do. She'll have to help you to catch up with your studies some other day."

Barbara and I finished putting everything back into the drawer without a word. I couldn't imagine what she was feeling. When we were finished, we stood up, facing each other.

"Paula," Barbara whispered.

"What?" I whispered back.

"What's a antique?"

Chapter Thirty-Nine

"It's your funeral."

Those may have been the truest words Barbara ever said to me since she told me that Elvis was the greatest singer in the world. After Barbara left, the minute she closed the door behind her, my mother charged into the living room like a bull into the arena. She was screaming.

"How dare you bring a cheap tramp into my house!"

"She's not a cheap tramp. She's nice. Really nice. That's just how she dresses."

"'Just how she dresses.' Have you taken complete leave of your senses? How dare you have anything to do with such a person. Haven't you learned anything from me? From us?"

"Well, yeah, I learned not to be prejudiced and not to judge people by how they look."

Her eyes opened wide with a rage worse than when I knocked her grandmother's china pitcher onto the floor. She swung her hand back over her head like she was getting ready to smack me with all her might. I braced myself. But she stopped herself in mid-swing. Her arm stayed there, in the air, over her head. She opened and closed her hand and bit her lips. I thought maybe she was trying to decide whether to slap me or punch me. But she turned around without saying another word. She went to the kitchen, and I went to my room. It wasn't unusual for my mother to not talk very much.

But that evening, she was still not talking very much. She was not talking very much . . . even more than usual. Since she didn't say anything about it, there was no way to know for sure what she was thinking and whether she believed my story about Miss Polatsek asking me to help out a new girl. I doubted it. But it was possible.

As I left for school the next morning, she said, "Please come straight home from school this afternoon, Paula. Alone." That certainly wasn't her usual way of saying, "Goodbye now, Paula, have a nice day," and my little bit of hope got littler.

"Okay. I don't have any club meetings or anything today, so I'll be home right after school. Maybe we could—"

She walked out of the room.

Even after my mother walked out of the room in the middle of my sentence, something she'd certainly never done before, I still thought it was at least a little possible that she believed my story about Barbara. Was that totally stupid? Or just desperate? Maybe both. But my hope wasn't altogether gone until the next morning and Margaret came running down the path as I tried to slip past her house, shrieking, "You brought Barbara home! To your house. Oh, my God, Paula! Oh, my God!"

"This is the way the world ends
This is the way the world ends
This is the way the world ends
Not with a bang but a whimper."

Those words, from a poem we read in school that nobody liked and I didn't understand before, filled an empty space left in my brain after Margaret said what she said. It felt like all my thoughts fell out. I knew the way my world ends. Not with a bang or a whimper. But with Margaret shrieking, "You brought Barbara home!"

Chapter Forty

I don't remember anything about that morning. Barbara wasn't sitting at our table at lunch. I searched the cafeteria, and sure enough, there she was. Sitting with them. The cool kids. I kept my eyes on my tuna fish sandwich and nibbled it slowly. It was making the sick feeling in my stomach worse. But I had to do something because if I was just sitting there doing nothing, I would seem like a pathetic jerk. Which was what I was, but I didn't have to let the whole world see it.

"Psst. Hey. Listen."

I jumped a little. Barbara had snuck up to the table while I was watching mayonnaise ooze through holes in the Wonder Bread my mother still used for my sandwiches. She never bought the raisin bread I had asked for after I stayed at Margaret's, and I never brought it up again after she went crazy the first time I mentioned it.

She leaned over the table. "Did you get in trouble?"

"I don't know yet. Probably. My mother told me to come straight home this afternoon."

"I don't want to get in trouble, you know?"

"You? But you . . . I didn't think you cared about getting in trouble."

"Well I don't. Usually. But. Do you think your parents would maybe like call my old lady?"

"I don't know. I didn't think about that. Why would you get in trouble? All you did was come to my house."

"Yeah, right. I just don't want them to call her up, you know?"

"Well, I don't know what they're going to do. I don't understand what you're so upset about."

"You don't, huh. Well, how would you feel if some stuck-up bitch called up your old lady and told her you weren't good enough to be friends with her precious daughter. How would that make your old lady feel?"

I had only been half paying attention to what Barbara was saying because it seemed stupid. I mean, I was the one in trouble, not her. But what she just said came as a total shock. I jerked my head up. Barbara had an expression on her face I'd never seen before. I couldn't really figure it out.

"But, Barbara. I mean . . . that's not . . . you know . . ."

In a voice that was almost a whisper, she said, "She looked at me like I was dirt, Paula."

This was a Barbara I'd never seen before. She was close to crying. When she said the word "dirt," it was filled with feelings I didn't even know she had. Hurt. Pain. How could my mother have been so mean?

"I don't think it had to do with you. It had to do with her being . . . surprised . . . to find the papers all over the floor and to find me with someone she didn't know. I don't think I'm supposed to see those papers. And I don't think I am ever supposed to be with someone she doesn't know. She thinks she knows every minute of my life."

Barbara's voice was almost a whisper as she repeated, "She looked at me like I was dirt, Paula."

She straightened up and walked away.

Chapter Forty-One

"Paula. Please come in here."

The time had come. I walked out of my room and down the hall to the living room like I was walking to my execution. The only thing missing was a priest. I wondered if Jewish people had rabbis walking with them when they got executed. They never showed that in the movies. It didn't matter. I wouldn't feel any better if I had some guy walking next to me mumbling, "The Lord is my shepherd."

My parents were sitting next to each other on the couch and motioned for me to sit down in the armchair facing them. That was already a first. They never sat next to each other.

My father turned to my mother, who nodded. He turned back to me and started talking in this strange, hesitating way. He always seemed so sure of what he was saying. Now he sounded like he was reading from a script someone had just given him, and he didn't have time to memorize his lines.

He cleared his throat. "Well, Paula, apparently you have a . . . friend whom we didn't know. Of course, that by itself is not wrong. You are not a little child. But it appears that you have been spending a significant amount of time with her. And you never told us about her. You never gave us the . . . opportunity to meet her."

I waited for him to say something else. But he seemed to be done talking. My mother bent her head over her hands when I tried to see her face to see what she was thinking.

"Is that all? You just wanted to meet her? Well, now you've met her. So, everything is okay now, right?" I was going to get up to show that we were finished talking. Luckily, I decided not to.

My mother hissed through clenched teeth, "No, Paula, everything is not okay. And you know that very well."

My father continued, "Paula, from what we have seen and learned about this girl, she does not seem to be . . . suitable."

"Suitable?"

My mother hissed again. It was like a duet. "Yes, Paula. Suitable. She's a tramp. A cheap tramp." She turned to my father. "You should have seen her, Martin. You wouldn't have believed it. Bleached hair. Green eyelids. A sweater so tight it looked like it was painted on. A skirt—"

My father waved his hand impatiently. "I get the picture. Be that as it may. Perhaps Paula simply has bad taste. She certainly has bad judgment. That is not my concern. You are free to waste your life in any way that you wish once you leave this house. But while you are living in this house, you will follow our rules. And you will tell us the truth. It appears now that for some months you have been lying to us. Spending time with a person you knew we would not . . . approve of. When we thought you were with the friends we knew, you were not. When we thought you were in appropriate activities, you were not. And this will stop. Immediately."

How does he know I wasn't where they thought I was? *Margaret.* She was a busy little bee, wasn't she? Busy little snitch. And then my mother chimed in. Not hissing this time but practically screaming. Her eyes were wild. Her face was twisted. She didn't even look like my mother. "I never want you to talk to that girl again! Ever! Do you understand?"

Do I understand? My life is falling apart. How hard is that to understand?

"No!" I cried. "Please. It's not fair. You can't! I won't!"

My father had been pretty calm up until now. Compared to my mother, that is. But I had definitely just said the wrong thing because he became the opposite of calm.

"We *can't*? You *won't*? You have a lot of nerve. We can and you will. You will have nothing more to do with that girl. You will go only to the afternoon activities of which we approve, or you will come straight home. For now, we will allow you to keep the radio and phonograph in your room. For the next month, you may listen to music for one hour a day. If you go to classes and activities for a month, we will lift the restriction. However, if we hear that you are still sneaking around, going to the record store, or seeing this girl, the radio and the phonograph will be removed from you room. And the records."

"But Aunt Carol gave me the record player. For my birthday. And I bought the records with my own money."

My father laughed his mean laugh and looked at my mother. "Her own money. Did you hear that?" He turned back to me. "Earned by the sweat of your brow, no doubt. Where did you work to earn your own money? In the coal mines perhaps. We gave you an allowance. Your own money is our own money. Which we will keep if you lie to us again. I will not have you sneaking around, keeping secrets. So long as you are living here, in our house, there will be no secrets. Do you understand?"

Secrets. If only he hadn't used that word. When he said the word "secrets," it was like letting an evil genie out of the bottle. I jumped up.

"Secrets. You are angry with me because I had a secret. My secret was a friend. A wonderful friend. My only friend, really. And I knew you wouldn't let her be my friend because you're prejudiced. Just because of how she dresses." I turned to my mother. It was my turn to hiss. "You were so rude to her. All those years you told me not to be rude to anyone. Not to hurt anyone's feelings. Well, you didn't care about being rude to her. You didn't care about hurting her feelings. And now you say there will be no secrets. Well, if you don't like secrets, where are Lena and Sophie?"

Chapter Forty-Two

*M*y parents sprang off the sofa, towering over me in a silence that was the loudest noise I'd ever heard. And then my father exploded. He raised his arms and moved toward me. His face was unfamiliar, twisted. His eyes blazed with rage.

He wants to kill me.

I was freezing . . . shaking. I stepped backward. If only I could take the words back. If only I could turn this monster back into my father.

My mother grabbed his arm. He wrestled it away and turned and grabbed her by the shoulders. He shook her. "Did you tell her?"

My mother knew about Lena and Sophie.

She shrieked, "No! No!"

I ran forward and tried to get between them, screaming, "It was Margaret! It wasn't her, it was Margaret!"

My father let go of my mother and stared at me as if he had never seen me before.

"Margaret? Leo's Margaret?"

"Yes."

His mouth twisted and his jaw stiffened. His eyes were slits.

"That son of a bitch. He couldn't keep his damned mouth shut."

He's going to kill Dr. Feldman.

I couldn't stop trembling. I screamed, through chattering teeth,

"No! No! It wasn't his fault. Margaret found . . . It was nobody's fault."

He turned to me again, and only when I fell into the chair did I realize that I'd been running backward. I jumped up.

"Wait. Wait. I'll show you."

I ran back to my room, took the picture out of my book bag, and ran back to the living room. My parents hadn't moved. It was like they'd turned into statues. I held the picture up to show them. The terrible energy drained out of my father, and he seemed like he might collapse. He stood still, squeezing his eyes closed, his chest moving in and out like he had been running. He left the room without looking at the picture or at me.

A hand clamped my arm. My mother didn't look like she was going to kill me. She just looked like she never wanted to see me again.

"You stupid, stupid girl. Where are they? Where are they? Where do you think they are? They're dead, of course. How could you do that to him? Do you hate us so much?"

She grabbed the picture out of my hand and put it in her apron pocket, as if she could make it disappear. She started to walk toward the kitchen, but suddenly she swung around and gaped at me with a combination of surprise and dislike on her face, which was the worst thing I ever saw.

"Is that . . . is that what you were searching for in the papers?"

I sort of nodded.

"You idiot. What's wrong with you? Are you stupid? It was in Germany. Before he came here. It was in Germany."

The word echoed in my brain. Germany. I'd spent my whole life walking around a giant pit in the middle of our lives called Germany. Germany. A dark place where people died.

We hardly dared say the word out loud. But it didn't stop me from thinking about it. For years, I imagined that we'd find out it had all been a mistake. That the terrible things my mother told me about hadn't really happened. My father's parents were actually alive. They would come to America and move to a beautiful house in the country. We would be a regular family, like the ones in the schoolbooks, with grandparents to visit and Thanksgiving dinners. And my father would laugh and tell jokes that were funny because he would be like other people's fathers. Fathers who were American and Christian and lived lives where nothing terrible had happened. And he'd love me more because he was so happy.

That's what I thought before. Ever since I was little. Before Lena and Sophie. But Lena and Sophie changed everything. If Lena and Sophie were alive, my father wouldn't love me more. He wouldn't love me at all because there wouldn't be any me. He'd be living with them and wearing a dopey smile all the time. My mother would probably be happier, too. Married to someone else. But I would never have been born.

Is that what he thinks when he looks at me? *Sophie would've done better than Margaret on the French midterm. Sophie wouldn't listen to music that sounds like a broken furnace. Sophie would be taller and prettier and play the piano and get into every good college in the world.*

And that was when my heart broke. I know it sounds like a stupid thing to say. But it was a real feeling. A pain I could hardly stand started in my heart and filled my whole chest until I couldn't breathe.

I threw myself down on my bed and cried until I fell asleep in my clothes on a wet pillow. And that was how I woke up the next morning. Because my mother never came in to make sure I had turned off the light.

Chapter Forty-Three

J didn't know if I was still forbidden from talking to Barbara. My parents were so angry with me, it didn't seem like they cared what I did. And I didn't care what they said. Talking to Barbara was the only thing I wanted to do.

She was waiting at the table.

"You don't have to worry about my parents calling your mother," I began before I even sat down, "they're only mad at me."

"Yeah? Did you get a beating?"

"A beating? No. But they yelled and now they're not talking to me at all."

Barbara started to laugh. "Not talking to you. Is that a punishment?"

"Yeah, it's awful."

Barbara shrugged. "Doesn't seem like much of a punishment to me. But your parents . . . they said you can't talk to me anymore, right?"

For a minute I didn't believe I'd heard her. I mean, it was one thing for Barbara to know more than me about being cool. But it was another thing for her to know more than me about being me.

"Why would you think that?"

"Oh, come on. Your old lady hated the sight of me. Did she ever talk like that to Margaret? Or your other fancy friends. 'Go away, girlie. Paula's too busy to bother with you.'"

Fancy friends? Sometime, but not today, I would ask her about why she called them that.

"Well, what seemed to really bug them was that they thought I was lying to them because I never told them about you."

"Well, you were."

"I guess. But when my father talked about how important it was to be honest and how you should never keep secrets in a family, it made me really mad."

"Yeah?"

"Yeah. I mean. Honesty? Not keeping secrets? What a hypocrite."

"Hypo—what?"

"Hypocrite. Someone who tells people not to do stuff and then does it themselves."

"Really. There's a special fancy word for that? Doesn't everybody do it?"

"No! Well, maybe. I guess. But it made me so mad that I couldn't help it. It just slipped out. I asked him about Lena and Sophie."

"Oh, my God. What happened?"

"He went crazy. He wanted to kill me. Then he wanted to kill whoever told me. So, I showed him the picture and told him it wasn't anybody's fault."

"But your mother. She didn't know. What'd she do when she found out?"

"Well, it turns out that she did know. He thought she was the one who told me. He grabbed her shoulders and started to shake her. She was crying. It was awful. So, after he left the room, she called me an idiot and looked at me like she hated me. Then she told me they were dead."

"Dead? So that explains everything. Right? I mean, it's okay for a guy to marry another wife if his wife is dead and you don't have an older sister after all. Too bad. I mean, maybe. I don't know what it's like to have an older sister. I can tell you what it's like to have a younger sister. It stinks to high heaven."

"Barbara. What are you blabbing about? Don't you get it?"

"Get what?"

"Get that if she didn't die, I wouldn't have had an older sister. If she didn't die, I would never have been born."

"Why would you never have been born?"

I don't know what reaction I was hoping for, but this definitely wasn't it. "Because, dummy. If his first wife didn't die, he wouldn't have married my mother. And if he didn't marry my mother . . ."

"Oh. I see. Wow. A world with no Paula in it. What would I do for a good laugh?"

"A good laugh? Is that all I am to you? What about me?"

The more upset I got, the calmer Barbara seemed. She was looking at me like we were talking about the price of canned peas. She shrugged her shoulders.

"What about you? If you never was, there wouldn't be any you to miss not being you. But there would still be me. And I would still need someone to make me laugh."

The fact that what she just said made some sort of crazy sense made it hurt even worse. I stood up and started to walk away.

Barbara stood up, too. "Where are you going?"

"Just pretend I was never born, Barbara. Okay?"

Suddenly, Barbara looked really upset. I couldn't believe it.

"Oh, for God's sake, Paula, lighten up. I'm joking. Of course,

I'm glad you were born. I mean without you, I wouldn't have anyone to talk to. You know, really talk to. Other people like you, who are . . . you know . . . smart, and know about Holden and books. I mean, they don't want to talk to me. Be my friend. They look at me like your mother did, you know. Like I'm not worth talking to."

She'd never said anything like that before. I knew why I wanted Barbara for a friend. She was cool. But I never really thought about why Barbara wanted me for a friend. I certainly never thought that she might want me for a friend because I wasn't cool. Or that maybe Barbara didn't think that being smart and reading books wasn't cool. Maybe she thought it was cool. I sat down. Barbara smiled and sat down, too.

Chapter Forty-Four

*A*s soon as we were both sitting down, Barbara said, "How come they're dead? They weren't old. Did they get sick?"

"No, they didn't get sick. They must've gotten killed. In Germany. By the Nazis. Didn't you ever hear of Nazis?"

"Yeah. A little. It was in World War Two, right? When we were born. Tony was in the army. But it was the end of the war, and he didn't have to fight or anything. What do the Nazis have to do with your father? And his wife?"

"My father lived in Germany. The Nazis lived in Germany. And they killed the Jews that lived there. Millions of Jews."

"Millions? How come?"

"How come? Because they were Jewish. And because the Nazis were really bad people. I mean—"

"Is that what happened in Germany? Millions of Jews got killed?"

"Yeah. Didn't you know that?"

"Yeah. No. Not exactly. Oh, man. What a bastard."

"What? Who?"

"Tony. This one night, Tony came home madder than hell. And he says to my old lady that one of his bosses, Mr. Goldsomething, cut his hours. And Tony says, 'That skinny little Yid. Too bad Germany lost the war. They had the right idea.'"

"He said the Nazis had the right idea?"

"Yeah. I didn't know what he meant. But now I do. I told you Tony was a no-good bastard.

Chapter Forty-Five

After Barbara left, I stood up and turned around and smashed into Margaret, who was standing behind my chair. I had no idea how long she had been there. She hadn't said a word, which was strange for her. In fact, she hadn't made a sound.

"What are you doing standing here like some kind of stupid statue?"

And then I realized. "Were you spying on me?"

Margaret sighed and started talking in one of her many annoying ways. The one where she was about to tell you a sad story that she had to tell you and wished that she didn't.

"Well, your mother told my mother that you weren't supposed to talk to Barbara ever again and that you had to go to all your extracurricular activities. So, they agreed that I should, you know, keep an eye on you to make sure."

I stared at Margaret. She was smiling. As if everything was going to be all right now that I had her to keep an eye on me. As if she had no idea that "keeping an eye on me" was another word for spy and snitch and traitor. As if she had no idea that I wanted to strangle her or run away or just lie down on the sticky cafeteria floor and die.

I sank back down into the chair. I closed my eyes and put my head down on the table, cradling it in my arms like it was nap time in nursery school.

From far away, I heard Margaret's voice. "Paula, what's the matter? Are you sick? Do you need to go to the nurse?"

When I didn't answer, Margaret put her hand on my shoulder and gently pushed it back and forth. "Paula, Paula. What's wrong? Are you sick?"

I couldn't remember anything in my life feeling more terrible than Margaret's hand on my shoulder. Worse even than the Novocain injection the dentist gave me, which was the worst pain I'd ever felt in my life. A strange wave of energy rose up from my feet and filled my body. My teeth clenched tightly together, and I could hardly breathe. I stood up and looked at her.

My teeth were still clenched. I didn't know how to open my mouth any farther. My voice slipped out like a hiss. "Get away from me."

Margaret's smile slid off her face like it weighed a million pounds. She stepped back, looking scared, and started to splutter.

"But. What?"

"Shut up, Margaret. Shut up. Get away from me. You, you, traitor. Benedict Arnold. If this was a hundred years ago, they'd shoot you. Or hang you."

Margaret and her scared face took a couple of steps backward. "What are you talking about? She's your mother. Not the British. So maybe you'd better think about that before you hire a firing squad."

"She's the enemy. And you're a traitor. You're going to betray me to her."

Margaret kept backing up until she seemed to find courage waiting behind her. She started to move back toward me, slowly but proudly, and started talking in her "you don't understand anything" voice.

"Look, Paula. I don't know why you're getting mad at me. I mean, it's not like any of this is my fault. You're the one who brought Barbara home."

The strange energy drained out of my body, and I felt like I might be able go on living, even if I hadn't figured out how yet. Margaret's words slowly sank in.

"Are you crazy? It's all your fault. I would never have brought Barbara home if you didn't give me the picture. And showing my parents the picture was what got them really mad."

"Don't be ridiculous. They didn't get mad at you for the picture. They got mad at you because you lied. My parents are the ones who got mad about the picture. They got really mad at me for showing it to you, and I'm not getting my allowance for two weeks. But your parents were mad because of all your lies."

Because I lied? She knew the entire conversation between me and my parents. There didn't seem to be any dirty linen my mother wasn't willing to air in public. What was she going to do next? Take out an ad in the *New York Times*? I could see the headline: "Paula Levy Lies to Her Parents." I didn't have anything more to say. But Margaret did.

"But Paula. She was right. The first thing you did was to break the rules and talk to Barbara."

I thought I would have time to figure things out. But I didn't. Margaret was going to tell my mother that I talked to Barbara today. This very afternoon. Maybe she'll leave school early so she can tell her sooner. I started walking toward Margaret, feeling the gentle tug of my shoe sticking to the floor and pulling it free. My mind raced.

I can't kill her. Here in front of everyone. I have to trick her. Help me, Holden. King of tricks.

"Look, Margaret, you don't have to tell them about this."

"Why not? Because telling her would be treason? You would have me shot?"

"Yes. I mean no. Because this meeting didn't count. I was just being polite. That's a rule, too. I had to tell Barbara that I wasn't allowed to talk to her anymore. I mean, what was I going to do? Just walk past her with my nose in the air? What would that look like?"

Margaret looked at me like she was thinking about believing me, although she didn't.

"You were just saying goodbye?"

"Right. I was just saying goodbye."

"But you were talking to her for the whole lunch period."

"You were watching me the whole lunch period?"

"Pretty much."

Great.

"Were you standing behind me the whole time?"

"No, silly, only after I finished eating my lunch."

At least she hadn't been listening. I don't know why that made me feel better, but it did. A little.

"Well, Margaret, you have to understand. I mean, Barbara and I are friends. I mean, were friends. So, we had to, you know, like, finish up talking about some things."

"So, you finished talking about them?"

"Yeah."

"And you won't talk to her again?"

"No. Of course not."

"Well, okay. And if I don't tell, then you won't be mad at me, right?"

"Right."

She smiled. "Okay. Then I won't tell. No hard feelings, right?"

Is that what Benedict Arnold said?

"No hard feelings, Margaret."

"Good. Let's go outside then. Together. Like friends."

As Margaret and I walked outside together, like friends, my mind was working. Working. Working. I had to figure out where I could meet Barbara without Margaret seeing us. I had to figure out how I was going to tell Barbara to meet me there, wherever it was, without Margaret or the cool kids seeing us making the arrangement. And I had to figure out how to tell Barbara my parents wouldn't let me talk to her without hurting her feelings so badly that she didn't want to be my friend anymore.

My life was like the monster that grew two new heads every time you cut one off.

Chapter Forty-Six

I found out that afternoon how busy my mother had been. Mrs. Kirschner gave me a gigantic smile when I walked into Chemistry Club.

"Nice to see you again, Paula. Your mother called this morning and said you would be coming back today."

Like I'd been on a trip or in the hospital or something. I nodded and sat down. I couldn't find words like, "I'm glad to see you, too." Because I wasn't. The whole valence thing had always been a major puzzle. Not to mention a total bore. I couldn't wait to see what would happen when I "came back" to the orchestra the next afternoon. Maybe they'd play "Hail, Hail, the Gang's All Here."

During class break after third period the next day, Barbara and I passed each other in the hallway pretending, as we always did, not to see each other. Sheila gave me the evil eye, as she always did, her eyes becoming narrow slits under her mascara. She jerked her head back and forth trying to catch me and Barbara looking at each other. I couldn't see Margaret, who was walking behind me, but I imagined her doing the same thing. Except that Margaret's big bug eyes could never be narrow slits. Maybe Margaret and Sheila could work together to make sure Barbara and I never talked to each other again. If I were ever going to smile again, which I doubted, I would have smiled at the thought of Margaret and Sheila comparing notes at the end of the day.

I could hear Margaret telling her mother, "Paula doesn't talk to her juvenile delinquent friend anymore, but now I have one of my own. She's my spy assistant."

Chapter Forty-Seven

S tanding on the lunch line, I saw Margaret saving me a seat and Barbara sitting alone, on the other side of the cafeteria. I put my tray back on the tray pile and walked in a big circle to where Barbara was sitting.

"My parents are crazy. Really crazy," I began as soon as I was close to the table. I couldn't sit down.

"They said you couldn't talk to me anymore, right? I told you they'd do that."

"You were right."

"So how come you're standing up? Did they say you can't eat lunch anymore, either?"

"No. But they made Margaret a spy. If she sees me talking to you, she'll tell."

An angry look spread over Barbara's face. "Well, then, what're you waiting for? Get lost."

Who was she angry with? I hoped it was only my mother and not me, too.

"And I can't come over after school, either, because I have to go to all that junk after school that I was missing. My mother is checking on them."

"Well, I certainly hope you get into a good college."

"Look. Don't be like that. I'll figure out something."

"Look. I told you already. Get out of here before Goody Two-Shoes rats on us. I don't want your old lady calling my old lady."

"I know you don't. But I don't think she's going to. I mean, she's already called up half the world and she didn't call her. So, we just—"

"We just nothing. Get lost. Actually, it wouldn't have worked out so good for me to meet you after school anymore, anyways."

The floor started opening up under my feet. Any minute now I was going to fall through a giant hole to the other end of the world and disappear forever. My eyes burned. But when I looked back into Barbara's face, she was smiling. And her eyes were kind of twinkly. She didn't look like a person who was about to tell someone she never wanted to talk to them again.

"That's why I came over here today. That's what I wanted to tell you. I met a guy."

A guy! She was going out with a boy. She wasn't so insulted she never wanted to see me again. I let out a long breath that I didn't know I was holding onto. The floor became solid and firm under my feet again. It was the best thing she could have said, other than that the boy had a friend who wanted to meet me because he liked girls who dress like creeps but are really cool.

I wanted to know everything about this. I wanted it more than anything. But I didn't dare sit down. If Margaret saw us and told my parents, I couldn't imagine what they would do. But they'd think of something. They'd find a way to make my life even worse than it was now.

"I'll figure something out, and I'll let you know."

Barbara smiled and nodded, but the smile wasn't for me. She was already thinking about something else. Something she cared about a lot more than she cared about me.

Chapter Forty-Eight

I know. I didn't handle that very well. Especially the not hurting Barbara's feelings part. I was pretty depressed about it as I walked back to the lunch line until, like a flash of light breaking through the ceiling of the lunchroom, a solution popped into my brain.

I'm sure you know what study hall is—a free period when you don't have a class and can sit in the auditorium and do your homework or read a book. Or if you're cool, you can throw what's left of your lunch at someone trying to do their homework and fly paper airplanes whenever the teacher is yelling at someone on the other side of the room for flying paper airplanes. Actually, there was so much lunch throwing and paper airplane flying in the study hall that honor students made "better use of the time" by helping out in the school offices, filing and putting things in alphabetical order and stuff like that. They told us this would look good on our college applications, although I never knew why. Anybody applying to college knew the alphabet.

Barbara and I both had sixth period study hall. M&MM (Margaret and my mother) didn't know that because Margaret and I never went to study hall. We had always made better use of our time. Fortunately, though, not in the same place.

That afternoon I told the school clerk, Miss Siegel, that I had this really big project and would need to go to study hall for a few weeks. Miss Siegel was nice and never had much work for me, anyway, since I wasn't allowed to see the students' secret records, which was most of what she took care of. She smiled and nodded and wrote out a pass.

I almost felt like I was flying as I climbed the stairs to study hall, although I knew that if Sheila had sixth period study hall, the whole plan was down the drain. As I handed my pass to the study hall supervisor, I looked around. There was Barbara. She was sunk down in her seat looking at the floor. When she looked up and saw me, she almost jumped out of her chair. Sheila was nowhere to be seen.

Maybe I do have a fairy godmother.

"How the hell . . . ?" Barbara asked as I sat down next to her.

"Never mind. Tell me about the guy. Are you, like, going with him?"

Barbara smiled. "I didn't believe you when you said you'd figure out a way to get around the cops. I didn't think you had the guts. But here you are. If I didn't see it for myself, I would never have believed it."

"Right. I told you I would figure it out and I did. That's why I am an honor student and in all the honor classes and made the honor society, Junior Arista. And I will make Senior Arista. And I would have made Freshman Arista and Sophomore Arista, if there were such things. Now tell me. Are you going with him?"

"Well, not exactly. I mean, I just met him."

"No kidding. What grade is he in?"

"No grade. He doesn't go to school."

"Really? What school does he go to?"

"He doesn't go to any school. He left school when he was sixteen and joined the navy."

My heart pounded and slid into my throat. What kind of future would Barbara have with a boy who didn't even finish high school? My parents would kill me if I even talked to someone who . . . All of a sudden, it was like there was someone else inside my head looking at my thoughts. I realized that my immediate thoughts weren't mine at all. They were my mother's. Before I got a chance to think anything, my mother jumped into my head and thought for me. He didn't finish high school. She wouldn't have a future. That wasn't me. That was my mother. I didn't really care about any of that. I didn't really care, at that moment, what kind of future Barbara was going to have. What I cared about, what I really wanted to know about, was *boys*. Not the pudgy, pimply boys in my class. I wanted to know about the cool, handsome boys who wore pointy shoes and had slicked-back hair. The ones who never looked at me but who Barbara hung out with. I never had the nerve to ask Barbara about them. And this was my chance.

"How old is he?" I asked in a low voice because my throat still felt like it was full of my heart or something else that didn't belong there.

"Nineteen."

"Nineteen! Almost as old as Elvis. And he doesn't mind going out with a girl who's only fifteen?"

"Are you stupid? He thinks I'm seventeen."

"You told him you were seventeen? And he believed you?"

"Of course, he believed me. I told you I could go out with a guy who was older than me. You didn't believe me."

Barbara looked older than I did, of course. I mean, for one thing she *was* older. For another, she tweezed her eyebrows and put

159

blonde streaks in her hair with peroxide, and most of all, her sweaters stuck out pretty far from her chest. But I didn't think she looked seventeen. Seventeen was practically a woman.

"How did you meet him?"

"I was at the roller rink, and he came up and asked me to skate."

She picked him up. At the roller rink. Didn't she know how dangerous that was? He could be anybody. He could be . . . There they were again. My mother's thoughts. I did not have to think them.

When my mother's thoughts fell out of my head, the empty space they left was filled with the most beautiful picture I'd ever seen. I saw a handsome sailor putting his arm around my shoulder and skating with me. I started to get the feeling I got when Richie, the record store guy, looked at me with his blue eyes and said, "Thanks, doll." And I knew that if what happened to Barbara had happened to me, if a handsome sailor came up to me and put his arm around me and started skating with me, that would be better than . . . getting a hundred on the History Regents. Better than making Senior Arista. Better than getting into the best college in the world.

"Are you okay?" Barbara's face was close to mine. "You look strange."

The skating rink disappeared, and I was back in study hall.

"Oh, sure. I'm fine. But where does he live? I mean, what does he look like? Is he really cute?"

"Pretty cute. Why all the—"

"Twenty questions. I know. I'm sorry. It's just that I never had a boyfriend, and I just wanted to know, you know, what he's like."

"Well, he's nice. And he's, you know, mature. He holds the

door for you. And he has money to pay for pizza and stuff. So anyway, I'm going to be seeing him in the afternoons. Because he's home on leave and wants to see me as often as he can."

I nodded and tried to smile. It was hard. Not because I was worried about Barbara picking up a stranger who dropped out of high school and might be dangerous . . . not because I was afraid that she wasn't going to have a great future with a boy who dropped out of high school. It was hard because I was jealous. Completely and totally jealous. More jealous than I had ever been of anyone in my life.

Chapter Forty-Nine

Y ou know what they say about mailmen.

"Neither rain nor sleet nor dark of night will stay these couriers, blah blah." Well, that was me! So far nothing had stopped me and Barbara from being friends. Or maybe I was like a Greek hero, cutting off the monster's heads with his sword. Barbara and I met every day in study hall, safe from the peering eyes of M&MM. Every day we had forty-five whole minutes to talk. The only thing we couldn't do in study hall that we could do at Barbara's house was smoke. And I never really liked smoking anyway.

There was only one thing Barbara wanted to talk about, and it wasn't Elvis anymore. It was Billy. That was the sailor's name. She acted like everything Billy said was the funniest thing she ever heard.

"I was laughing so hard," Barbara was saying, her eyes looking past me, as if she were watching the best movie in the world on the wall behind me and couldn't take her eyes off it for a second, "I almost pissed in my pants."

I didn't usually think the things Billy said were very funny. But of course, I never said it. I tried to picture Barbara and Billy in the bowling alley and in the movies and in the pizzeria. I knew that he held her hand when they were walking and put his arm around her when they were sitting in the movies. I was dying to know about the kissing. I mean, there must have been kissing. But she never talked about it.

Whatever they were doing, she wasn't the same Barbara. She was calm. And happy. It seemed like if she had a chance to meet Elvis, she wouldn't even bother. She stopped worrying that my mother would call her mother and seemed to really like having a friend who was willing to spend her whole study period listening to every not-very-funny thing Billy said.

One time, I even got the courage to say, "Gee, Barbara, he sounds so great. I would really love to meet him," in a voice I practiced in the bathroom in front of the mirror so that it would sound like I didn't care too much about meeting him.

She looked surprised, like it was the strangest idea in the world, and said, "Yeah, you'd like him. He's a great guy." But she never suggested a time or place. Of course, I didn't think I could escape M&MM long enough to meet Barbara and Billy anywhere, but it was nice to think about.

I spent a lot of time imagining Barbara and Billy and me and Billy's friend at the luncheonette, listening to Elvis and having ice cream sodas. Billy's friend looked like Richie in a sailor suit. They had their arms around our shoulders, and we were all smiling like we had the best secret in the world. But I didn't say that to Barbara, who just kept smiling and looking past me at her private movie playing on the wall behind me.

$\mathcal{M}$ y parents didn't seem to be able to forgive me for the sin of Barbara. Like she was the eighth deadly sin. If we had been Christian, they probably would've been telling me that I was going to go to hell. Since we weren't, it seemed like they were trying to make me feel like I was already there. The only time they talked to me was to ask me what I did in school. And when they did, it was more like taking attendance than really caring. It was like I'd stopped being a person and turned into a list of stuff to be done.

All day long I felt the weight of Margaret's eyes on me, as if I were wearing a heavy coat. Except for study hall. Being able to see Barbara every day made life tolerable. Even if all she talked about was a dopey sailor who even I was getting tired of hearing about. Until one Monday afternoon when everything came crashing down. Barbara was sitting in study hall with red eyes.

"What happened?"

"My ol' lady went shopping Saturday afternoon like she always does. So, Billy came over. But she came home early. And we didn't hear her come in because the brats were in their room yelling. And when she walked in, we were in my room, you know, we were, like, kissing."

"Kissing?"

"Yeah, Miss Goody Two-Shoes. Kissing. It's what people do when they love each other."

"I know what . . . Oh, never mind. What happened?"

"What do you think? She went crazy. Because . . . see . . . we weren't like . . . all buttoned up, you know."

"You weren't . . . buttoned? You mean . . . you had your clothes off?"

"No. Not really. Well not so much."

"But you weren't in, you know, like, in the nude?"

There were lots of different magazines with stories about movie stars. Sometimes I would sneak into the candy store to look at them. It seemed like movie stars were always "in the nude." It was exciting to say the word out loud. But it was a mistake. Barbara's face was suddenly filled with anger.

"In the . . . What're you, nuts? Who do you think I am? Marilyn Monroe? Never mind. I can't talk to you."

"No. I'm sorry. Go on. Please."

"Okay. But don't keep interrupting. So then like my old lady, she grabbed Billy and shook him. And she screamed at him, 'She's only fifteen, you bastard!' and, 'My husband's going to kill you!'"

"So, Billy looked really shocked and scared and said, 'I'm sorry, lady, I'm sorry. She said she was older. I'm sorry. I'll never come back. I swear to Christ I'll never come back.'"

"He ran out. He didn't even look at me. He didn't even say goodbye."

Barbara could hardly say the last part. Her lips were trembling, and she really looked like she was going to cry.

"He ran out? What a coward."

"Coward? What does that have to do with it? You should've seen her. She was crazy. Anyway, he already told me that his leave was almost over and that it would be hard for him to write to me when he left because he was going to be training to be the captain of a spy ship. He was going to be working with the president. It was very secret."

"The president of the United States? Oh, Barbara. That sounds like baloney to me."

I know it would have sounded like baloney to my mother, who read a lot of books about unhappy lovers and sailors who go back to sea and never write to the girls they met on leave, which she left in the trash can and didn't know that I took out. Maybe she wasn't always wrong.

"You never help me. You make it seem like it was Billy's fault. And it wasn't. It was her. She screamed at him like a crazy woman. After he left, she slapped me in the face and called Tony and told him to come home right away. She started tearing my room apart. They found a towel under my mattress that was full of, you know, goo."

Well, of course, I didn't know. I didn't have the faintest idea what she meant by "goo." But if I asked her what it was, she wouldn't tell me and would stop talking to me. So, I nodded and didn't say anything.

"I said, 'I love Billy and we're going to get married.'

"Tony screamed, 'Nobody's marrying a fifteen-year-old tramp like you.' He took off his belt and chased me all over the house smacking me wherever he could reach me."

Barbara rolled up her sleeves. Her arms were covered with ugly red marks shaped like the end of a belt.

"I ran to my room and locked the door. In a little while, they said I better come out. Of course, I didn't come out until they promised not to hit me anymore. They took turns yelling at me about how I was selfish and a tramp and didn't care about anyone but myself, and how they gave me everything and raised me in such a nice home, and I didn't care about them, and I didn't care about what people thought about them. And then they yelled at each other over who made me such a selfish tramp. My mother told Tony it was his fault because he was always hitting me. And he said it was her fault because she let me do whatever I wanted. And they both agreed that the problem was that I was running around with wild trampy friends. So anyway, they made an appointment with this doctor to see if I'm pregnant."

"Pregnant. Barbara. Did you . . . do it?"

I figured Barbara and Billy kissed. But I never thought they did "it." Whatever exactly "it" was. Was that what the "goo" was from? I wondered how I could find out more about "it." I was pretty sure none of my other friends knew any more about "it" than I did.

"No. Not all of it. He really wanted to. I wish I had. Now I'll never see him again. And he'll just find a new girl who'll let him, and he'll never even think about me again."

"Barbara, don't think that. My mother told me lots of times that if a boy really loves you, he won't want to do it until you're married."

Oh God. Why on earth did I say that?

"Your mother's an idiot. And so are you. What do you know about anything? No one's ever loved you."

My eyes burned. She was right. No one ever did love me. Not even my parents.

"Well, I know, but maybe. Maybe you could, like, go back to the skating rink or someplace like that and you know, meet somebody else."

"That just proves you're an even bigger idiot. Billy was my one and only true love. I'll never love anyone else ever again."

"Ever? Not even when you're old? Like in your twenties?"

"Not even then."

"But what about Elvis?"

"What about him?"

"He's going to be on *Milton Berle* again."

"In California. Anyway, my parents said I can never go out again. My whole life is over. And I'm not even sixteen."

Chapter Fifty-One

*W*hen I sat down next to Barbara in study hall the next day, I almost fainted. No red lips. No green eyelids. If I'd seen her on the street, I might not even know it was her. I was embarrassed. It felt like I was seeing something I wasn't supposed to see.

She started to talk in a quiet voice that was practically a whisper, and I had to really strain to hear her.

"You know, right, that you're like my best friend, I guess. I mean, the only person I can talk to."

Am I dreaming?

"You're my best friend, too, Barbara."

"Yeah? Well anyway, I wanted to tell you that. And to say goodbye."

My eyes started to burn.

"Goodbye? What're you talking about?"

"You have to promise you won't tell. You can't tell anybody what I'm going to tell you."

"Of course. I promise."

"And you have to promise you won't try to change my mind."

"Of course not."

"Well. My old lady and Tony called up Tony's aunt. She's this big shot nun who runs a convent school. I never met her, but Tony was always talking about how scared he was of her when he was a little kid."

"What's a convent school?"

"You never . . . ? It's like a jail for girls. There are these nuns who watch you every minute. And everybody wears an ugly uniform, and you have to pray all the time."

"But . . . why?"

"Well, you know, Tony always hated me. So, I guess he figured this was his big chance. When I came home from school yesterday, they're both there waiting for me. "Tony kept yelling, 'That little tramp ain't staying under my roof no more!' And in a little while, his aunt came over."

"Where does she live? Is it far away?"

Barbara looked annoyed. "Who cares? Are you going to let me tell you or what?"

"I'm sorry. I'm just . . . I mean, go on."

"Anyway, she's like about four feet tall and five feet wide and I'm like, 'Gimme a break. Who cares about this little fatso.' Until she starts to talk. She sounds like a tuba. You have to hold your ears to keep from having your eardrums busted. She says, 'You give her to me, Tony. I know how to handle her. My school's full of girls just like her.'"

"Like what?"

"Will you let me finish, for Chrissakes? So Mother Brian—"

"Mother Brian?"

"That's her name. Nuns get these weird names. I swear, if you interrupt me once more—"

"I'm sorry. I'm sorry. Go on."

"So, Mother Brian puts her face next to mine and she's got this black mustache and hair on her chin and one thick eyebrow all across her face and stinky breath. 'I know you, missy,' she says. 'You think you're so smart. Wearing makeup and doing God only knows what with the boys. By the time I'm through with you, you'll never do any of that dirty stuff again. You'll want to be a nun. Like me.'"

"Oh, my God. Sister Barbara."

"You think that's funny?"

"No, no. Of course not. I'm sorry."

"So, there's my mother, right? And she's not saying anything. And I'm crying. 'I'll do anything. Please don't make me go.' And she's crying, too. You know, she doesn't want to send me. Not really. But she's afraid of Tony. So fatty went back to her school to make a bed for me, or whatever, and she's coming to get me in two weeks."

"Where is the school? Can I visit you?"

How exactly I would manage that I didn't know, since I wasn't supposed to even be talking to her.

"Don't be a birdbrain. I'm not going to any damn school."

"You're not? But you said—"

"But you said. But you said. Will you stop babbling all the time? I'm not going to any damn school. I'll die first. I swear I will."

"But . . . what are you going to do?"

"I'm going to go to Memphis."

She was so calm when she said it, I thought maybe I heard wrong.

"You're . . . what?"

"Memphis. I'm going to go to Memphis."

"But . . . your parents . . . how?"

"My parents?" She said the word "parents" like it was the funniest word in the English language. "What're you talking about? This has nothing to do with my parents. I'm running away. Like Holden did."

"What're you going to do in Memphis?"

"I knew it. I knew you were going to try to talk me out of it."

"No. No. It's a great idea. But—"

"But. But. What're you? A goat?"

"I'm just trying to think. I mean Memphis. Why Memphis?"

"Why Memphis? Well, there's this singer. I guess you never heard of him. But he lives in Memphis."

"I know Elvis lives in Memphis. But you can't just go to Memphis and knock on his door. I mean, first of all, he travels a lot. And second of all, there's a zillion girls trying to see him all the time and he probably has guards and stuff."

"And third of all, I know all that. You don't have to be an honor student to know how to count, you know. I'm not going to just show up at his door and ring the bell. 'Hey, Elvis, it's me, Barbara.' God. I'm going to, you know, get a job. And meet people who know him, find out what he does. You know. Be smart about it."

"Be smart about it. That's good. What'll you do for money?"

"Well, like I said. I'll get a job. But until then, Tony does this work sometimes, you know, like on the side. And people pay him in cash. And he hides the cash in the back of his drawer. He thinks nobody knows, but I saw him sneaking it in there and the next day I pulled out this sock with more than four hundred dollars in it."

"Barbara. That's stealing."

"Ohhhh, Goody Two-Shoes. So what?"

"So what? They could call the cops, is what. You could—"

"They'll never find me. Unless you tell them where I am. Are you a dirty snitch?"

A picture jumped into my mind of me sitting in a chair with policemen standing all around shining a light on me.

Where's Barbara?

We know you know.

Things will go a lot easier for you if you tell us.

"Of course I'm not a snitch. But what kind of job are you going to get?"

"I don't know. Like being a waitress or something like that."

"What about school?"

"I hate school."

"I know. But I think there's laws that kids can't work. And they have to go to school."

All of a sudden, it was like Barbara had been holding a million tears in her eyes and couldn't hold them for another second because waterfalls started to roll down her cheeks. Waterfalls. I used to think that nothing bothered cool kids.

"I knew I shouldn't talk to a spoiled brat baby like you. You pretend to love *Catcher in the Rye*. You pretend you think like Holden. That everything is fake and phony. Well, you're the phony. Holden got thrown out of school all the time. He ran away. He didn't care. He didn't care about laws. Where in that book does Holden say, 'Oh, no. What will I do? It's against the law for a kid to stay in a hotel all by himself'?"

My brain felt like a merry-go-round. Words kept flying by, but I couldn't grab them. They didn't make sentences.

"Look, Barbara. I know you think I'm just a stupid baby and I don't know anything. And it's true. But I'm just trying to understand. Like, I mean, how're you going to get to Memphis?"

"There's a Greyhound bus that goes there. From the terminal on Thirty-Fourth Street."

"What about your mother?"

"What about her?"

"Don't you think they'll look for you?"

"Maybe. But they'll never find me. I'll change my name."

Barbara had an answer for every question. They weren't good answers, but she held them up in front of her like a shield.

"When are you leaving?"

"Couple of weeks."

I didn't have much time.

Chapter Fifty-Two

y mother was sitting in her chair when I came home from school that afternoon. As usual. She didn't look up when I came in. As usual. But she was holding something in her hand and looking at it with this big smile on her face. Not usual.

I hope I've made it clear that neither of my parents had ever been big smilers. And I didn't remember her smiling even a little smile since the Sophie and Lena disaster. So, instead of walking to my room without saying anything, as usual, I decided to take a chance. I held my breath and said, "Hi, Mama. What's that?"

She looked up in surprise, like she wasn't expecting me. She started to look away, like she still didn't want to talk to me, but then changed her mind and held her hand out to me. In it was a snapshot. My stomach closed like a fist remembering what had happened the last time someone handed me a snapshot.

She said, "Isn't that the cutest thing you've ever seen?"

It was the longest sentence she'd said to me in weeks that wasn't asking what I did in school. I started to feel warm all over and realized that I was happy that my mother was talking to me again, and I'd been really lonely. I missed her. I would never have thought that I would.

I reached out to take the picture. I wasn't afraid. It couldn't be a picture of Lena and Sophie if my mother smiled at it and said it was cutest thing.

It was a picture of a baby propped up on a sofa.

"Your aunt Carol just sent this. Isn't she adorable? Look at the dimple in her chin. And she's such a good baby. She never cries. The picture makes me realize how much I miss that little thing. If only Carol hadn't moved so far away."

I frowned at my mother. I didn't know she was such a big baby lover. I handed the picture back to her.

"Was I a good baby?"

"You? Oh, my God. You never stopped crying. Your father was always saying, 'Can't you do something? She sounds like a foghorn.' And I would say, 'Too bad we didn't buy her in Macy's. Then we could return her and get our money back.'"

She was laughing while she talked and stared at the picture.

I said, "Is that so," trying to make my voice sound like I didn't care about what she just said. "Crying all the time. Sounding like a foghorn. Funny, you never told me any of that before."

She looked at me, and her big dopey smile froze on her face. If I weren't working so hard to keep from crying, I might've laughed to see her looking so confused, realizing what she said and wanting to take it back. She felt bad about hurting my feelings even though she still hated me. It felt like someone lit a match in the front part of my brain. I pressed my lips together and sucked them into my mouth.

My mother sputtered like a balloon someone was slowly letting the air out of. "Oh . . . but . . . I . . . you know . . . that was . . . joking. You were a beautiful baby. You've seen the pictures."

The fire behind my eyes was still there. But the rest of me was cold and empty. I knew I was going to cry. But not yet.

I turned around and walked to my room. I slammed the door behind me and fell down on my bed, crying, trying to untangle my thoughts. *Pictures*, I thought, *I hate pictures*. Everything bad in my life had come from pictures. People who lived before cameras were invented didn't know how lucky they were. Dead people stayed dead. People who moved away were gone. Not like now. You could take Sophie's pictures and my pictures and Aunt Carol's pictures and mix them all up together and you would never know the difference. Who was alive. Who was dead. Who lived in Cleveland. Who lived in Germany. Pictures made everything the same. No time. No place. Everybody's picture lying there on the floor in front of you.

And now, because of a picture, I've had the first conversation with my mother in weeks, and she tells me she and my father couldn't stand me when I was a baby. It was true that my parents never treated me like Margaret's parents treated her. They never looked at me like I was a precious jewel or acted like anything I said was the most brilliant thing they ever heard. But I always figured that, deep down inside, that was how they really felt. I was their only child, after all. But now I knew the truth. They didn't feel that way at all. They never said they loved me because they didn't. I rolled over and buried my face in the pillow, moving only when I needed to find a drier spot.

Chapter Fifty-Three

*T*he next day I went to study hall to meet my only friend in the world, "you're my best friend, Barbara." My head throbbed and my eyes were scratchy. I'd hardly slept.

But Barbara wasn't in study hall when I got there. I sat down and opened a book, so no one would see how worried I was. But I was terrified. What if she had run away already? I would never be able to find her. I might never see her again.

In a few minutes, Barbara came in and sat down on the other side of the room. She looked down and wouldn't catch my eye. So much for "you're my best friend, Barbara." Why on earth wasn't she talking to me? I couldn't imagine. I had to talk to her. I quietly gathered my things and started to walk toward her.

Mr. Ryan's voice boomed across the large room. "Where do you think you're going?"

Was he talking to me? Of course he was. I looked at the red-faced giant standing in front of the room. Generally, I was petrified of him. I mean, all of us honor students were. We never wanted to get in trouble. But now, I didn't care. I wanted to get to where Barbara was sitting, so I needed a reason.

"Um. It was a . . . drafty over there. And I have a cold."

I hardly recognized my voice, sounding so loud in the large

quiet room and making up such a silly story. How exactly a room without windows could be drafty, I'm sure I don't know, but I made some sniffling sounds and he nodded. Probably because I was a mousy creep who never gave him any trouble rather than because he believed me. Anyway, at that moment, a crumpled-up lunch bag flew across the room, and he had more important things to pay attention to. I sat down next to Barbara, who smelled of cigarettes. Actually, she reeked of cigarettes, like she had rolled around inside a cigarette pack. I grabbed her arm.

"We have to talk."

She jerked it away. "No, *we* don't. You better not have told."

"Told? Are you crazy? Of course, I haven't told. But anyway, there's another reason. I've decided I'm going with you."

She faced me. But not in friendship. "Very funny. What are you, now, a comedian? Like Milton Berle? Did Elvis tell that joke on *The Milton Berle Show*?"

"It's not a joke. I'm going with you."

She looked like an iceberg that was starting to melt. A little. Around the edge. She stared straight into my eyes as if she could look into my brain to see if I was telling the truth.

"But Mommy and Daddy—"

"Shut up. I don't want to talk about them."

I started to cry. Barbara stared at me in disbelief. But only for a minute, and then the cold, angry "drop dead Barbara" came back.

"What's with the waterworks? Cut it out. Who do you think you are? My little sister, Phoebe? Holden didn't take his little sister with him, and I'm not taking mine with me. Why should I?"

When Holden told his little sister, Phoebe, that he was going to run away, she showed up with a suitcase and wanted to go with him. He didn't let her. I hadn't thought about that part of the book in a long time. I was surprised Barbara thought of it right away.

"I'm not Phoebe. You're not Holden. And I'm coming."

"You really mean it? I mean, you really want to run away from home? But why would you want to do that? Your parents would never send you to a nun-prison. They're Jewish, for Chrissakes. And, I mean, you're rich. You've got a room and an allowance, and they never hit you."

"So what? I mean, I'm not rich. And what difference does that make? You have a room. Holden was a lot richer than me. And he was just as unhappy at home as we are. We're all in the same boat, Barbara. You, me, Holden."

"I guess, but what about your perfect attendance award?"

I started to punch her, but she caught my hand and shrugged.

"Okay. You can come if you want. But you better not try to get to Elvis first."

"You don't have to worry about that. We're not going to Memphis."

She threw my hand down like it was on fire. It would've smashed on the ground if it wasn't attached to my arm.

"Get lost. You come here crying, begging me to take you along. And now you're bossing me around. Get lost. I don't need any spoiled brat baby bossing me around."

"Goddamn it, Barbara. Shut up and listen to me for a change."

We stared at each other in surprise. I'd always been so sure that cool kids knew more stuff than I did that I never told Barbara what I thought or what she should do. Even when I was pretty sure she was making a mistake. Like with Billy. Like with Memphis. But I'd been up all night figuring this out. And I had to convince Barbara to listen to me.

"You've got to listen to me, Barbara. I've been thinking about this all night. See, the thing of it is, you're not even sixteen years old. You can't live on your own. No one's going to hire a fifteen-year-old girl. No one's going to rent you an apartment. They'll just . . ."

"But if—"

"I know what you're going to say. You're going to say you don't look fifteen. Well, you don't look eighteen, either. And that's how old you have to be to live by yourself."

Her eyes opened wide, and she almost swallowed her lips. She turned away, sniffled a little, and turned back. Her voice sounded calm, although she didn't look calm.

She nodded. "You could be right."

"You know I'm right."

"But . . . then . . . what are you saying? I knew I shouldn't tell you. I knew you'd try to talk me out of it."

"I'm not trying to talk you out of it. It's the opposite. I'm trying to help you. Just because we're too young to live by ourselves, it doesn't mean we have to stay with our parents. It just means we have to find a grown-up who'll let us stay with them."

"Are you crazy? Grown-ups all stick together. If we talk to a grown-up . . . any grown-up . . . they'll call our parents so fast it'll make your head spin."

"I know a grown-up who might help us."

Her face twisted. I could tell she didn't believe a word I was saying.

"Who?"

"My aunt Carol."

"Who the hell is Aunt Carol?"

"My mother's sister. The one with the baby my mother went to help out with."

"Your mother's—"

"Listen. Please. Let me finish at least. Aunt Carol is a lot younger than my mother, and she was always really nice to me. I know she really liked me. And, you know, she has this little baby. People who have babies need a lot of help. So, if we go to Cleveland and explain everything to her, I think she would understand and want to help us and want us to help her with the baby. And if she wants us to stay, maybe our parents would go along with it."

"You want us to go to Cleveland? What's Cleveland?"

"It's a city. It's in Ohio."

"Is that like a foreign country? Like France?"

"No. It's a state. It's closer to New York than Tennessee. The state that Memphis is in. Didn't you even know what state Memphis was in?"

"I know enough to know that Ohio sounds like Nowheresville to me. So, you stay up all night figuring out that we should go to this state that's got no rock and roll but is closer to New York than Tennessee. And we're going to show up at your aunt's house in Cleveland, and she's going to open the door and say, 'Oh, Paula. How nice to see you. Won't you and your friend come in and have cookies and milk?'"

Barbara made it sound like a really dumb idea. I tried to remember why it had made so much sense last night.

"Well. It's like I told you. She's nice. I think if we explain everything to her and tell her we won't make any trouble for her. We'll go to school and get jobs and—"

"School?"

"Yeah. Of course."

Barbara looked away and was quiet for a long time.

"You know what I think, nosebleed? I think you've lost your

mind. If you ever had one. Aunt Carol doesn't know me from a hole in the ground. She'll take one look at me and think the same thing your mother did. There's no chance she'll let me stay, even if there was a chance she'd let you stay. Which there isn't. And there's no chance our 'parents' would agree to let us stay there if Aunt Carol did call them up and say, 'Guess who's my new babysitter?' And I'm not going to school. And I'm not talking to my old lady and Tony ever again. I'm going to Memphis. That's it. You can come with me if you want."

"Sure. Great. We'll go to Memphis. And you know what's going to happen? We go into a soda fountain and tell them we want a job, and they ask us how old we are and where are our working papers and where are we from because we talk so funny they know we're not from there. And then they call the police. And the police call our parents, and they put us on the first bus going back to New York. You know, this is a whole different thing from what Holden did. Holden only ran away for a couple of days."

"What happened then?"

"Don't you remember? He went home, and he got sick and went to, like, a hospital. And he doesn't want to talk about it because his parents sent him to another school. And he's just another boring kid going to another boring school."

Barbara stared at me like she never realized that was how it ended. After a minute or two, she said, "Another school. Yeah. I guess maybe that is what happened to him. But it doesn't mean that'll happen to us."

"So, you'll think about it? About going to Cleveland?"

"No, birdbrain. I won't."

Chapter Fifty-Four

Maybe Barbara was right about Aunt Carol. Maybe she wouldn't help us. I knew I was right about Memphis. I racked my brain trying to think of something. I hated everything about my life. I wanted to leave it so much I could hardly breathe when I thought about it. But it didn't seem like the world gave four-teen-year-old girls a lot of choices. It was like my life was a big gray wall, and the only bright spot on it was study hall. Forty-five minutes out of every twenty-four hours when I got to talk to Barbara. And one way or another, that was going to end. But a few days later, when I had all but given up hope, Barbara actually had a good idea.

"Cheer up, sourpuss," Barbara whispered, as she slid into the seat next to me. "Today is your lucky day. We don't have to go to Dweebland."

"What?"

"I said, we don't have to go to Dweebland. Are you going stupid? Because I sure don't want to run away with some stupid girl."

She was getting more and more annoying.

"Don't tell me you're back to the stupid Memphis idea."

"No, I'm not back to the stupid Memphis idea. Even if it's a million times less stupid than your Dweebland idea. I figured out a completely new place to go. And it's perfect. We can go to Hoboken."

"Hoboken?"

"Yeah. It's in New Jersey. That's a state, too. And it's even closer to New York than Dweebland."

"I know where New Jersey is. But why?"

"'Cause that's where my old man lives. This guy that you would call my father."

"I didn't know you had a father."

"What'd you think? I was like Jesus? There was this big star shining when I was born?"

"Don't keep making dumb jokes. Did you change your mind? Just tell me."

Barbara looked shocked.

"Are you crazy? Of course I haven't changed my mind. It's just I was thinking about what you said. About needing a grown-up to help us. And I figured, your family isn't the only family with secrets. I have a secret, too. My secret is that I found all this stuff about my old man. I never met him, you know, or maybe when I was a baby and can't remember. But I found all these papers hidden in my old lady's dresser drawer. And I know who he is and where he lives, even though no one ever said one word about him to me. If there's any grown-up in the world who might help us, it'd be my old man, right? I mean, he is my old man, after all."

The study hall seemed to rock like a ride in the amusement park.

"But why do you think he'd help us? My father—"

"Is married to your mother. It's different. My old man doesn't care what my old lady thinks. She's not his wife. And he must hate Tony. I mean. Anybody would. Especially him."

"But did you ever meet him? I mean, how do you know him?"

"Well, I don't know him. Like I said, they split up when I was little. But I found this bunch of papers about the divorce and stuff. So that's how I found out about him. His name is Sean Dougherty, and he lives in Hoboken."

And then, for the first time since I decided to run away with Barbara, I started to feel scared. It was one thing to think about going to Aunt Carol's house. Somebody I knew. But this was different. We were going to a strange place to ask a man neither one of us had ever met to help us.

As if Barbara was reading my thoughts, she said, "Don't worry. I know lots of stuff about him. There were these pages from newspapers in the drawer, too. So that's how I know. He's a musician. He plays the piano in a band. Like a jazz band. They call him 'Doc' Dougherty, and he's played all over the world. England. Paris. He's famous."

"How come you never told me about him?"

"Why didn't you tell me about your sister? Nobody ever talked about him. It wasn't like I was going to meet him or anything. Until now. I think it'd be pretty cool to live with a guy that plays in a band. I mean, maybe he even knows Elvis. He's probably rich. A famous piano player. Must make more money than a dumb truck driver like Tony."

He couldn't be too famous. I'd never heard of him. Of course, jazz was the music my mother liked. Too bad I couldn't ask her if she'd ever heard of him.

"Do you know what he looks like?"

She shook her head.

My hands were all sweaty. I rubbed them together and felt them shaking. I remembered a kid show that had a puppet named Slugger, who was a piano player. He was skinny and had big ears and a cigarette hanging out of his mouth. Maybe that was what Barbara's father looked like.

I sat back and turned the idea around in my head. It made a lot of sense, even if it was scary to think about going to someone I didn't know. A father would have to want to help his daughter, even if he didn't know her. And even if my father never helped me very much. If I started to make plans, I was sure I would start to like the idea more.

I asked, "What're you going to use for a suitcase?"

"A suitcase? I didn't think about it. There's an old suitcase in the closet. We could use that."

"How can I get my stuff over to your house?"

"What stuff? You weren't planning to go to my old man's house in your creep clothes, were you? I mean, what's the matter? Can't leave home without your poodle skirt?"

"Oh, shut up. You know very well that I haven't worn a poodle skirt since I was a kid."

"But you had one, right?"

"Well, yeah. Everybody had one. Didn't you?"

"No. My old lady said they were too expensive. I mean, I didn't want one. They were fruity."

"No, they weren't. I really . . . Never mind. What should I bring? I can't exactly go naked, you know."

Barbara laughed. "No. But you have to get cool clothes. So I won't have to be embarrassed. You got any money? I mean, you must have money. You're always buying records."

"Yeah, but they don't cost as much as clothes."

"Come on. I bet you can get some money."

I'd been putting money into a bank account every week since I was in first grade. The money was for my future. I didn't know exactly when the future was, but I was pretty sure it wasn't now. One day my whole life might be ruined because I didn't have that money.

"Well," I said, "there is this bank account."

A big smile spread across Barbara's face.

"I figured. We'll go shopping after we're settled."

Chapter Fifty-Five

By the next day, Barbara was really cooking. I mean, she was planning.

"We can leave on Tuesday, when my old lady leaves early for work. Then she won't see us carrying out the suitcase."

"But what if your father is at work on Tuesday? Shouldn't we go on a weekend when he's home?"

"Are you going to argue with me about everything? You think I'm some dummy that needs an honor student telling me everything? Musicians work at night, birdbrain. And anyway, everyone is home on the weekends. Tony sits on the couch all day in his undershirt drinking beer and belching. So, like, I think he'll notice me walking out the door with a suitcase. Any more bright ideas?"

"Well, just one. Don't get mad, but how do you know that he still lives at the address that was in the papers?"

Barbara looked at me and smiled the biggest smile I had ever seen her smile.

"Because, Miss Honor Student, I called information in Hoboken and gave the operator the address and asked for his number. And what do you think? She gave it to me!"

I had to admit that for a person who started out wanting to become the world's youngest waitress in Memphis, Tennessee, without even knowing that Memphis was in Tennessee, Barbara had made a lot of progress.

"Okay, Barbara. Tuesday it is. But . . ."

"I knew it. You're chickening out. I knew you wouldn't go."

I answered her impatiently. I wasn't used to Barbara whining. She was starting to sound like Margaret.

"I'm not chickening out. I'm just trying to work everything out. It's a little complicated. Like how am I supposed to get the money out of the bank?"

"What do you mean?"

"I mean, the bank is only open while we're at school."

"It is?"

"Don't you know anything about banks? They're only open until three in the afternoon."

"Then how did you put the money in?"

"They collect the money at school with your bankbook. Then I guess someone goes to the bank because in the afternoon they give you back your bankbook with a stamp in it saying you put money in that day and how much you have altogether."

"Where is the bank?"

"I don't know exactly. The address is on the bankbook."

"Give it to me, and I'll get the money."

I froze. *Give her my bankbook? Let her go to the bank and get my money?* My thoughts raced, and I felt cold all over. I must've had a strange look on my face because Barbara looked at me with surprise.

"What's the matter? You said they don't know you at the bank, right? So, if I say I'm you, who's going to know any different? I can go when I'm not in school. Nobody's following me around all day."

I hated it when people said stuff that sounded logical but had nothing to do with the problem. I wasn't worried about the bank. I was worried about my money. I mean, how could you just give somebody your bankbook and let them take your money? I mean, how . . . It was my mother again. In my head, thinking my thoughts. My mother's world was filled with crooks and kidnappers waiting to jump out of their dark hiding places and do terrible things to you. Steal your money. Steal your child. But my world wasn't like that. I had a friend I could trust with my life, let alone with my bankbook.

The next day I gave Barbara my bankbook. The day after that, she wasn't in school. She wasn't in study hall, and I didn't see her walking around the cafeteria pretending not to see me at lunch. There was enough of my mother left in my head that all through the Reconstruction era and "The Tell-Tale Heart," I wondered if Barbara had run away with my life savings. Whenever I noticed the thought bubbling up into my thinking, I would tell myself that I was pathetic and go back to a serious consideration of the impeachment of Andrew Johnson. But the thought was like the beating heart the narrator heard in Edgar Allan Poe's story, and I wondered if I was crazy like he was. I could be. The beating heart wasn't there, and Barbara hadn't run away with my money. Probably.

But I would be lying if I didn't tell you that I breathed a sigh of relief, quietly so no one could hear me, when I saw Barbara wandering around the cafeteria pretending not to see me the next day.

She sat down next to me in study hall and whispered, "Open up your briefcase."

When I looked at her curiously, she rolled her eyes and looked impatient. My briefcase was lying on the floor under my seat. I pulled it out and undid the clasp of the strap that went over the top, holding it together. After I sat up, Barbara slowly bent over, looking around her like the first day we met, like a spy. She had her little black purse in her hand, and I saw her take a fat envelope filled with money out of her purse and slip it into my briefcase. I saw the corner of the top bill sticking out. It had the number "50" on it.

Without sitting all the way up, she whispered, "I didn't take out all the money in the account because there were more forms to fill out if you closed the account, so I took out $285. There's $25 left."

"Two hundred—"

"Shhhhh."

My heart beat so hard inside my chest, it felt like it was trying to break out of my ribs. I felt icy cold. I'd never had more than twenty dollars at one time before and that was only once, when I took my birthday present money to the store to buy the poodle lamp. I had been terrified walking down the street, passing all these strangers who might have been robbers.

I kept thinking it would be just my luck to be attacked on the one day that I was carrying a fortune instead of all the other days of my life when all I had with me was my lunch money. I know that was my mother thinking. But it did seem like it was dangerous to have so much money with you. My parents never carried that much money around or even had it in the house, as far as I ever knew. I would have to carry it in the hallways and in the street and on the subway. I would have to leave it on the floor during class and during orchestra practice because I would look ridiculous holding my briefcase during class, and it was impossible to hold it while I was playing the violin.

Keeping my face turned to the front of the room so it wouldn't look like we were talking, I leaned my body closer to Barbara and whispered, "How could you carry so much money around? Weren't you scared?"

She did the same, leaning closer to me and whispering, "I didn't exactly make an announcement about it. 'Hey, everybody. Guess what I've got in my purse?'"

We snuck a sideways look at each other. My eyes felt like they were opened so wide they must have been bigger than Margaret's. We both turned our faces away and Barbara whispered, "If you walk around looking like a normal human being and not like you just robbed a bank, which is how you look now, nobody knows how much money you're carrying, birdbrain."

"But. I mean. What if—"

Barbara hissed, "I can't believe I'm running away with such a birdbrain. If you're afraid to carry money around school, what're you going to do on a bus full of strangers going to a place you've never been to before?"

It was like a bucket of cold water dumped over my head. I couldn't catch my breath. I think I may have started to shake, but I wasn't sure because I didn't feel my body. Barbara was talking softly, but I could hear the panic in her whisper. She was just as scared as I was.

"I knew it. I knew you would chicken out. I knew you'd never come with me."

"Don't keep saying that," I whispered back, trying to make my whisper sound calm and brave. "I'm not chickening out."

I wouldn't. I owed it to Barbara not to. But there was a little part of my brain that was starting to wish I could. Maybe not so little. And maybe not just starting.

Chapter Fifty-Six

F or the rest of the day, until I got home and hid the money in my desk drawer, I was in a sort of trance. I kept repeating to myself, *Nobody can tell I'm carrying around a fortune.* Nobody would dream that I took the money I'd been saving since I was in first grade out of the bank or that in a few days they would never see me again because I was going to run away. Nobody I knew had ever done anything like that before. That's why it was so scary. I felt cold all the time, even with a sweater on.

Waiting was harder than I thought. There were so many things that could go wrong, I didn't think I could keep from going crazy. What if there weren't any buses going to Hoboken? What if there was a bus but we missed it? What if all the tickets were sold out? What if they wouldn't sell us a ticket because we were too young? What if we couldn't find Barbara's father's house? What if he didn't want us to live with him?

I couldn't talk about my feelings with Barbara because she would get angry if I tried to talk and say, "I knew you were a spoiled brat baby," or "I knew you'd never really go."

It was amazing how much you could get done if you didn't have to go to school every day. Barbara had gone to the bank. She went to the bus terminal on Thirty-Fourth Street by subway and found out that it was easy to get to the bus terminal by subway, that buses went to Hoboken every hour, and that round-trip tickets cost seventy-five cents. We only needed a one-way ticket, and that would be forty cents.

Everything started to seem different. The most ordinary things were suddenly special in a way I could never have imagined. I kept thinking things like, *Is this the last time I will ever run into Mrs. Jamison outside the bakery? Is this the last Elvis magazine I will ever buy at Sammy's?* And of course, whenever Margaret gave me one of her "I know more than you do about everything in the world" looks, I wanted to shout, "You don't know anything! You don't even know that after next Tuesday you'll never see me again."

I was afraid to look at my mother. She always said she could tell I was lying by looking at my nose. I know. She said strange things. Even when I was little, I didn't think my nose really changed when I lied. I mean, it wasn't like I was Pinocchio or something. But I didn't want to take a chance. It was safer not to look at her, which wasn't that hard, because she wasn't talking much anyway, except to say, "Your dinner is ready," and "Did you finish your homework?"

Chapter Fifty-Seven

I t was hard to figure out what I could take with me. I couldn't talk about it with Barbara. Thanks to her idea of taking money out of the bank, I had a fortune hidden in my desk drawer. It was more than enough to buy a cool wardrobe. I knew exactly what I wanted to get. A fuzzy white sweater. A tight black skirt with a slit up the back and flat black shoes with a strap around the back. I didn't know if there was such a thing as cool underwear or pajamas. If there was, I'd never seen them, so it seemed like I could take some underwear and a pair of pajamas. I would take my garter belt and stockings, of course, since I wouldn't be wearing socks. And my toothbrush and toothpaste. Maybe I could take a few pieces of my favorite jewelry. They wouldn't take up a lot of room.

It was harder to think about the things I would be leaving behind. Because the more I thought about it, the more I realized there were a lot of things I really loved. My radio. My record player. My records. Books and magazines. Pictures of me when I was little. The rest of my jewelry. The big girls' bed I'd been so excited to be big enough for. The poodle lamp. It was better not to think about it. After all, I might get to see these things again sometime. I might come back to visit.

My briefcase was pretty roomy when I took out the loose-leaf notebook and textbooks and hid them under the bed. Barbara and I carefully worked out our escape plan. I would go to school on Tuesday, wearing my ordinary clothes and carrying my ordinary briefcase. M&MM wouldn't notice anything that would make them suspicious. Nobody would know I carried a briefcase full of money and underwear. When Margaret and I were walking down the hall to class, I would tell her I had to go to the bathroom. I would walk back up the hall and out the door I came in and down the block to the subway, where Barbara would meet me.

On Tuesday, Margaret was waiting for me in front of her house as usual. I smiled and tried to act normal. Unfortunately, I couldn't stop thinking about the money. It was hidden underneath some underpants and bras and stockings and a nightgown. I'd started out folding things neatly but finally just stuffed as much as I could into the briefcase. $285! It was enough to buy a television set. It was equal to 380 days of school lunch. More than a whole year's worth of lunch every single day, including weekends and vacations when you're not in school.

Margaret leaned her face close to mine and asked, "What's the matter?"

"Nothing's the matter. Why did you say that?"

"You look strange."

Maybe my mother was right. Maybe Margaret could tell from my nose that I was only pretending it was an ordinary day.

"Well, I'm not strange. I'm just the same old Paula."

She shrugged. But she seemed satisfied and didn't ask me anything else for the rest of the trip.

Chapter Fifty-Eight

*E*verything was going according to our plan. I walked a little way into school with Margaret before I turned away saying, "I have to go to the bathroom, Margaret. I feel sick."

Margaret nodded and kept going. After she was swallowed in the crowd of students, I walked back toward the exit.

"Hey, you, girlie, where do you think you're going?"

Not according to our plan. How could we forget about the teachers standing by the doors in the morning? I turned around and saw a teacher I didn't know walking toward me. I didn't have much time to figure out an answer. What would Holden say? Something crazy that no one would believe. What would Barbara do? Run out without saying anything. I was on my own.

I smiled my most honor-student-good-girl-I-did-all-my-home-work smile and said, "Good morning."

Her expression didn't change. "You're going the wrong way."

"I know that's how it looks. But just before I got to my home-room, I looked in my pocket and saw that I had only one glove. I need to go back to look for it. I'm pretty sure I know where I dropped it. It's just a little ways down the block."

She looked like she didn't believe me. She kept shaking her head and walking toward me. I couldn't believe how dumb she was.

I knew she didn't know me. But anybody could tell from my clothes and my manners that I was an honor student, and honor students don't lie or get into trouble. Well, I mean they don't usually lie or get into trouble. Because I was lying and was about to get into a lot of trouble, if only she would let me.

I kept smiling, trying to look like an honor student who always did her homework and never lied to a grown-up for a second.

"I'm pretty sure I dropped it when I stuck my gloves into my pocket. And that was just by the gate. My parents gave them to me for my birthday. They'll kill me if I lose it. Please. It'll just take me a minute. If I go now, I'm sure I can be in homeroom on time."

I thought that was a good touch. The birthday present part. And it seemed to work. She hesitated, looking hard at me like she was trying to decide whether I was lying. Like she was waiting for my nose to tell her I was lying.

What if she looks inside my briefcase?

I pushed that thought quickly out of my head as it started to make me feel cold all over and forced my face back into the dopey smile.

She finally nodded.

"You'd better hurry. You have less than five minutes to get to homeroom."

"I will. I will," I said, turning as I spoke and running out the door.

"No running!" I heard her yell.

I slowed down and walked out of the building. The sun was blazing so bright, I had to squint. The day was cold, luckily, since I don't know what I would have said if I hadn't had a glove to look for. The sun warmed my face. I felt like it was shining just for me. The whole world was shining just for me. I could have been a queen, walking across the yard, knowing the school behind me was getting smaller and smaller. How happy I was to be outside of it. In the yard. On the street. Moving toward freedom.

Barbara was standing under the pole that held the glass globe, by the stairs leading down into the subway, next to a suitcase. She was twisting and turning and moving from one leg to another. I could tell she was nervous. I wasn't. For the first time since we decided to run away, I wasn't scared at all. Everything was going to work out fine. Barbara's father would be home when we got there. He would be living in a big and beautiful house, with lots of bedrooms and maybe even a swimming pool. He'd be so happy to see his daughter again, his long-lost daughter, he would welcome us with open arms. He'd love to have us live with him. We'd each have our own room, next to each other, and piles of records and cool clothes. Barbara's father would drive us around in a big convertible car, and we would go to parties with his cool musician friends.

Barbara didn't smile when she saw me, but she did look relieved.

"I thought you weren't coming. You're so late."

"I'm not late. I'm exactly on time. How would you know, anyway? You don't even have a watch. I got stopped going out of school. I was—"

"We can't just stand here talking all day. Let's go. We'll miss the bus."

"We have plenty of time. Just let me tell you something cool. I—"

"Tell me on the bus."

Barbara picked up the suitcase and started walking down the stairs. It was old and beat-up, and looked like it was made out of cardboard, covered with tiny black and white checks. It wasn't very big, so I could see that Barbara hadn't brought a lot of stuff with her, either. I wondered if she had taken Tony's money. We would be going on the biggest shopping spree in history if she did. I wondered what kind of stores they had in Hoboken.

I called after her, "Is the suitcase heavy? Do you need help?"

She just shook her head and kept walking.

Chapter Fifty-Nine

*W*hen Barbara and I were standing next to each other on the subway platform, with the suitcase in between us, I felt like I was in one of those movies where the camera picks a person up in one life and puts them down into a different one. If you'd told me a few months ago that I would have a cool friend, I would have said you were crazy. I'd never heard of Elvis Presley, and my mother knew where I had been every minute of my life. And now, I was running away from home to live in Hoboken, New Jersey, with a famous musician. The father of the girl my parents had forbidden me to have anything to do with. I was on a great adventure. Like Magellan. Lewis and Clark.

I hadn't exactly worked out how my parents would know that I'd run away. I didn't leave a note because Barbara told me not to. I told her I would just say goodbye. I wouldn't tell them where I was going or anything. But Barbara said my house was so neat and clean that my mother would find a note right away, and they would start looking for us before we got the chance to get away. So, it wouldn't be until I didn't come home for dinner that my mother would realize there was something wrong. She'd call Margaret for a report on my whereabouts. And Margaret would say I went home because I didn't feel well.

"As soon as we got to school," Margaret would tell my mother, "Paula said she felt sick and went to the bathroom. She never came to homeroom and wasn't in class, so I figured she went home. We all thought that," she would add, because she was beginning to worry that she might have failed Paula-spying, the only thing she had ever failed in her life.

"No," my mother would tell Margaret, "Paula didn't come home. I haven't seen her since she left for school this morning."

Now Margaret would freak out, as she heard fear creeping into my mother's voice. Two different grown-ups had given her the responsibility of keeping an eye on me, and she had failed. I could see her eyes opening to the size of dinner plates as she tried to figure out how she was going to get out of this.

And my mother would think I'd been kidnapped by a maniac on the GG train. She'd wring her hands and repeat, "I knew it, I knew it," and start to cry and call my father. Of course, he wouldn't cry. He'd be his usual logical and impatient self.

"She left school and didn't come home? But where could she go? Is she hiding or something?"

"Maybe she's been kidnapped," my mother would say.

And he'd say, "I very much doubt it."

And she'd say, "We better call the police."

"The police?"

"Yes, Martin, please call them. I'm afraid something terrible may have happened to her."

And he'd agree and call the police and tell them his daughter was missing. Maybe by now he'd be starting to get worried, too, and start to feel sorry for the things he said to me. He'd hurry home to be with her because she was so upset, and they would sit together wondering where I could be and if maybe I'd been kidnapped or murdered. They might start to realize they really did love me and wished I was home.

Or maybe they would be glad that I was gone.

"Remember how she sounded like a foghorn when she cried," my father would say, laughing. And my mother would start to smile, too, and stop being so sad.

I decided I would call them after we were settled and tell them I was okay and that I had a new life and they should tell the police to stop looking for me if they had called the police. I wouldn't tell them where I was. Maybe I would tell them I would come to visit sometime. Or maybe not. I would have to see.

Chapter Sixty

T he subway train thundered into the station. I had been so lost in thinking about my parents, I'd forgotten where I was. The noise scared me into remembering. My legs went numb. My feet felt glued to the platform. This was it. The big moment. I could still turn around and climb the stairs and go to English class. I'd be late, and I'd get detention. I'd never had detention before, but that was no big deal. I could put the money back in the bank, and no one would ever know I'd been about to run away from home with the girl I wasn't supposed to talk to. But once I got on that train, there would be no turning back.

"What're you waiting for?" Barbara demanded, pulling on my arm. She looked into my face. "Hey. You're not changing your mind, are you?"

I saw fear in her eyes. She was pulling on my arm so tight, it was starting to hurt. She'd accused me of changing my mind a lot of times during the past two weeks. And she could never hide the frightened look in her eyes when she said it. I always got mad when she said it because it meant that she didn't have any faith in me. She didn't know what a good friend I was and that I wasn't a baby, and I wouldn't let her down. But just now I did almost change my mind. Right now I felt scared to death at the thought of what we were doing.

In comic strips, they sometimes showed a character trying to make up his mind while a little devil was talking to him in one ear and a little angel in the other. I could hear two voices talking to me now—one saying, "Get on the train," and the other saying, "Go back to school." Freedom, adventure, Barbara on one hand. Safety, Chemistry Club, a good college on the other. I didn't know which was the devil and which was the angel, but I knew I had to choose.

I pulled my legs until they came unstuck from the platform and followed Barbara onto the train, and the doors closed behind me. That was it. My life would never be the same again.

I looked around and saw, to my surprise, that we were in an ordinary subway car. It wasn't the nightmare train with no windows and crowds pressing all around so I couldn't breathe. And there didn't seem to be anybody who looked like a maniac, either. Just a few ordinary people reading newspapers, looking at their wrist-watches, or just staring straight ahead.

I turned to Barbara. "What's your mother going to do when she finds out?"

"Who cares?"

"But, I mean, didn't you think about it?"

"Yeah. Sure. She'll cry, and Tony will yell at her."

"He'll yell at her because you ran away?"

"Yeah. That's just what he does. Whatever happens, he yells at her and takes the strap to me."

"You mean he hit you more than just that time with Billy?"

"Yeah. He did it all the time. Doesn't your old man?"

"No. He never hit me at all."

"Then why are you running? Oh, yeah. Your sister died. I don't know. If they would let me stay home and not hit me . . ." Her voice trailed off for a minute. Then she looked me hard in the eyes.

"You're not going to change your mind, are you? I mean, just keep thinking about how great it's going to be living with a famous piano player. Maybe he lives in, you know, a mansion. Maybe he's got a swimming pool. Cool people coming over and having parties. We'll never miss home for a second."

In another minute, Barbara was going to tell me her father lived in Buckingham Palace with the Queen of England. And Elvis came to dinner every Thursday. But she was right, even if that part probably wasn't. It was freedom that was the important thing. Getting up in the morning and deciding what you want to eat for breakfast. Choosing your own clothes. Never having someone tell you your grades weren't as good as Margaret's. Never looking into your father's eyes and knowing he wished you were his other daughter.

I smiled at Barbara, and I could see it made her feel better. I mean, it wasn't just me here. I had to remember how much Barbara needed me. Without me, she'd be riding in the back of a police car in Memphis on her way to a bus back to Queens. Maybe even wearing handcuffs. Well not yet, of course. Not until she got there. It was the least I could do for the person who had given me everything. At least, that's what I always thought. But was it true? Did I really owe Barbara everything? Elvis. I definitely owed her Elvis. Cigarettes. Yes, but they made me sick. *Catcher in the Rye.* I read it before I met her. Rock and roll. I found that before I met her. Elvis. Was that all? Well, that was enough. Wasn't it?

The train we took from school was a local. I'd never taken it except from my house to the school, so I didn't know all the stops after it passed my station. When it reached Queens Plaza, I told Barbara we should get off and switch to the express train. She agreed, without any argument, which was pretty unusual, and we crossed the platform and waited for the E train, which would take us to the Thirty-Fourth Street station. That was our stop. I'd been to this stop lots of times. I'd never been to the Greyhound bus terminal. I only knew where it was because we passed it every time we went to Macy's.

Chapter Sixty-One

There was a bus going to Hoboken in twenty minutes, and there were plenty of seats. The man selling tickets was bald and wore glasses. He took our money and handed us our tickets like we were nothing special, like we were just like anybody who walked into the bus terminal and bought a ticket, which I guess we were, even though it didn't feel that way to me. I wanted to grab the tickets and run, before the ticket man had a chance to say something like, "Why aren't you kids in school?" or "You can't ride the bus without a grown-up," but Barbara just stood there and smiled at him. She actually stuck her chest out a little, and I saw his eyes move down to look at it.

"Do you know where Second Street in Hoboken is?" she asked in the sweet voice I'd only heard once before . . . when she was talking to my mother. It didn't work then, so I was afraid it wouldn't work now. But I was wrong.

"Sure, I know where that is, miss," the ticket man answered quickly, without looking up from Barbara's sweater. "What's the address?"

He called her "miss" and talked to her like she was a grown-up. Maybe Barbara did look as old as she thought she looked and older than I thought she looked. Anyway, it turned out that Barbara's

father's house was only a few blocks from where the bus stopped, and the ticket man explained exactly how to get there. He even drew us a little map on a piece of scrap paper.

Barbara gave it to me to hold, and I looked down at it and smiled. Now I was a real explorer. I even had a map. Of course, I didn't have a compass, but it wasn't like I was going to drive the bus or that I even knew how to use a compass.

When we stepped up the stairs onto the bus, the driver smiled at us and helped us with our suitcase. I was relieved there was another grown-up, besides the ticket man, who didn't wonder why we weren't in school. Maybe things weren't the way I thought they would be. Maybe no one would wonder why we weren't in school. Or care. People always told stories about truant officers driving around in paddy wagons looking for kids who weren't in school. Maybe they weren't any more real than the bogeyman.

The bus was old, and there were crumpled newspapers on the floor. The plastic seats were torn and scratched the backs of my legs. But the Lincoln Tunnel was only a few blocks away from the bus terminal, and there wasn't a lot of traffic, so it only took a few minutes to get there.

"This is weird," Barbara said, looking out the window. "Have you ever been in this tunnel before?"

"Yeah. A few times. With my parents when we visited their friends. And once we went to Atlantic City for a vacation."

"Atlantic City? What's that? You mean the Atlantic Ocean?"

"No. Atlantic City. It's a city by the Atlantic Ocean. It's got this really nice beach with a big boardwalk with games and rides and stuff to eat."

She smiled. "Yeah? Is it nice? I bet he'll take us there. Buy us stuff to eat and stuff."

I smiled. I really liked cotton candy and the bumper cars. I was afraid to go on the roller coaster.

"Great."

"How long is this tunnel? It's kind of creepy."

I wondered if she was scared of the tunnel. I hoped not. We were going to be doing a lot of things scarier than riding through a tunnel.

"We'll be out of it soon."

"Good."

I had just said that to calm her down. I didn't really know how long the Lincoln Tunnel was. But it turned out, I was right. It didn't take very long, and then it turned out that Hoboken, which I didn't know anything about, was by the end of the tunnel.

The driver helped us carry our suitcase out of the bus, and we were there. I looked around. It was a strange kind place, not like the country or the beach, places I'd visited in New Jersey before. It wasn't really like any place I'd seen before because it wasn't exactly the city, either. There were a lot of buildings, but they were small. Bigger than my house but smaller than an apartment house. And I couldn't see any skyscrapers anywhere.

I held up the ticket man's map, and we started to walk along what we thought was the street on the map. It was exactly right, and we found the street that Barbara's father lived on. It was lined with wooden houses about three or four stories high. Most of them hadn't been painted in a long time. Some of them had trash in the yard or an old car parked in front of it. I'd never been to a famous musician's house before, but I was pretty sure it wouldn't look like this. I kept on walking, trying not to think about anything. But my stomach kept moving up into my throat, making it hard to breathe and even harder to swallow. I looked over at Barbara on the other side of the suitcase and caught her eyes looking around.

"You know," she said, "sometimes there are nicer houses at the end of a street."

I nodded like I understood what she meant. Which I didn't. You could see pretty far down the street, and as far as you could see, the houses were all the same.

"Sometimes people fix up the inside of their house but not the outside," I suggested, and Barbara nodded.

Before we got very far down the block, and near any nicer houses, if there had been any nicer houses, we came to the number of her father's house. It was a small wooden house, not much bigger than my house. I mean, my parents' house. We opened the screen door and saw a metal plate on the side of the door with six buzzers on it. They were like the buzzers in the apartment houses near us, like the one Barbara lived in, for example. But those buildings were five or six stories high and half a block long. I wondered if all those buzzers meant that six different families lived in this little house. It seemed impossible. I never thought that our house, my parents' house, was too big for three people to live in. We seemed to fill it up without a lot of room left over. I couldn't imagine how we would share that space with even one other family, let alone five.

Barbara looked around and frowned.

"I wonder if I wrote down the wrong number."

There were little metal squares next to the buzzers for people's names. Most of them were empty.

I frowned, too.

"No one seems to put their name on their buzzer."

"Look," Barbara said, pointing. Sure enough, one of the little squares said, "Dougherty." We didn't see it at first because the name was written by hand, in pencil, and it didn't show up very well against the card, which may have been white when he wrote it but was grimy and gray now.

Barbara looked at me. "I guess this is it." Not exactly enthusiastic.

She pressed the buzzer for a long time. Nothing happened.

He wasn't home. I knew it. What were we going to do now, carrying a suitcase in Hoboken where we didn't know anyone?

And then I heard noises coming from inside, like someone walking down a creaky staircase in a ghost movie. The door opened and a man was staring at us. He was skinny and had baggy black circles under his eyes, which sunk back into his head. The opposite of Margaret's. He was wearing a crumpled shirt. The top buttons were unbuttoned, and the collar curled under, like it wasn't starched or ironed. He actually did look a little like Slugger, the puppet piano player I told you about before, except he didn't have big round ears or a cigarette hanging out of his mouth. He was blinking very fast, like the light hurt his eyes, and when he looked at us, he looked confused, like we were a life-form he had never seen before.

"Sean Dougherty?" Barbara whispered. A loud whisper. I knew she was whispering because her voice wasn't working right.

He didn't answer right away. He narrowed his eyes like he was trying to decide whether to tell the truth or not. Finally, he nodded slowly.

"Maybe. Who wants to know?"

"Barbara. I'm Barbara. Your daughter, Barbara."

He stopped blinking and his eyes opened wider. He still looked confused. You could almost see little wheels turning in his head trying to make sense of something that someone just said in a foreign language.

"Barbara? Barbara? But . . . how? I . . . You're . . . grown-up."

"Yeah, well. That's what happens when you don't see a person for fourteen years."

Her voice was working again. I wondered if this guy would like having a fresh daughter. And then he smiled. Not a big smile. But a growing smile. Like he was starting to understand that something great was happening.

"Fourteen years? Fourteen? Really?"

I looked over at Barbara. I only saw the side of her face, but it seemed like she might be starting to smile, too.

"Yeah," she answered, "really."

Barbara's father was really smiling now and leaning over to look closely at her like he was making up for years of not seeing her.

"Wow. Man. Just look at you. You're beautiful." He stepped back to get an overall view and noticed me.

"But who is—"

"My friend. Her name is Paula."

He nodded. Slowly. I smiled and started to hold out my hand. Like I'd been taught. I was waiting for him to smile back. But he didn't. I thought about a teacher who used to say, "Wipe that smile off your face." I wished I could. I mean, of course he was surprised and confused and wanted to know about his daughter. But he could've smiled at me a little.

He stared at Barbara for a few more seconds, or hours, I don't know. It felt like a long time to be standing not knowing what to do. Finally, he said, "Do you want to come in?"

"Yeah. That'd be nice. Unless . . . That'd be nice."

I knew what she was going to say. She was going to say, "Unless you want to bring the chairs out here." But I guessed she didn't know him well enough. We picked up the suitcase. I guess he hadn't noticed it before. He frowned and looked from one of us to the other. But he turned and walked up the stairs without offering to help us.

Chapter Sixty-Two

I guess you've figured out by now that, even if Barbara's father was a famous musician, which he probably wasn't, he definitely didn't live in a mansion. There was a sharp pain starting behind my eyes, and I knew exactly what it was. Disappointment. Like when my parents bought me something I really wanted but it was the wrong one.

But if I was feeling disappointed, I could imagine how Barbara was feeling. This was *her* father. Her big secret. I knew, without her telling me, that she'd spent her whole life thinking that no matter how bad her life was, she had a better life waiting for her, and someday she would pack her bags and go there. I looked over to see if what she was thinking showed in her face, but she was staring straight ahead and didn't look at me. It seemed like maybe her teeth were clenched tight together because her cheek looked like it was solid.

We got to the top of the stairs on the second floor, and Barbara's father opened one of the doors with a key that I hadn't noticed he was holding in his hand. We walked into a kind of living room. I say kind of living room because it wasn't like any living room I'd ever seen before. The kitchen was part of it. On the side wall, there was a small refrigerator, stove, and sink with a table and chairs. Most of the room was taken up by a piano and piles of sheet music and black posters that said THE LIONEL JACKSON QUARTET in silver letters with notes and treble clefs scattered around the letters. At least he was a musician. Barbara had gotten that part right.

We sat down on a sofa, and Barbara's father pulled out one of the chairs from the kitchen table and sat down facing us. He looked from one of us to the other but didn't say anything. He opened his mouth and closed it again a few times. He looked like he was lost or something. I never saw a grown-up look like that before. But of course, I never saw a grown-up looking at a daughter he hadn't seen for fourteen years.

He tilted his head to the side and said softly, "Did Connie send you?"

"Connie" was a name I'd never heard before. It must've been Barbara's mother. Barbara never called her anything but "my old lady."

"Connie? Yeah, sure, she says hello."

He frowned. "Is she . . . okay?"

"Yeah. Sure. She's great. I mean, why don't you call her if you're so interested?" Barbara sounded angry.

Barbara's father heard the anger in her words and frowned.

"But then . . . she didn't . . . Does she know you're here?"

I half expected Barbara to ask him if they were playing twenty questions. That's what she would have said to me.

She shrugged. "Yeah. Maybe."

"How did you find me?"

I was leaning as far back into the soft, lumpy sofa cushions as I could so I could look at Barbara without twisting around and looking stupid, even though no one was looking at me.

Barbara shrugged again. "I heard her talking about you on the phone with her friends and how she kept your letters and stuff. So, I looked for them, and I found them. Wasn't hard."

He nodded. "Yeah? She was talking about me? What did she say? I mean, what do you want? I mean. What would you like? Would you like some milk or something?"

Barbara's father's apartment smelled funny. Like smoke and sweat and I'm not sure of what else. I looked around and thought that his maid didn't do a very good job. My mother would've fired her. Unless, of course, he didn't have a maid. But that was impossible. He couldn't clean the house himself. He was a man.

The smell wasn't a strong smell, but it made me feel sick. I mean, maybe it was the smell, maybe not, but I was definitely feeling sick. About everything. I didn't want to live here. I didn't even want to be here. I knew, even though I'd never seen it, that Aunt Carol's house would be clean and wouldn't smell funny. And it wouldn't have a funny-looking old refrigerator on the side of the living room. It would have carpets and drapes that matched the slipcovers on the sofa, and chairs that weren't lumpy. It wasn't that I cared about stuff like that. Those were things my mother cared about. Not me. But I couldn't help wishing we'd gone to Aunt Carol's house.

I didn't know if I was included in the milk offer or if it was only for Barbara, so I smiled and shook my head a little bit, hoping that if he wasn't offering me any milk, it wouldn't look like I thought he was. Nobody said anything for a minute, and I looked around, trying to figure out where we were going to sleep, but I couldn't even figure out where he slept.

Barbara said, "No. We don't want any milk."

She was trying to sound like herself, but she sounded like her voice was sticking in her throat. Her rouge looked like bright, round red spots, and I realized that it was because she was pale, like all the blood was running out of her face.

"That's good," Barbara's father said with a little laugh, "because I don't think I have any. I don't usually have company. I mean, maybe, you know, if you'd called or something."

"Called? Yeah. I guess I forgot my manners."

Barbara turned to me. "Hey, Paula, how come you didn't remind me about, you know, being polite? You just let me drop in on this guy that hasn't called me in fourteen years."

Chapter Sixty-Three

I stared at Barbara and opened my mouth. Nothing came out. Barbara's father seemed to feel the same way. He opened his mouth, too, but nothing came out for a minute, and when it did his voice was loud and strange.

"Barbara, that's not what I meant. You know that's not what I meant."

He took a few breaths. They were deep, and I could hear them and see his skinny chest filling up and emptying out. When he talked again, his voice sounded more normal.

"Look, kid . . . Barbara, I mean. I don't dig what you want me to say. Am I glad to see you? Oh, my God, yeah. I am. But you can dig that I'm surprised. I just meant if I knew you were coming—"

"You'd have baked a cake," Barbara interrupted him, using the words of a corny old song.

He smiled. And she smiled. And even I felt a little better.

Barbara said, "How about a cigarette?"

"You smoke? Oh. I forgot. You're all grown-up."

He pulled a crumpled cigarette pack out of his pocket. It was smaller than the ones I was used to because it was the kind of cigarettes that didn't have filters. He held the pack out to Barbara, and she took one. He held it toward me, but I shook my head. I already felt like I might throw up. I'd never smoked a cigarette without a filter before. It might not make me throw up, but it sure wouldn't make me feel any better.

He pulled a cigarette out of the pack with his mouth like cowboys and detectives did in the movies. It looked very cool, and I thought that maybe I could get to like him if I got to know him better. He pulled a crumpled pack of matches out of one of his pockets and lit Barbara's cigarette and his own. He went to the kitchen area and came back with an ashtray, which was empty but not clean. It said *FREDDY'S DINER* in red letters around the side.

The cigarettes seemed to be relaxing Barbara and her father. They sat back in their chairs and smiled. A little. The way they both smiled. After a little while, Barbara said, "So. You play the piano, right?"

Her father answered quickly, like he was happy that someone thought of something to say. "Yeah. How did you know?"

Barbara looked over at the piano.

"Oh, right. But I mean, did Connie tell you? Did she tell you about me?"

"Not really. When I found the letters, I found the newspapers and stuff. Do you still play?"

"You saw the clippings? About how I played gigs in Europe and England and stuff like that?"

"Yeah. I saw that. Where do you play now?"

"Now? Well me and three other guys, we're a quartet. We play gigs in different places. Right now we play on Friday and Saturday nights at this club, you know, like a nightclub. It's in Newark. The Golden Note."

He seemed happy to have something to talk about. He kept looking at Barbara, like he was trying to be sure that she was listening.

I felt like I'd walked onto the stage and into a play when I was supposed to be in the audience. I had nothing to say, and no one was paying any attention to me. I looked around again, as if maybe I'd missed something. Like the door leading into a big empty bedroom for Barbara and me. I looked at Barbara again. She raised her eyebrows at me and looked away so her father wouldn't see.

"Maybe you could come and hear us play sometime. That'd be cool."

He's going to take us to a nightclub? Wow. That would be cool. If they let us in, of course. Which I doubted.

He continued, like he was reading my thoughts, "Maybe you have to be older to get in. I don't know. I've never seen kids there."

Barbara nodded. Like she was giving great consideration to his words. But, for the first time, I noticed she was blinking kind of fast, and her nose was turning a little red.

"Do you, like, still travel and play in different countries?"

A big grin lit his face. "You saw that in the papers, right? I'm glad Connie kept them. We went all over. Europe. Japan. Morocco."

"Used to? Not anymore?"

"Not so much. It's hard, you know. I don't really play, you know, like rock and roll. What people mostly listen to now. I bet you like rock and roll."

Barbara shrugged. "It's okay. Yeah. I like it. Couldn't you learn to play it?"

He shrugged back. "I guess. Maybe. I mean, I play jazz, you know. Do you know what jazz is? There's still jazz clubs. Just, you know, not so many."

And then I surprised everyone, including myself, by saying, "How is rock and roll different from jazz?"

Chapter Sixty-Four

*B*arbara and her father both turned to look at me with the same expression on their faces, like they had both forgotten I was there and wondered who had said something and why. It was funny because they really looked alike. But I didn't stop because I really wanted to know.

"I mean, how come you can't play rock and roll if you can play jazz? Is it harder?"

"Harder?" Barbara's father answered quickly, like I had insulted him. "No, it's not harder. It's different. But it's easier. Much easier."

By the time he said the second "easier," he was walking to the piano.

Did I tell you that I knew how to play the piano? Probably not because it was just another one of those lessons my mother made me take so I would get into a good college, or something. I never played anything good. Only stuff like Bach and Mozart.

Barbara's father sat down at the piano and suddenly looked different. While we'd been talking, he'd sat with his shoulders slouched forward, the way my mother always told me not to sit. But when he sat down and leaned over the piano, it didn't look like slouching. It looked like he was about to take the piano into his arms and hug it. He put his hands on the keyboard and turned to look at us.

"So, see, rock and roll is like jazz for beginners, you know. It's easy stuff. All the songs are just three or four chords, with like this three-fourth or four-fourth rhythm."

He leaned over the keyboard and started to do what looked like pumping his arms up and down. I wished I could see his hands because it wasn't anything like what my teachers taught me to do.

Bah bah bah bah bah bahbah
Bah bah bah bah bah bahbah
Bah bah bah bah bah bahbah
Bah.

At first what he was playing sounded like banging. Lots of notes played at the same time with both of his hands. Not one or two at a time like I'd been taught. But I heard melodies. I heard songs. Songs I knew. "Earth Angel," "At the Hop," "Heartbreak Hotel." It was amazing. I didn't want him to stop. But he did.

He turned around and held his hands out. As he spoke, he shrugged his shoulders.

"See, that's it. That's really all there is to rock and roll. The songs are all the same few chords. And the same rhythm. And they're written out in sheet music and always played the same way. Even when they're played by different people at different times. But when cats play jazz, it's different. Completely. Jazz has lots of chords. More than one key at a time and fifths and sevenths and diminished. The rhythms change. And you never, never play a tune the same way twice. Never."

He started to play a song I knew. It was called "Stardust." After playing a little, he started saying the words, not really singing, exactly, but not talking, either. Then he stopped saying the words and just played, and the music started to move away from the melody I knew. I got up and walked over to the piano, so I could see his hands. His fingers looked alive, like they were moving over the keys . . . dancing over the keys . . . by themselves.

"See," he said, "even a standard, like 'Stardust.' Everybody knows it. Everybody plays it. I've played it, I don't know, maybe a thousand times. But every time, it's different. Depending on stuff. You know, like today, for example, it has seeing my daughter after a long time in it."

The music moved in and out of the melody. Sometimes you could hear it for a while. But just when you thought you knew what was coming next, it surprised you and moved away. I was so lost in the music and trying to hear what he was saying about it, that I jumped when Barbara was suddenly standing by the piano talking in a loud voice.

"What do you do the rest of the week, Sean? When it's not Friday and Saturday?"

He looked surprised, too. He stopped playing and looked up at Barbara with a hurt look on his face. I knew what he was feeling. Today was a day of disappointment. Barbara was disappointed because Sean didn't live in a mansion. And now Sean was disappointed because Barbara didn't want to listen to him play.

"Well, yeah, sometimes we play during the week. You know. At a party or in a church. Otherwise . . . um . . . drive a taxi. You know. It's not the greatest gig in the world, but it puts food on the table. Gives me time to take care of my stuff."

The word "taxi" was like a punch in the stomach, even though I guess I already knew our plan wasn't going to work. I looked at Barbara. It was the same for her. Her eyes opened wide and got really shiny. She looked at me and shook her head. This morning

I'd felt like Columbus, setting out on a grand adventure. Now I felt like Columbus would've felt if he'd reached the edge of the world and came to the black pit everyone told him was there. My world was flat.

And it wasn't even lunchtime.

Chapter Sixty-Five

*B*arbara turned her face away from me to look at her father. I could see the side of her face. One eye. Half her mouth. The eye was filling with tears, and the lips were pressed together. I looked back at her father and wondered what he was thinking. When he woke up this morning, the last thing he could ever have imagined was that his daughter, who he hadn't talked to in fourteen years, was going to show up at his door. Just like he never thought that all this time she was dreaming about him. And he certainly never thought he wasn't anything like the father she'd been dreaming about. And her world and her dreams had just fallen apart in front of him. But maybe he was beginning to know that, because he looked uncomfortable, squirming in his chair and turning his head back and forth from me to Barbara. He finally started talking really fast.

"You know, Barbie, your mother's a good person. Really good. It wasn't her fault. She was a good wife. I really dug her. You know. But it was just . . . it was the music. You know what I mean. The music. I just loved it too much."

Barbara sat up straight. I was afraid she was going to cry. Her mouth was moving funny, and she spoke very softly: "Yeah. You loved it. More than you loved me."

He sat up straight. I was looking at both of them, so I saw something they couldn't see. The way they moved their faces and their bodies. They moved the same way. Exactly. And they'd never seen each other before today. I wondered if my parents and I moved the same way. I never thought so. And we lived together every single day of my life.

"No, Barbara. I loved you a lot. I guess it doesn't seem that way to you. And I can understand it. What it must look like to you. But I never forgot about you. Really. That day, in the hospital, you were all red and wrinkly. Closing your little fingers around my finger. I said, 'Look at those fingers. She'll be a piano player.' I . . ."

His voice trailed off, and he pulled a greasy, worn-out leather wallet from his back pocket and opened it. *He's not going to offer us money, is he?* I wondered, feeling a little panicked by the idea. But instead, he pulled something out of one of the little sections in front of where you keep the money. It was—oh, my God, no—it was a little snapshot. From where I was sitting, it could have been the snapshot Margaret had given me. He handed it to her.

I jumped up and walked over to see it without worrying about whether I'd been invited. It was amazing. Was there some kind of rule, I wondered, that when people had babies, they had to take a certain kind of picture? Because this picture looked just like the picture of Lena and Sophie that had wrecked my life. There was Barbara's father, disguised, like my father was, in his young face, wearing a big smile. His arm was around the shoulders of a pretty woman holding a baby. They looked really proud, wearing old-fashioned clothes like the ones my parents wore in the pictures with me as a baby. Not so old-fashioned as the one with Lena and Baby Sophie and not in a strange place. It had been taken near where Barbara and I lived. I recognized the drugstore and the bakery across from the field where they stood. I remembered playing in that field. There was an apartment building there now.

Barbara was crying. She wasn't trying to hide it. Tears washed her mascara down her cheeks.

She whispered, "Is this . . . me?"

There were tears in Barbara's father's eyes, too, but he was smiling. "'Course. I only ever had one daughter."

Barbara and her father both started to look blurry because I was crying, too, especially when he said, "I only ever had one daughter." He reached up to touch Barbara's arm, but she pulled away and thrust the picture toward him. She started to wipe away at her tears, angrily, as if she wanted to tear them off her face. When she finally started to talk, her voice was quiet.

"You only have one daughter. Yeah, right. One too many, I guess."

All I could think, looking from Barbara to her father, was how much alike they looked. His face was covered with a lot of different feelings, and when he spoke, his voice was angry.

"Look, Barbara. You don't understand. I mean, you're just a kid. My life is hard, you know. Music is hard. I loved you and your mother. I did. But I wasn't good at having, you know, like a regular life. I work all night. I don't make money. I travel if I have to. Music is hard."

"Yeah. You loved us. But you chose the music."

"Chose? Oh, yeah, you mean I could have gotten a different job, like working in a store or something."

"Or driving a cab."

She was like a detective. She was looking at him through eyes that were slits in a face smeared red and black with mascara and rouge. Her father shook his head and looked up at the ceiling like he was hoping somebody up there would come down to help him. He bent his elbows and turned his hands to the ceiling to catch whatever it was he hoped was going to fall.

"I wanted you to have a good life. A better life than you would have with me. Connie thought . . . we thought . . . it would be better if you just never knew me. It was hard for me, Barbara. You gotta believe it. It was hard for me to never see you again. I did it for you. So you could have a good life. Did it work, Barbara? Do you have a good life?"

Barbara put her head down and didn't answer for a long time. I could hear her breathing, loud and deep. The kind of breathing that seems like if you forget to do it, you won't breathe at all.

Finally, she started talking, without looking up. "You seem like a bright guy, Sean, and if you just think about it a little, I know you can understand this. My friend and me—Paula and me—we're sitting here in your living room with a suitcase. So, what do you think? Do you think that means I have such a good life?"

Chapter Sixty-Six

When Barbara said the word "suitcase," her father jerked in his chair like he'd stuck his finger into an electric socket. He turned his head to stare at the suitcase where we'd left it by the door, like he'd forgotten there was a poison snake slithering toward him.

"What're you doing with a suitcase?"

"What do you think we're doing with a suitcase, Sean? Selling brushes? We're running. I mean, we're moving away."

I couldn't believe any person could recover so fast from being so upset. But there she was. The tough old Barbara I hadn't seen since before Billy. Maybe even before missing Elvis on *The Milton Berle Show*.

"But . . ."

He looked away from us and shook his head.

"Yeah, Sean. We're moving to Cleveland. We got jobs there and a place to live with Paula's aunt. Babysitting and stuff. It's not the greatest gig, but it'll put food on the table. Give us a chance to do our stuff."

"Cleveland?"

Barbara's father and I said the word at the same time and with the same shock in our voices. We turned our heads to look at Barbara. She stared into my eyes, nodding her head up and down hard. I knew she was telling me to shut up and agree with whatever she said no matter how crazy it was.

"Yeah, *Cleveland.*"

She turned back to her father. "And I figured it like this. I mean, I don't know when I'll be back. If ever. So, I thought that I'd come by and say hello before I left."

She turned back to me. "Before *we* left. Right, *Paula?* Isn't *that* what we *figured?*"

I had to hand it to Barbara. She made up better stories than I could ever have thought of. And I was the one who wanted to be a writer when I grew up. If I couldn't be a movie star. I wondered what Barbara wanted to be. She never said.

I nodded in agreement.

She continued, "So now, I think it's just about time for us to go. If we're going to catch the bus to Cleveland. *Right, Paula?*"

She smiled and stood up and began to walk toward the suitcase. I stood up and hurried after her.

Sean Dougherty stood up, too. "But, but . . . you just got here. Are you hungry? We could go to Manny's for burgers. You like burgers, don't you? Of course. Everyone like burgers. Manny makes the best burgers."

"Thanks anyway, Sean. But we have to catch the bus. You know, Paula's aunt is waiting for us."

I didn't want to contradict Barbara in front of her new father, especially after she'd given me a really terrible you'd-better-agree-with-me-or-else look. And maybe he believed what she was saying about going to live with my aunt. It sounded like it could be true, if you didn't know that it was the opposite of true and the opposite of everything Barbara'd ever said before about Dweebland. And if you didn't know that Barbara had made so much fun of the idea of going to Dweebland that I hadn't even bothered to find out my aunt's address. And if you didn't know that we didn't even have a ticket for the bus back to New York.

So maybe Barbara's father believed her because he didn't know any of that. But I knew all of it. I knew we were like people in the middle of an earthquake who had nowhere to go and nowhere to stay. All my life I had known what I was supposed to do every second. Now I was looking at a future that was like a blank sheet of paper. I didn't have anything I was supposed to do ever. Was that really what I wanted, when I decided to leave home? I didn't know. I didn't know anything except for one thing. I knew that I was starving.

"It's okay, Barbara. We have time for lunch. Thanks, Mr. Dougherty, I'd love a hamburger."

I knew it was my voice saying those words, although I didn't exactly remember deciding to say them. But I was glad someone said them because I really was hungry. Barbara looked at me with her face twisted in anger. She opened her mouth. But before she could disagree with me, which I knew she was going to do, I said, "Really, Barbara, it's okay. Let's just go to lunch. We'll take everything with us and go straight to the bus station. There's time."

Like the rest of our lives.

I could tell she was trying to make up her mind. Maybe she was hungry, too. I hadn't eaten anything that day because I was nervous. And Barbara had told me that she never ate breakfast. Of course, she hardly ate lunch, either. Actually, she never seemed to eat, but she never died of starvation, so she must've eaten something when no one was watching. I prayed this was one of the times that she would eat something. I didn't normally pray, like for help on a math test or something, but right now we needed all the help we could get. And I remembered my manners. I breathed a prayer of thanks when she said, "Okay. I mean, I'm not hungry or anything, but Paula, man, you should see her put it away. She's got like this hollow leg."

Barbara's father looked like he'd just won the Irish Sweepstakes. A huge grin spread over his face.

"Great. Great. I'll just get my jacket." He reached for the suitcase. "Here, let me take that. Manny's is just down the block. We can walk."

Chapter Sixty-Seven

J wish I could tell you that Manny's hamburgers solved our problems. Or maybe I just wished I could tell that to myself because you probably already knew that even the best hamburger in the world couldn't rescue two girls in Hoboken on a school day with a suitcase and no place to go.

Manny's was around the corner from Barbara's father's house. It was in an old bus that someone had taken the wheels off of and put on cinder blocks in an empty lot . . . maybe Manny, whoever he was. But they'd taken out the seats, too. There wasn't enough room inside for tables. Just a long counter with stools. A couple of men sat at the end of the counter. They smoked cigarettes and drank coffee and talked to a skinny man with a dark-red leathery face that looked suntanned, even though it wasn't summer, who stood behind the counter scraping the grease off the grill in long, straight strokes.

He smiled when we came in and said, "Hi, Doc, who're the beauties?"

Barbara's father grinned and answered, "My daughter and her friend, Artie, so you'd better button your loose lips, my man, and mind your p's and q's."

Artie stopped grinning and looked confused but quickly smiled again. I thought maybe Barbara's father, who was standing behind us, gave him some kind of signal.

"The usual, Doc? Or should I call you Daddy-o?" Artie asked after we sat down.

"Nah. I'll just have some coffee. But these young ladies here, they came all the way over the river to see me this morning. Can you dig it? All the way over the river from New York City. And they are hungry, man. So, you'd better put the pedal to the metal and feed them something really boss."

"Yeah, Sean, but actually we came under the river," Barbara muttered. She was sitting in between me and her father and didn't say it very loud.

I thought maybe I was the only one who heard it until Artie burst out laughing and said, "She got you there, Doc. Got you good. She's your daughter all right, Daddy-o."

Barbara's father laughed, too. Barbara was looking down at her hands, and if I didn't know her better, I would have thought that she was blushing because her face was almost as red as Artie's.

Artie handed us menus, but we didn't really need them because everything they served was written on the signs hanging on the back wall behind the counter. I ordered a hamburger, since Barbara's father had said they were the best, and a glass of milk. Barbara said she didn't want anything. Her father had to practically beg before she agreed to let him buy her a hamburger, too. It really was a good hamburger, and Barbara surprised me by eating the whole thing. I guess she did get hungry.

I liked Manny's. The customers who came in all knew Artie and each other. That never happened in the restaurants we went to at home. I mean, where I used to live. We hardly ever saw anyone we knew, even in the restaurants that were near our house and we went to all the time. I started to like Barbara's father more, too, because with his friends he was funny and friendly, and everyone seemed to like him. They all knew about his music and asked him where he was playing and stuff. One guy said he was learning how to play the saxophone and asked him all these questions like what key he played different tunes in. In Manny's, at least, Doc Dougherty was a famous musician.

I ate my hamburger slowly, chewing each bite thoroughly. I wasn't in any hurry. But Barbara was.

"I swear to God, Paula, if you don't finish that damn hamburger, we'll be here till dinner."

I knew Barbara had finished her hamburger and that her father was on his second cup of coffee. I turned my head to smile at Barbara's joke, but she wasn't smiling. She was looking at me really hard, and I knew that she wanted to leave.

"It's okay. I'm done." I drank the last drops of my milk, wiped my mouth with the napkin on my lap, and folded it up next to my plate.

"How about some dessert, ladies?" Artie smiled. "You like chocolate cream pie? Huh? Maybe some ice cream?"

"No," Barbara answered quickly, "we've got to get going."

"You sure?" Barbara's father added. "Manny's chocolate cream pie is famous."

Barbara shook her head and stood up to end the conversation. Barbara's father pulled a couple of crumpled dollar bills out of his pants pocket and slapped them down onto the counter.

"Keep the change, Artie."

"Thanks, Doc. You bring these lovely ladies around here again, mind? Have a nice trip, girls."

The other customers joined Artie in a chorus of goodbyes. I

smiled and waved at them. Even Barbara looked around and nodded. Maybe her idea of being a waitress somewhere might work. It would be nice to work in a place like Manny's, where everyone was so friendly. I bet Artie would give us a job. Maybe he would even teach us how to make hamburgers and grilled cheese sandwiches and chocolate cream pies. I mean, how would they know how old we were if nobody told them?

Chapter Sixty-Eight

"Aw, come on. You really have to go, huh? Well, at least let me drive you. The cab's right outside the house."

Barbara's father seemed to really be getting into the whole father thing. Even after only a couple of hours, it seemed to me he was better at it than my father, who'd had years to practice. Twice.

Sean didn't seem like the kind of guy who would care about things like French midterms, so he wouldn't make you feel bad because someone else did better than you did. And he would certainly never say that the music you loved sounded like the furnace exploding. If only he had a bigger house, it might not be bad to stay here. Waitresses wore cute uniforms. Black and white with an apron. Sometimes a little hat. Maybe a pretty decoration, like flowers or birds.

Unfortunately, Barbara wasn't getting into the daughter thing at all. It was like she couldn't tell the difference between Tony and somebody who loved her.

"No, man. It's no trouble. We'll get the bus."

"But shouldn't you call your mother? Tell her you're okay?"

Barbara spun around and walked over to where he was standing. She looked him in the eyes and poked his chest with her finger.

"Look, Sean. I don't want to call her. And I don't want you to call her, either. Do you understand?"

"But . . ."

Barbara turned toward me. Her eyes were little slits, and she looked, like, ready to kill someone, probably me.

"I told you grown-ups all stick together."

Suddenly, it was like a light went on inside her head and she realized she was acting like her mother didn't know where she was, which was the truth but not what she'd told her father before and not what we wanted him to think.

She turned back to him. He was looking at us with a puzzled look.

"Look, Sean. I'm sorry. It's just that, it's like she's at work right now. And if we tried to call her when she's at work, she'd get like all upset and think that something was wrong and get all worried. And nothing's wrong. Everything's fine. So, we'll just take the bus back to New York and get the bus to Cleveland. And everything'll be cool, just like we planned."

Planned?

Barbara's father looked like he might cry. "Look, Barbara, I'm glad you came. Really glad."

"Yeah, right."

He smiled. "You really have a Dougherty temper, don't you?"

"Yeah, well, I don't know what I have. Just don't call her. Okay?"

He held up his hands like someone was pointing a gun at him. "Okay. Okay, Barbie. But, you know, maybe you could, you know, drop me a line. Let me know how you're doing. Okay?"

He moved his arms toward Barbara like he was going to hug her. But she ducked away.

"Sure, Sean, I'll write. As soon as we get to Cleveland. And don't call me Barbie."

Chapter Sixty-Nine

We walked back down the street with our suitcase. The street didn't look as bad as it did when we first saw it and were walking in the opposite direction. I mean, I know it was just as shabby and dirty as it was before. But now it looked sort of friendly. Even homey. Barbara was looking away from me. I wondered if she was crying. I was.

We turned the corner, and I sank down on the suitcase. We had no place to go. Our great plans had failed. Maybe they weren't such great plans after all. Was there anything else left for us to do? Did we have to go home after all? No adventures. No worried calls to find me while my frozen dinner, hot from the oven, sat on the table getting cold. No tearful parents begging me to come home. Barbara sat down next to me. Her face was wet and red.

I asked, "Do you really want to go to Cleveland?"

Barbara's face was red. "No. But you said you wouldn't go to Memphis. And I can't leave you here."

"But . . . how?"

"There's a bus that goes there. It leaves a couple of times a day. I checked it out when I went to the terminal."

"But—"

"But, but, are you some kind of—"

"Goat? No. It's just—"

"It's just nothing. Are you going to help me, or do I have to drag the suitcase with you sitting on it?"

The bus to New York was leaving in a few minutes after we got back to the terminal. We bought a ticket from the driver, and soon we were back in the tunnel. More stuff had happened to me in that one day than usually happened to me in a year. And it was only half over.

I turned to face Barbara. "You know what I was thinking?"

"No, genius, what were you thinking?"

"I was thinking that if your father had a room for us, it wouldn't be so bad living there."

Barbara made a terrible face. "Are you kidding? Live in that dump?"

"Well, I mean, if we lived there, we could fix it up. You know. Curtains. Pictures. A maid who did a better job of cleaning."

Barbara shook her head while I talked about the curtains and the pictures, her mouth pulled all the way over to her ear in a sneer that made her look like Sheila. But when I said "maid," she almost fell out of the seat. Her voice was so loud it was almost a scream.

"A maid? You think he has a maid?"

I was glad there weren't many people in the bus because a woman who was sitting five or six rows away from us turned around to look at us.

Barbara stared straight into my eyes. "What do you think? You think everybody has a maid who comes to their house and makes it look all shiny and perfect like yours?"

"Why are you talking like that? Like I insulted you or something. I mean, I guess everyone I know does have a maid. But so what? Who cares?"

She spun her head around and looked out the windows on the other side of the bus. But not before I'd seen her eyes starting to fill with tears. Tears! About maids! I reached out and touched her shoulder. "What is—"

But she jerked away from my hand. She stood up and walked toward the back of the bus. I started to get up to follow her but changed my mind and sat down. There was no point trying to talk to her until she wanted to talk to me. I was getting tired of trying.

In a few minutes, she came back and sat down. She gave me a sad-looking smile.

"You've been thinking about your father for a long time, haven't you?" I asked. "For your whole life, right?"

Barbara turned and looked at me suspiciously. Her eyes narrowed, but she didn't say anything, so I kept talking.

"I bet it was like me with my grandmother. I mean, she's dead, she died in Germany. I knew that. But I kept imagining, for a long time, hoping, I guess, that we'd find out it was all a big mistake, and she wasn't dead at all. She was alive. And she was coming to America. And she'd live with us, and everything would be great, I mean, really great, because she'd love me so much. And my father would be happy if she wasn't dead, and he'd love me more. And if my father was happy, my mother would be happy, and she'd love me more, too. I thought about it so much. How great my life would be if only my grandmother wasn't dead."

"My old man wasn't dead. He was in Hoboken."

"I know. I know. But didn't you think that someday you would find him? And your life would be so much better. I mean, it's like what you told me. You told me he was a famous musician. That he lived in a big house and had cool friends. So, weren't you thinking about that? For a long time?"

Barbara looked away and didn't say anything for a while. When she started to talk, she kept looking ahead. Her voice was so soft, I had to lean over to hear her.

"Yeah. I thought about it. Whenever Tony was beating on me. Calling me names. I'd think that somewhere I had a real old man, not like this bastard my stupid old lady got messed up with. And someday I would find him. My real old man. And yeah, I guess I thought I'd go live with him, and we'd have this really great life. Parties and nice clothes. But it was all a lie. Right. You dig it, man? It was all a lie. He lives in a dump. He drives a taxi. He's got an even worse life."

"Worse? Why? Because he doesn't live in a mansion? Or have a maid? You don't know how lucky you are. You have a father who loves you. Not like me. Your father's like the total opposite of my father. My father lived with me and took care of me. But he never loved me. So maybe your father didn't take care of you. But he always loved you."

Barbara shook her head slowly. She looked sad.

"You really don't understand anything, do you? You think I care about that? You really think I'm going to . . . what? Dance a jig? Because now I know that all these years Sean Dougherty was in some dump in Hoboken carrying a picture of me in his greasy old wallet. Fat lot of good it did, Paula. Fat lot of good. Because all that time, I was living with Tony. And he hated me. And he was always whaling on me with a strap and calling me names. He didn't care that somebody in Hoboken loved me, and I don't either."

All the energy seemed to drain out of Barbara's face, and she hung her head. She closed her eyes and took deep breaths, like she'd been running.

I leaned back and closed my eyes, too. My thoughts raced. I'd left home because I thought my parents didn't love me. Maybe they just didn't love me the way I wanted them to love me. Maybe Barbara was right.

Chapter Seventy

T he bus to Cleveland left at five thirty. The bus to Memphis left at six o'clock. It was three fifteen.

We were back in the Greyhound terminal.

"Barbara. Why do you want to go to Cleveland? It doesn't make any sense. I don't even know my aunt's address."

"That's okay. You can get it from information. She has a phone, right?"

Barbara had become the master of telephone directories.

"I guess. But why do you want to go there? You never did before. And you're probably right that she'd just call my mother and wouldn't let us stay."

"Well, what's your big idea, Miss Genius? You never wanted to go to Memphis. Where do you want to go?"

"I don't know."

"Well, I don't, either."

We left the suitcase in a locker that cost a quarter and went out to the street. While we were trying to decide which way to go, three sailors came over, smiling at us like they were our long-lost friends.

"'Scuse us, miss. 'Scuse us. Y'all have a minute?"

They were really cute, especially the one who was talking. He had curly blond hair and the bluest eyes I'd ever seen. He didn't look too old. Maybe not even as old as Elvis. And he was looking at both of us. Both of us! How your life can change when you don't wear socks.

Barbara must've thought they were cute, too, because she moved in front of me and said, "Yeah. I got a minute. Maybe."

I moved next to her. "Me too. Maybe."

I'd never talked to a strange man on the street before, let alone three of them, and of course, my mother always told me not to. But these sailors didn't seem scary. They seemed nice. They were smiling these big happy smiles and looking at us, looking at *me*, the way the cool boys look at the cool girls. The way you smile at the world's most delicious chocolate layer cake covered with whipped cream and bright red roses on the top. I felt like I had butterflies in my stomach. Except that they were all over my body.

The sailor continued, "Thas jus' wonnerful. I was sayin' to m' buddies, here, I was sayin', 'These here women, they sure do look to me like real honest-to-God New Yorkers.'"

He was from the South. Or at least, he wasn't from Queens. Or Hoboken. He had a slow, dreamy way of talking, kind of like Elvis on *The Milton Berle Show*. And he called us women!

"Yeah," Barbara said in a not very friendly way. "We're from around here. So what?"

"Well, see, we're not from around here. No indeedy. In fact, we jus' landed here this mornin'. And we really wanted to see that there Empire State Building. The really tall one? Do y'all know where that building's at?"

Before I could say anything, Barbara said, "Turn around, sailor. It's right behind you."

They turned.

I said, "It's the pointy one, right over there." I pointed to the pointy one, but no one was looking.

"Just over there? Why lordie lord. Why we coulda been walkin' 'round for hours lookin' for it. We do surely need us a guide. D'y'all have a lil' bit a time?"

I smiled and shook my head, but he didn't seem to notice.

"My name's Billy Bob. And this here is Jimmy Ray and Buddy."

What strange names. I said, "Where are you from?"

He turned and looked at me with a smile. "Why thankee for askin', lil' lady. We all is from Memphis. D'y'all know where tha's at?"

Suddenly, Barbara and I started to have a who-can-talk-faster contest.

Before I could say anything, Barbara said, "Memphis? Tennessee? Do you know Elvis?"

Billy Bob's smile got even bigger, which I wouldn't have thought was possible. It was like it spread above his eyebrows and down his chin. Jimmy Ray and Buddy were grinning, too.

"Elvis? Y'all like Elvis?" He turned to face Jimmy Ray and Buddy. "Y'all see that? Even heah in the big city they all be likin' our homeboy. Why sure, we know Elvis. Everybody in Memphis knows old Elvis." Jimmy Ray and Buddy nodded their heads up and down like they might fall off.

"Yeah. Me and Elvis. We was real gud buddies, weren't we?" He turned to face Jimmy Ray and Buddy again. They kept grinning and nodding like they were some kind of dolls and not real people.

"Let's take us a little walk, and we'll tell y'all all about old Elvis. We had us some good times together. Good times. And that's a fact."

Barbara and I looked at each other. I wondered if she believed that they knew Elvis. I wasn't sure. I didn't know if Memphis was a big city or a small town. If it was a small town, it was possible that everyone in Memphis knew each other. But even if they didn't, these guys seemed nice. I was feeling warm all over. It was like their bright smiles and starched white uniforms were spreading a curtain of light across the whole, dirty-gray street, and I was warm inside of it.

I looked at Barbara. "Do you want to walk down to the Empire State Building?"

She shrugged. "I guess we have time for a short walk."

She started walking. I followed her. Billy Bob eased in next to her as we walked, and I was in between Jimmy Ray and Buddy.

"Hey, sweet thing," Jimmy Ray or Buddy said to me. I wasn't sure which was which. "Have you lived in this here big city your whole life?"

Sweet thing! I'd never heard anybody call anybody "sweet thing" before. Is that how southerners talked to each other? If all southerners were as nice as these guys, maybe we should go to Memphis. There was still time to change our minds.

I smiled and nodded. "Yes. I've lived here my whole life."

"Do tell. And where do you live? Do you live nearby?"

"Not so nearby. I live in Queens."

"Queens?"

"Yeah. You have to take the subway for a little while to get there."

"The subway?"

"Yeah. A train. It goes underground. And under the river, too."

"A train that goes under the ground. You hear that, Buddy? They got themselves a train that goes under the ground. And under the river."

So he was Jimmy Ray.

Jimmy Ray was a little cuter than Buddy, although they all could have been brothers with their curly hair and blue eyes. Buddy's hair was darker brown than Jimmy Ray's, and Billy Bob's was the blondest. While I was looking at Jimmy Ray, I felt Buddy take my arm and squeeze it gently. I turned to look at him, hoping he couldn't tell that I was starting to feel burning hot all over and had a sort of flutter that kept going up and down from my stomach. Buddy smiled at me and then talked to Jimmy Ray over my head.

"So, Jimmy Ray, looks like we been here in this big city for only a couple of hours and right off the bat, we meet ourselves a couple of queens. Isn't that right, honey? A couple of queens from Queens."

We all laughed. Queens from Queens. That was really funny. And then I felt Jimmy Ray take my other arm. The warm feeling stopped. I liked how it felt when one sailor was holding one arm. But two sailors holding two arms didn't feel very good. Billy Bob was trying to put his arm around Barbara, but she kept pushing it away.

"Say, darling," Jimmy Ray said, "you must have yourself a whole lot of friends. Isn't that right? Seeing as how it's such a big city and you've been living in it your whole life."

"Friends? Why?"

"Well, there's three of us and only two of y'all, know what I mean."

"Well, no, I don't exactly know what you mean."

"Well, sweet thing, I mean, what kind of party can we have with three of us and only two of you?"

"Party? We were just walking you over to the Empire State Building."

They both laughed, and one of them said to the other, "You see, I done told you these big city girls had a sense of humor."

I didn't laugh. I was starting to like "Paula and Barbara's Sailor Adventure" less and less. Although, when I thought about it, the thought of calling Margaret or any of my friends and asking them to meet me at the bus terminal to go to a party with some sailors was the funniest thought I ever had. Barbara and Billy Bob suddenly seemed to be very far ahead of us. Far enough that they wouldn't hear me unless I raised my voice.

So I did. "Hey, Barbara. Wait up."

She and Billy Bob both jerked around in surprise. Barbara gave me an angry look. An angry look! So much for never caring about another boy again.

"What's up?" she said in an angry voice. "What's with the yelling?"

They were all staring at me.

"No. Nothing. I just wanted to, you know, stay together."

We moved into a little circle. "You know what this pretty thing just told me?" Jimmy Ray said like he was making an important announcement. "She just told me she didn't have any friends she could get to come party with us."

I tried to explain. "No. That's not what I said. I said we don't have time. We have to catch a bus, right, Barbara?"

Barbara didn't answer right away. She looked like she was trying to decide. Boy. I started to pray that she would agree with me because I was afraid that she wouldn't. I held my breath. She finally nodded and I let out a long breath.

"Yeah, we got to catch a bus."

I figured that explained everything and waited for Jimmy Ray and Buddy to let go of me. Jimmy Ray did, and I started to move away when Buddy put his arm around my shoulders and pulled me backward, close to him. He looked down into my face, and I could feel his breath. It smelled of onions.

"Hey, little cherry," he said to me with a kind of smirk.

"Where you going, huh? Why you running off? I can show you a real good time." He pushed his body against my leg and rubbed it from side to side. I tried to pull away from him, but his arm tightened around my shoulders. It felt like steel.

"Let me go. My name's not Cherry."

I wasn't sure exactly why I said that. My name wasn't "sweet thing," either, or any of the other names I'd been called in the past few minutes. But they'd seemed like nice names and "Cherry," whatever it meant, didn't.

Barbara started walking toward us. "Cool it, sailor boy. Get your mitts off of her."

Billy Bob grabbed Barbara from behind and turned her around. "Never you mind them, honey. We got business here of our own."

Barbara shouted, "Get your damn hands off of me, you lousy gob!"

Barbara was pushing against Billy Bob's chest, but he was holding her tightly. Hands grabbed me from behind, tightly, hurting me, pulling me backward. I couldn't catch my breath. I struggled against the hands, but they pulled me closer and held me tighter. A voice hissed in my ear, "Shut up." Only my toes were touching the ground, and I lost my balance and fell against whichever sailor it was who was holding onto me. I swung my feet, trying to find the ground.

Suddenly, Barbara pulled one of her legs backward and kicked Billy Bob in the shin. It wasn't very hard. He didn't look like it hurt, but he did look surprised. He loosened his grip and looked down at her, smiling. She leaned her head back and said, in a kind of strangled voice, "You idiots. She's only fourteen."

The arms holding me opened at the same time that Billy Bob let go of Barbara. I ran to stand next to her. The sailors moved together, backing away from us, holding their hands up like someone was pointing a gun at them. I figured it was because of what Barbara had said, but it didn't look like they were looking at us. And then a loud, angry voice thundered from somewhere behind us.

"Just a goldarned minute."

Chapter Seventy-One

I twisted my head and saw a huge policeman with a red face and a blobby nose standing a few feet away from us. His hands were folded over his chest, and he looked angry.

"What're youse lousy punks doing on my street?"

So that was what they were looking at. I could feel the cold draining out of my body as the sailors began to turn and walk away. But all of a sudden, the policeman's face was close to mine. He was holding onto me and to Barbara and yelling at us.

Yelling at *us*!

"You little tarts. You think you can come here and set up your dirty business on my street? On my street! Well, you got another think coming. You can turn yourselves right around and get on the first bus back to wherever it was you came from."

Barbara's face screwed up in annoyance, and she shook herself free. "Relax, flatfoot. You got it all wrong. We're not tarts. And we didn't come from anywhere. *We* come from here. And these hicks were just asking us for directions."

Was she crazy? To talk to him like that? Flatfoot? And to lie about what happened and not tell him that they attacked us? I wanted to tell him what really happened. But when I tried to talk, I started to cry. It was like I had been holding in a mountain of fear and disappointment, and now it all came bubbling up. Tears ran down my neck into my sweater. My nose ran into my mouth. It was awful.

The policeman looked at me and said in a mean and sarcastic voice, "What's the matter, sweetie? This your first arrest?"

My first . . . *arrest!?*

The three sailors were walking away. Not running exactly. But walking as fast as they could.

"That's right, sailors. You better scram. Maybe where you rubes come from it's okay to mess with fourteen-year-olds. But this is New York. If I see you on my street again, you just may not be on that ship of yours when it tootles out of the port."

I was working really hard to stop crying. It was really embarrassing. The policeman turned back to us.

"You girls is really from here? Youse didn't just get here on a bus?"

"No, sir. We're really from here."

"Where do youse live?"

"Queens. But we're here to catch a bus to Cleveland. We're going to my aunt's house. She—"

"I don't suppose either one of youse has any identification or nothing."

I looked at Barbara. She shrugged. I pulled out my subway pass and my student card. Barbara rolled her eyes when she saw the student card. I thought everyone had a student card, but I guess I was wrong. She did have a subway pass, though.

He studied them and put them in his pocket. He pulled out a pad and pencil. He looked at Barbara. "Okay. Starting with you. I want your name. Your address. Your parents' names and your phone number."

"Come on, Flanagan, give us a break. We're going to Ohio to work for her aunt. It's all arranged. You're going to make us miss our bus."

I wondered how Barbara knew his name. Then I saw that it was written over his pocket. He walked over to Barbara and leaned over her, menacingly. She looked tiny next to him and started backing up.

"Number one, my name is 'Officer Flanagan.' Number two, I done already told you what number two was."

Barbara slowly gave him all the information he'd asked for. As soon as she was done, I gave him all of my information before he asked for it again. He studied his notepad for a minute and looked up.

"All right, ladies, now we're all going to take a little walk, over to the Fourteenth Precinct. Are you going to come quietly, or do I need to use handcuffs?"

Chapter Seventy-Two

T he sidewalk in front of the bus terminal was crowded. People pushed in and out of the revolving doors. In the street, traffic roared by. For a minute, I thought maybe I should just throw myself under a car. I looked at Barbara. She looked the same way. And then it hit me. Like someone had thrown a bucket of cold water at me. This whole thing was a mistake, and all I had to do was explain it to Officer Flanagan.

"Excuse me, Officer. Could I just talk to you for a minute? Because I think maybe you have us confused with someone else. We're just high school students. I mean, I'm like in honor classes and Junior Arista. I always do my homework, and I've hardly ever even kissed anybody, except like at parties, and there was always a grown-up watching. But my parents lied to me, and my father had another daughter and they never told me about her, and he loved her more than he loved me even though she was dead. But I didn't know she was dead. And this is my friend, Barbara. She's my best friend and a really nice girl, too, even if she doesn't always, you know, do all her homework. She's not a criminal, though. Neither one of us is a criminal. It's just that her parents got divorced, which wasn't her fault, of course, and her mother's husband doesn't like her, and they want to send her away. And my mother's sister, my aunt Carol, she just had a baby. So, we thought that, you know, we could go out to Cleveland, where Aunt Carol lives, and help her with the baby and stuff. But we had a little time until the bus left, so we came out to take a walk. And those sailors, at first they seemed nice, but then they got terrible. And then you came. And at first I was glad because I thought you were going to protect us."

I said that all in only one or two breaths because I was afraid he would interrupt me and not listen. But by the time I got to the part about how I thought he was going to protect us, I was crying again and couldn't say any more. Barbara was staring at me. She rolled her eyes. Officer Flanagan looked from one of us to the other and smiled. Smiled! It made him look like a completely different person from mean Officer Flanagan.

"Is that so, little lady? And here I thought youse two were runaways. Well, my, my. I guess I'll have to tell Mrs. Flanagan when I get home tonight about how I made such a terrible mistake about the two nice young ladies I met assisting members of the armed services at the bus terminal. So, let me see." He looked down at his wristwatch.

"But here's my little problem. It's two thirty on a Tuesday afternoon. And Tuesday is a school day. And you tell me that you're students. Only you're not in school. You're at the bus terminal. You say you have permission to be out of school. You tell me that your parents, they know exactly where you are. And they know exactly where you are going? Maybe they even bought the tickets."

I didn't know how to answer that. I was so relieved that he was being nice, I didn't want to spoil it by lying to him. Because then he would stop being nice. But if I told him the truth, he would stop being nice. There didn't seem to be any way out of this mess. Suddenly, from somewhere behind us, there was a scream.

"Barbara. Oh, my God. Barbara."

We spun around and Barbara groaned, "Oh, no. My old lady. The bastard told."

A woman who didn't look anything like what I'd pictured Barbara's mother looking like ran toward us. From the things Barbara had said about her, I thought she would be this sad and timid little thing who worked as something like a waitress or a hairdresser. This woman was crying and looking pretty hysterical. She had neatly curled dark hair and wore a navy dress with a belt, a white collar, and high-heeled navy shoes. Barbara never told me where she worked, but it must have been in an office, from the way she was dressed. She was talking the whole time she was walking toward us.

"Oh, my God, Barbara, what have you done now? Officer. Please. That's my daughter."

"Which one is your daughter, lady?"

She pointed at Barbara.

Flanagan pointed to me. "What about this one?"

Barbara's mother turned toward me and studied my face like she couldn't figure out what planet I came from. Like my father did. Maybe I'm not from this planet. That would actually explain a lot.

"I've never seen her before. Who is this, Barbara? Is this the girl your father was talking about? What the hell were you thinking showing up at his house?"

Barbara glared at me with anger spreading all over her face. She hissed, "I told you they all stick together."

I stared at her in confusion until I realized that the "they" she was talking about was grown-ups, and that she was angry with me. With me!

"Don't tell me that you think this mess is my fault."

"Who else, Miss Junior Arista? Who said we needed a grown-up to help us? I told you they all stick together."

"Well, you didn't have to listen to me, Miss I'm-Smarter-Than-Anybody-in-the-World. Anyway, it was your idea to visit your father."

Barbara's mother and Officer Flanagan were moving in between Barbara and me like they thought we were going to start throwing punches at each other, which maybe we would have, except that we heard a man's voice shouting, "Barbara, Barbara! Thank God I found you. Connie, is that you?"

We all turned around and looked down the street in the other direction and saw Sean Dougherty running up the block.

Barbara threw her hands up into the air. "Oh, great. A family reunion."

I started to giggle, although there were still tears running down my face. Barbara glared at me. She was crying, too.

Officer Flanagan roared, "Who're you?"

He pointed to Barbara. "I'm her father."

Officer Flanagan pointed to me. "What about her?"

"I never saw her before today."

Barbara's mother let out a loud, snorting sound. "You never saw your daughter before today, either, Dougherty. Officer, you have to understand—"

Officer Flanagan looked at me. "Are you some kind of orphan or something?"

"Orphan? No, of course I'm not an orphan. My father is Dr. Martin Levy, and my mother is Mrs. Helen Levy, and we live at—"

"Okay. Okay. It's just that your friend here seems to have so many parents, and nobody's ever seen you before."

Barbara was laughing. Tears still glistened on her cheeks. But she was laughing. Before I could say anything, noises started to come out of a big, black walkie-talkie that hung from Officer Flanagan's belt. He raised his hand and held it to his ear.

"All right. That was the precinct. The boys called the numbers youse girls gave me, and a Mr. and Mrs. Levy and a person named Tony are on their way to the precinct. So, I suggest we all walk over there and wait for them."

Chapter Seventy-Three

"Officer, can't I please just take my daughter home? She won't give you any more trouble. I promise."

Barbara's mother stood in front of Officer Flanagan and smiled at him with the smile I'd been trying to use—a smile that said, *You don't have to concern yourself with us. We're law-abiding citizens.*

"Who's Tony?"

"My husband," Barbara's mother answered. She gestured to Barbara's father. "We're, you know—"

"Divorced," Officer Flanagan finished her sentence.

"Yes. I wish you hadn't gotten Tony involved in this," she continued.

"You got him involved when you married him, lady. We only called him."

Barbara's mother looked shocked, then she repeated, "Officer, please, can't I take my daughter home?"

An icy fear spilled out of a terrible thought. If Barbara went home, I would be alone in a police station with my parents. I looked over at Barbara. I was going to plead with her to stay with me if I had to. But I didn't have to.

She looked back at me and shouted, "Oh, no, you don't. I ain't leaving Paula. And I ain't going home with you. Ever."

Barbara's mother started to answer her, but Officer Flanagan shouted, "All of youse, shut up! And follow me to the precinct."

We walked single file, following Officer Flanagan down the street, like a weird parade. I once read about running the gauntlet in a scary comic book. Everyone lined up in two lines, and the person being punished had to run in between them while they threw stuff at him. That's how I felt. It was like everyone I'd ever met was lined up on the sidewalk, watching me. No one threw anything. But there they all were. My teachers. My friends. My neighbors. Mr. and Mrs. Singer. Kids from school I never talked to. I saw them with my eyes opened or shut. It made no difference. I was so tired, I felt like I could fall asleep standing up and walking. I wondered if I was being arrested. I wondered if being arrested was put on your "permanent record card." My teachers always warned us that everything we did, like talking during a fire drill or cheating on a test, was written on our permanent record cards. I wondered if this meant I would never get into a good college. And I wondered if I cared.

Chapter Seventy-Four

O fficer Flanagan led us into a back room of the police station and told us to shut up and wait. I sat on a bench and watched Barbara's parents trying to talk to her on the other side of the room. Her mother was holding her arm. She pulled away and came over to sit next to me.

I moaned, "What're we going to do?"

"Do? What exactly do you think we can do? There isn't much you can do in the middle of a cop station, genius."

She was trying to sound like her tough old self, but the word "genius" caught in her throat. When my eyes locked into hers, I saw the tears spilling out of them. She leaned closer and touched my arm.

"At least we tried, Paula."

I took her hand and held it with both my hands. Was that all there was? Trying? I suddenly understood what I never thought about before. Holden didn't escape. He was only gone for a couple of days. It seemed longer. But today seemed longer, too, although it was only a few hours. And then Holden wound up in a mental hospital. After the book ended, he just went home and grew up. And so would we.

"Oh, my God. She *is* here!"

My mother's shriek rattled the room. I turned toward the door to see the parents I thought I would never see again. My mother was crying into my father's handkerchief. He had his arm around her and was talking into her ear as they walked. I'd never seen him put his arm around her before.

She pulled away and looked at him.

"She's here," she repeated, in an astonished voice, "in the police station."

The sympathetic expression froze on my father's face and was replaced by his more familiar look of impatience.

"Well, what did you expect? Did you think the police called us at random with inaccurate information?"

But my mother didn't seem to hear him. She moved toward me, her head moving on her neck like it would fall off while she examined the room.

She's making sure that there's no one here who knows her. She would be so embarrassed.

Her eyes settled on Barbara with a flash of recognition.

"I knew it. I knew it was that little tramp. Get away from her, you bitch. Get away from my daughter."

My father tried to catch up to her and pull her back.

Barbara's mother jumped up and yelled, "Hey! Don't you talk like that to my daughter! Who the hell do you think you are?"

My mother turned to face Barbara's mother, her face twisted with unfamiliar anger. In a voice I'd never heard before she shouted back, "Who the hell do you think *you* are?"

While I stared at this stranger walking inside my mother's body, my father put his arm around her again and tried to lead her back toward the bench where Barbara and I sat, speaking softly into her ear. Maybe there was a stranger in his body, too.

Officer Flanagan filled the doorway, throwing his shadow across the room. He looked around angrily and came in, followed by a man who was almost as big as he was, wearing a brown delivery man's uniform.

Barbara breathed, "Tony. Shit."

Tony walked over to Barbara's mother. Barbara's mother said something, and Tony and Barbara's father nodded at each other. They each began to put their hands out as if they were going to shake hands and then, at almost the same minute, they each put their hands down.

Officer Flanagan stood in the middle of the room and motioned to Barbara.

"Over here, young lady. With your family."

We looked at each other. I didn't want to let go of her hand.

"Paula," my father almost shouted, "you heard the man. Now get away from that . . . person."

"And what's wrong with our daughter, Mr. High and Mighty?" Tony stood defiantly next to Barbara's mother and put his arm protectively around her shoulder. As his arm touched her shoulder, she turned her head to stare at him in shock.

My father stood up very straight, pulling his shoulders back. He was about two feet shorter than Tony, but they were standing pretty far apart so it didn't show so much.

"If you wish to address me, sir, you may call me Dr. High and Mighty."

I knew he wouldn't have been so brave if Officer Flanagan weren't standing between them.

Barbara walked over to her parents and Tony, and my parents came to stand next to me. We stood staring at each other across the room like gunfighters about to start a battle.

My mother whispered to my father, "*Pruste goyim.*"

My father nodded and, indicating Tony with his head, whispered back, "*Lumpen proletariat.*"

My body shook with rage. The new rage I'd never felt until a few weeks ago. Who did they think they were to say such mean and insulting things about people? I hoped Barbara's parents didn't hear what they said, although they probably wouldn't understand what they said, even if they did.

Tony turned to his wife and evened the score. He said, in a voice that wasn't anywhere close to a whisper, "Kikes."

At least my parents whispered when they insulted people. Barbara's mother turned to him and said, "Shut up, Tony."

Officer Flanagan said, "I take it you people have never met before?"

They all shook their heads.

"Introduce yourselves."

Tony said in an angry voice, "You don't expect me to shake hands, do you?"

He didn't seem nearly as nervous as the rest of us. I figured he'd been in police stations before.

"Just names."

My father stepped forward and said, in a formal way, like he was being presented to the Queen of England, "Dr. and Mrs. Martin Levy." I almost expected him to click his heels and bow.

Tony stepped forward, mimicking my father's manner, hatred covering his face. "Mr. and Mrs. Anthony Montalvo."

Barbara's father stepped forward. "Sean Dougherty, Barbara's father."

We all stared at each other in silence, not knowing exactly what was coming next, when my father surprised everyone by saying,

"Excuse me, Officer. I beg your pardon. But if I may. Mr. Dougherty, are you, by any chance, Sean 'Doc' Dougherty, the jazz musician?"

Barbara's father, Sean "Doc" Dougherty, stood up straight and smiled.

"Yeah. Yeah. That's me. The Doc."

"I thought I recognized you. Well, I for one would be proud to shake your hand, sir. Your very gifted hand. I heard you play. Many times. In Berlin."

"You saw us jam? In Berlin?"

"At Haus Vaterland."

"We did a bunch of gigs there."

"Yes. We always went to see you. You are an exceptional musician, sir. It is a pleasure to meet you. Even in these, eh, unusual circumstances."

A big smile covered Doc Dougherty's face. "These circumstances are more unusual for a doc like you than they are for a doc like me."

We all actually laughed. Except Tony, who narrowed his eyes and pressed his lips together and glared. And then we all were quiet, surprised that we had laughed.

My father was smiling. Smiling? Jazz? It was such a shock, I forgot how scared I was. I even forgot how much I hated him.

"I didn't know you liked jazz." My voice sounded strange even to me. Meaner than I'd meant for it to sound. Almost like I was accusing him of a crime.

He looked at me in surprise. "Perhaps you do not know me as well as you think."

That was the kind of nasty thing my father always said to me. But the voice he said it with was kind. Well, almost kind. Kinder.

I couldn't stop myself from talking even though all I wanted to do was disappear and never see any of these people again. "I thought you liked Bach and those guys."

He smiled. "I do like Bach and those guys. If by 'those guys,' you mean who I think you mean. But that doesn't mean I can't like jazz. Does it, Doc?"

"No, Doc. It sure don't."

Officer Flanagan broke in. "Well, ain't this nice. I hope you didn't forget that I got me a couple of delinquents here. And I want to hear what you have to say before I book them."

"Book?" The word echoed around the room.

"Yeah. Book. I found these two, during school time, by the bus station, chatting with a group of sailors."

"Where are they?" Tony suddenly yelled. "Where are they? I'll kill them!"

Barbara and her mother looked at Tony in surprise.

"Relax, bud, I sent them back to sea."

"There's been some sort of mistake, Officer," my mother said. "You have to understand. It's not my daughter's fault. It's that girl over here. She is a very bad influence."

Barbara's mother stood up. "Your daughter's the bad influence, lady. My daughter never ran away from home before she met her."

Barbara and I grabbed our mothers' arms, but Officer Flanagan didn't pay any attention to them. It was like he hadn't heard a word they said.

"So, these two are looking at charges of solicitation, truancy, and disturbing the peace."

"How many times do I have to tell you, Flanagan," Barbara said loudly, bravely, "we didn't solicit nothing. We were helping out these hicks who didn't know their way around."

I pulled away from my parents and ran to stand next to Barbara. I figured if two people told the same story, they would have to believe us.

"It's true, Officer, sir, you've got to believe us. They started touching me and calling me 'Cherry' and . . ."

To my complete disgust, I started crying again and couldn't talk. Tears and snot kept slipping into my mouth, and I started to cough. I hated myself for being so weak. For not being able to stand up to everybody like Barbara.

"Look at her," Barbara said, pointing to me. "You see what I had to deal with, don't you? I had to protect her. You know what I mean?"

"Then there's the matter of lying to an officer of the law," Officer Flanagan continued, ignoring us as well.

"Did you," he began, looking around at our parents, "know that they were taking the bus to Cleveland? Did you arrange for them to have a job in Cleveland?"

The shocked faces of every adult there and the "what's" and the "where's" echoing around the room answered the question.

"No. I didn't think so. Lying. Vagrants. No visible means of support."

Barbara's father moved toward her. "Barbara, honey. Tell me what happened. Why were you running away?"

His voice was so sweet. I wished he were my father. But Barbara turned on him and hissed, "You promised not to tell. You bastard."

Barbara's mother stepped between them. "Don't talk to him like that. He's your father. Even if you never met him before. And you," she said, turning around to face him, "suddenly you're the big hero? The last time you saw her, she was pissing in her diaper. Now you come riding in like the Lone Ranger to save the little brat when she's arrested for hustling sailors."

"Connie, I—"

"Yeah, right." She turned back to Barbara. "Look, Barbara, this has gone on long enough."

"Yeah. Long enough," Tony echoed her, trying to move into the little group.

Barbara's mother put her hand on his chest to keep him back and said, "What the hell did you think you were doing, missy? Going to his house?"

Barbara was silent.

"Answer me."

"I had no place to go."

"What does that mean? Look at me when I'm talking to you."

Barbara turned to face her. "You were going to send me away. To that jail."

"What jail?"

"The school. The convent school."

"Is that what this is about? The school? Oh, Barbara, for God's sake. You're such an idiot. You're not going to any convent school."

"Whaddya mean?" Tony yelled.

"I was just going along with the idea until everyone forgot about it. I was never going to send you there. I couldn't. You're not . . ." She turned to look at Tony and said, in such a soft voice that I could hardly hear her, "She's not Catholic."

Chapter Seventy-Five

*T*ony and Barbara hadn't looked at each other the whole time. They were standing on either side of Barbara's mother, and they still weren't looking at each other. Which is why it was funny to see the same look of shock spread over both of their faces at the same time. Barbara's mother started to breathe these really deep breaths. I looked over at her because it was such a strange sound. Like she was underwater gulping for air. She was crying. Everyone in the room was watching her, so, after a minute that seemed like an hour, she started to talk again.

"I never baptized you, Barbara. And I never baptized me, either." She looked up at Tony and took a couple of steps backward, away from him, so she was more than an arm's length away from him. She looked frightened.

In a soft voice that sounded like she was apologizing for something, she said, "I'm Jewish, Tony. I mean, I was born Jewish, and I was never baptized or anything before Barbara was born. So, I think that makes Barbara Jewish, too. If your mother is Jewish, then you're Jewish. Isn't that right, Doctor Levy?"

She turned and directed this question to my father. Her voice was calmer now and made it sound like it was the most natural thing in the world for her and my father to be discussing questions of religious traditions in the middle of a police station. My father had been staring at her, like everyone else in the room, and obviously didn't expect to be spoken to at that moment.

He looked startled and stammered, "Uh. Yes. I believe that's true. That is how I understand it. Of course, I am no rabbi." My father turned to my mother and shrugged. "A *lantzman.*"

That was what they said to each other whenever they discovered that someone was Jewish who they didn't expect to be Jewish. They usually smiled when they said it, but they didn't smile this time. My mother leaned around my father to look more closely at Barbara's mother, like she was trying to see if she missed something.

Barbara and I stared at each other. She was Jewish. What did that mean? Was she still cool? If she was, she was probably the only cool Jewish kid in the world. I sure had never met anyone who was Jewish and cool. But before I could figure out if there was something about being Jewish that made it impossible to be cool, a sound like an angry elephant bellowed through the room. It was Tony.

"You hid that dirty secret from me. All this time?"

He was walking toward Barbara's mother, and she backed away, closer to Officer Flanagan. She began to sob.

"I was going to tell you. At first. But when I realized how much you hated Jews . . ."

Tony stopped walking and sank down onto the bench, like a balloon someone let the air out of all at once.

"Angela and Tony Junior. My babies. Are they . . . Jews?"

"No, Tony. They were baptized."

"But before that. When they were born."

She shrugged. "I suppose so."

Tony sounded like he was about to cry. "So, if they died . . . they . . . You devil. You'll be damned to hell."

Tears rolled down Barbara's mother's cheeks.

"I already have been, Tony, living with you."

For the second time that day, I felt like I was in the audience watching a play about Barbara and her family, who never turned out to be like I expected them to be. Barbara's famous father was a taxi driver. And her mother was Jewish. Of course, my family wasn't turning out like I expected them to be, either. My mother screamed and cursed. My father liked jazz.

Sean walked over to Barbara's mother and touched her shoulder. "Aww, Connie, I'm so sorry how things turned out."

He turned and looked defiantly at Tony, who had started to walk toward them but stopped when Sean looked at him, even though Sean was only about half his size. At least one thing was turning out to be exactly like Barbara had said. Tony was a big dumb bully.

Barbara had been staring at me, as if she was wondering the same things I was . . . about still being cool and all. She turned and looked at all of her parents—her mother and actual father talking quietly to each other and Tony sitting on the bench with his head in his hands. She slowly shook her head.

I tried to figure out what she was thinking. I mean, a lot of stuff had changed for her today. Nothing had really changed for me. But the thing that remained the same was we were still here with the people we never wanted to see again, and with no place to go.

Suddenly, Barbara spun around, stood up, and put her hands on her hips.

"Hey, Tony, how do you like them apples? The tramp's a Jew."

Chapter Seventy-Six

*B*arbara's mother walked over to Barbara and stood in front of her. Without a moment's hesitation, she slapped her across the face, hard, leaving a bright red hand mark on her cheek.

I told you, I think, that me and my friends never got hit. I mean, not like that. I'd seen fights in movies and on TV. But never in person. I'd never heard that sound in person or saw the redness spring up on someone's face in person. And not just someone. Barbara. My Barbara. The person I loved most in the world. My cheek stung as if I'd been hit, too.

Barbara's mother wasn't crying anymore. And she wasn't apologizing for anything. She was angry. Fire was coming out of her eyes.

"You listen to me, missy. I'm going to give you one chance. One last chance. From now on, you help with the housework. You help with the kids. You do your homework and get good grades. And you leave that mouth of yours in the garbage where it belongs. If you don't, so help me God, I will find a convent school that takes Jews."

Barbara was holding her cheek with both hands. It must've hurt. She was squinting at her mother, trying to make her eyes look angry. I could see tears in them. But her mouth twisted in rage.

"I got a better idea, Mommy. Why don't you take Paula home

instead? She's exactly the kind of daughter you want. And her parents don't want her."

My parents had been watching the drama of Barbara's family like it had nothing to do with them. But when Barbara said that, it was like someone had thrown a bucket of cold water on them. My mother gasped.

"Paula. What does she mean? How could—"

I turned to look at my parents. I walked away from them and over to Barbara and her mother.

"I'd be happy to go home with you, Mrs. Montalvo. I'll take care of the house. The kids. Whatever you want. Anything to not have to go back to their house."

I turned to face them. My mother's eyes were as wide as Margaret's, and the color had drained out of her face. She opened and closed her mouth as if she couldn't find the right thing to say. My father was holding her shoulders to prevent her from moving toward me.

My mother whimpered, "Paula. Why are you doing this to us? How can you insult us like this in front of these people? We've given you everything. Were you planning to stay out all night? Do you have any idea how worried we would have been? Did you care? Did you spend a minute thinking about anyone but yourself?"

My father said, "Please, Helen. Don't whine. While we have been playing out this melodrama, bailing out a delinquent adolescent, a patient has been waiting for me to save his life."

I walked toward them.

Suddenly, I wasn't crying anymore. I took a deep breath, which felt like the first one I had taken in a long time. I felt angry. And I felt cold. But I wasn't crying.

"Go ahead, Dr. Levy. Go back to your hospital. Go back to

your patients. Everyone is more important to you than I am. You don't love me. You never loved me. All you ever did was to make sure I got better grades than your friend's daughter. And you never even told me I had a sister. You never told me anything about her. And what happened to her."

"Why should I have told you that?" my father snarled. "It was none of your business."

"None of my business? Never to know what my own father was thinking. Never to know who you loved more than you loved me. Tell the truth. At last, tell me the truth."

The thoughts I had not dared to think came pouring out of my mouth. "How often did you think about her when you were with me? When it was my birthday, did you think about how old she would be? When you looked at me, did you think about how much prettier she would be? Smarter? More talented? Did you? Tell me the truth."

My father was looking more and more confused as I spoke. He kept looking around, as if hoping there was someone else who could answer these questions.

And, just as suddenly, I was crying again because a thought so painful, so terrible filled my whole body with a stabbing pain.

"Did you ever love me? Or did you hate me? Did you hate me for being alive when she was dead? Did you wish you could change me for her?"

My father's body jolted, as if he'd been hit by lightning, as if he was feeling the same terrible pain.

"Hate you? How could you think . . . Oh, my God. Could you really believe this? That I hated you? I just didn't want . . . I just . . . I didn't want that evil to be a part of your life. I wanted the past to stay in the past. I wanted you to have the future."

He turned to my mother and waved his arm in my direction. "Tell her."

My mother cried, "Paula, my baby. I always loved you. I did everything for you. How could you—"

"Really? You always loved me? Even if I didn't have a dimple on my chin? Even if I sounded like a foghorn when I cried and didn't do better than Margaret on the French midterm?"

Tears streamed down my face, and my nose ran into my mouth again. Suddenly, a big red handkerchief was in front of my eyes. I took it and wiped my face and saw Officer Flanagan walking away. But I wasn't finished. I looked back at my mother.

"How can you say you loved me? You didn't even know me. You didn't know anything about what I was thinking. What I wanted. How I really felt about anything. And you never cared. If I tried to tell you, you made fun of me. Sarah Heartburn. Posing for animal crackers. Or you talked about yourself. And the Depression. You two are the opposite, you know. A father who never told me anything about his past. And a mother who talked only about her past. What did you ever give me? Things you wanted. You picked out everything. A room that you decorated and clothes that I hate. Don't keep on saying you love me. Because I don't believe it."

Tears rolled down my mother's face as she stared at me, and I began to feel sorry for her. A little. But my father had recovered. He faced me with a cold anger in his eyes.

"I, for one, have had enough of this soap opera. Love has nothing to do with it. It has nothing to do with anything. It is a matter of duty and responsibility. Things you obviously know nothing about. You have a safe and comfortable home. You are warm in the winter and cool in the summer. If you are unhappy, it is a defect of character. Plain and simple, and Dr. Freud be damned. Helen, we will get her into therapy immediately. Officer, I would like to thank you for your service and your courtesy. You can count on a generous contribution to the Police Athletic Fund. This family will not waste any more of your time. Helen, Paula, we are going home."

"I'm not going. I'm going to live with Barbara."

"Well, yes, you are going, and no, you are not going to live with your coconspirator over there. You are fourteen years old. You have no choice but to do as I say. When you turn eighteen, you will be perfectly free to choose not to take any further advantage of my generosity. But not before that. I thought you were intelligent enough to know at least that. I guess not. Now let's go."

"I'd rather go to jail."

"Unfortunately, that is not your choice, either. You cannot check in and out of jail like it is a hotel. Now say goodbye to your erstwhile friend because you will certainly never see her again."

I looked over at Officer Flanagan.

"Aren't we under arrest, or something?"

He smiled for the first time. "No, young lady. You go home with your parents. And stay there."

He turned to Barbara. "Same for you. But I'll be keeping an eye out for the two of youse. I better not see youse hanging around the bus station when you should be in school."

"Connie," Barbara's father started with his sweet voice, "maybe Barbara can visit me. You know. On weekends sometimes. Would you like that, Barbara?"

Barbara shrugged. "Maybe. If we don't have to go to the syna-thing, the Jewish church with Paula and her parents."

Barbara's head was bloody but unbowed. Like the poem in my English textbook. The poem, "Invictus." Invincible.

"Under the bludgeonings of chance

My head is bloody, but unbowed."

Well, chance had certainly bludgeoned us today. But so what? Why shouldn't my bloody head be unbowed, too? After all, Barbara had never even read the poem.

Chapter Seventy-Seven

I walked to the door and turned around to face everyone.

"I don't care what you say. I don't care what any of you say. I am not going home with you. I'll sleep on the street. I'll starve to death. I don't care. Nothing is worse than being with you."

I ran out of the room and into the main area of the police station. It was crowded and noisy, and I blinked my eyes in confusion. It was like I had forgotten that there was a world outside the room where my life had fallen apart. There were people talking and walking, yelling and writing, and talking on the telephone. There were people thinking about all kinds of things that had nothing to do with me or Barbara or our parents. A world I was somehow going to live in from now on. For the rest of my life. Go home and grow up. Like Holden.

But maybe not yet. There was a group of six or seven policemen standing together and talking, next to the wall opposite from where I was standing. I ran over to them. They stared at me in surprise.

"Please," I said. "Please. Just let me stand here for a minute. Okay?"

"What's the matter, honey?"

"Is someone hurting you?"

I moved into the middle of the group. Policemen clustered around me protectively as I looked over to see my parents running out of the door, followed by Officer Flanagan. Barbara and all of her parents followed them, like it was their turn to be the audience and watch the Paula-and-Her-Parents play.

Although it felt like I had run a thousand miles, the room was not really very large, which is why, from across the crowded police station, I could see my father's face clearly, and his eyes filled with emotion. And that was when I saw it. The minute that the mask slid all the way off his face. I saw the tears that sprang into his eyes, and I saw his real face, the face of the photograph. Older. Terrified. But his real face.

"Sophie!" he screamed. "Not again. Please, God. Paula. My child. My heart."

My mother looked at him in horror and took him in her arms. He sank into her and rested his head against her shoulder. And there they stood. My parents. Holding each other. Weeping.

My father's head snapped up, and he sprang away from my mother. He looked as if he didn't know where he was. He touched his cheek and looked at his wet fingers, as if trying to figure out what the liquid was. He turned toward the wall and took the handkerchief from his pocket. He wiped his face, slowly and carefully. When he turned around again, the mask was back in place.

I had been standing totally still. Crying. Lost. Surrounded by men in uniform. As I guess Lena and Sophie had been once. When they were taken away. When they disappeared forever. Did he see them like that? Or only imagine it?

"Excuse me," I said. The policemen parted, like the Red Sea, and I walked away from them and toward my parents. They looked at me with eyes filled with longing. Both of them.

"I'll come home," I said, "but Barbara and I stay friends."

My mother screamed, "I won't have it! You're never to see that girl again. Never. I don't care if she is Jewish. I don't care if she comes from a family of famous rabbis."

"She's been my best friend for months, and you didn't even know that I knew her. We talked to each other every day and planned our escape, and you didn't know anything about it. Not even when you had creepy Margaret spying on me. She's the best friend I ever had. And I'm not going to stop being her friend. And you can't make me."

My mother turned to face me, and I looked into her eyes. They were cold, narrow slits. And so was her mouth.

If she ever loved me before, she certainly doesn't now.

And then, as if her face had been made out of ice, it melted. Tears streamed from her eyes, washing all the coldness from them.

My father turned to her and pulled on her arm. "For Chrissakes, Helen, let her see the girl. If it makes her happy. Apparently, we never did."

"Martin. Martin. How did this happen? How could she think we did not love her?" She turned back to me.

"Oh, Paula. I always loved you. I love you so much. What have I done?"

"Be that as it may, Helen. We can discuss this later. At home. Let us simply agree for now to let her see her friend, and we can go home. We can end this. All right, Paula. If that is your ultimatum, so be it. You can keep seeing her. Now let's go home."

My mother looked around as if she had forgotten where she was. She seemed confused and helpless. Her shoulders slouched and her head dropped, as if she was going to fall over. I almost felt sorry for her again. A little.

"All right," she said in a whisper. "All right. Just. Please. Come home. Please."

Chapter Seventy-Eight

The whole adventure, from sneaking out of school in the morning to coming home at night with my parents, was over in just twelve hours. I'd been in classes that seemed longer than that whole day did. With my clothes unpacked and the money back in the bank, it could almost have never happened. Except that it did.

We never did discuss it further at home, like my father suggested in the police station. I didn't expect to. I knew he was just saying that to get us out of there. My mother referred to the day, when she did, as my "escapade." It was her nasty way of making fun of it. Like calling me Sarah Heartburn. I'd never heard the word "escapade" before. What did it mean? Was it like lemonade? Orangeade? Was an escapade a drink, too? A drink of escape?

But something had definitely changed. Both my parents smiled at me more, even if they seemed more uncomfortable with each other. It seemed phony and forced. Like I had a fatal illness, and they were trying to be cheerful about it. But they were definitely trying. And when Barbara came over, my mother always made a point of saying hello and asking how she was and how her mother was and if she'd seen her talented father and if she wanted some milk. Barbara didn't groan or roll her eyes because I knew she was happy we'd been able to stay friends, too.

One night, as I was walking to my room after dinner, expecting that my family had used up all their conversation for that day, my father called me from his chair.

"Paula Levy. The very person I wished to see. Could you spare a minute from your busy schedule for your old father?"

He sounded like he was surprised to see me, like we were in some foreign city and he'd seen someone he knew walking down the street. He was smiling. My mother was sitting next to him, trying to keep a smile on her face.

"I have some information that I think may interest you."

I walked over, not knowing what to expect. When I was standing next to his chair, he continued. "You know that singer you like. The one with the funny name that you listen to all the time."

"Elvis Presley?"

"Yes. That funny name. Also, you remember, I told you I had a patient who did something or other in the music business?"

I nodded.

"Well, he tells me that your singer is going to be on *The Ed Sullivan Show*. Did you know that?"

I shook my head.

"Well, he remembered that I told him you had worn out this Presley's records, you played them so much, so he thought that you might like to see him in person. Is that something that would interest you?"

I felt like a pair of eyes floating in the air. My body was numb. My mind was numb. The words echoed in my mind.

See him in person.

I nodded. Unable to find my voice.

"So, he gave me two tickets. They are fairly close to the stage, he tells me, in the section where the reporters sit."

My head was like a great empty room. The words echoed in it over and over.

See him in person. Fairly close to the stage.

My father continued, in a matter-of-fact way, like he was telling me about his subway ride home. "My immediate thought was, you can go with Mama. But suddenly he was a mind reader. 'Look, Doc,' he said to me. 'Don't make her go with you or with your wife. Let her go with a kid. Someone who loves him. Like she does. You know? Let her really enjoy it.'"

How could he know that? A grown-up I'd never met knew how I felt. My parents didn't. My teachers didn't. But a man I'd never met knew me. The thought made me so happy. So hopeful. Maybe life would turn out better than I thought. Maybe there was a place where I would fit in.

"So, Mama and I discussed it. There was no sense asking Margaret to go with you. From what her father tells me, she does not care for him. So, we thought you could go with Barbara. Doesn't she like him, too?"

"She . . . loves him."

He nodded and continued, "That's what we thought. Mama was a little worried, of course. About your going to Manhattan without an adult. But I said, after all, you have gone all the way to New Jersey without an adult. Of course, you came home with a police escort. Hopefully you can avoid that this time. And no sailors!"

He stood and held the tickets toward me. I threw my arms around him. I felt him stiffen and then relax, and two arms pressed me to his chest.

Credits

SHAKE, RATTLE AND ROLL
Words and Music by CHARLES E. CALHOUN
© 1954 (Renewed) UNICHAPPELL MUSIC INC. and MIJAC
MUSIC
All Rights Reserved
Used by Permission of ALFRED MUSIC

Shake, Rattle And Roll
Words and Music by Charles Calhoun
Copyright © 1954 Mijac Music and Unichappell Music Inc.
Copyright Renewed
All Rights on behalf of Mijac Music Administered by Sony Music
Publishing (US) LLC, 424 Church Street, Suite 1200, Nashville, TN
37219
International Copyright Secured All Rights Reserved
Reprinted by Permission of Hal Leonard LLC

"The Great Pretender" by Buck Ram
Copyright 1955 by Panther Music Corp.
Copyright Renewed. Used by permission. All Rights Reserved.

Why Do Fools Fall In Love
Words and Music by Morris Levy and Frankie Lymon
Copyright © 1956 EMI Longitude Music and EMI Full Keel Music
Copyright Renewed
All Rights Administered by Sony Music Publishing (US) LLC, 424
Church Street, Suite 1200, Nashville, TN 37219
International Copyright Secured All Rights Reserved
Reprinted by Permission of Hal Leonard LLC

Heartbreak Hotel

Words and Music by Mae Boren Axton, Tommy Durden and Elvis
Presley
Copyright © 1956 Sony Music Publishing (US) LLC and Durden
Breyer Publishing
Copyright Renewed
All Rights Administered by Sony Music Publishing (US) LLC, 424
Church Street, Suite 1200, Nashville, TN 37219
International Copyright Secured All Rights Reserved
Reprinted by Permission of Hal Leonard LLC

About the Author

ENID WOLFE LANGBERT was not as adventurous as her protagonist, Paula, in high school, but she made up for it in the sixties by marching, sitting in, and raging against segregation and the war while, in her spare time, raising three children.

Divorced and disillusioned, she moved to the country with her kids, and eventually went to law school. She loved zealously advocating for her clients, whether they deserved it or not, until her husband became ill and she closed her practice to care for him. After he passed, she traveled widely and enrolled in an English literature master's program. She is now writing her thesis, tracing the influence of James Joyce's legal issues on his writing of *Finnegans Wake*—a topic about which she is unambiguously passionate. Enid lives in New York City.

Looking for your next great read?

We can help!

Visit www.gosparkpress.com/next-read or
scan the QR code below for a list
of our recommended titles.

SparkPress is an independent boutique publisher
delivering high-quality, entertaining, and engaging
content that enhances readers' lives, with a special
focus on commercial and genre fiction.